SHERLOCK HOLMES

The HAUNTING of
SHERLOCK HOLMES
and other stories

The HAUNTING of SHERLOCK HOLMES and other stories

DAVID MARCUM, EDITOR

JAICO PUBLISHING HOUSE

Ahmedabad Bangalore Chennai
Delhi Hyderabad Kolkata Mumbai

Published by Jaico Publishing House
A-2 Jash Chambers, 7-A Sir Phirozshah Mehta Road
Fort, Mumbai - 400 001
jaicopub@jaicobooks.com
www.jaicobooks.com

Published in arrangement with
MX Publishing Ltd
335 Princess Park Manor
London, N11 3GX

To be sold only in India, Bangladesh, Bhutan,
Pakistan, Nepal, Sri Lanka and the Maldives.

THE HAUNTING OF SHERLOCK HOLMES
AND OTHER STORIES
ISBN 978-81-8495-883-6

First Jaico Impression: 2016

Page design and layout: Special Effects, Mumbai

Printed by
Repro India Limited, Mumbai

Contents

COPYRIGHT INFORMATION

All of the contributions in this collection are copyrighted by the authors listed below. Grateful acknowledgement is given to the authors and/or their agents for the kind permission to use their work within these volumes.

The following contributions appear in this volume:

The Haunting of Sherlock Holmes and Other Stories

SP

PART I: 1881-1889

In 1874, while visiting the home of a University friend (see "The Gloria Scott"), Sherlock Holmes realized that his life's calling was to become a Consulting Detective. Moving to Montague Street in London, he commenced his career. A few years later, John H. Watson received his Doctor of Medicine degree and eventually joined the Army. After being wounded at the Battle of Maiwand, he returned to England, where he was introduced to Sherlock Holmes on New Year's Day, 1881. They agreed to take rooms at 221b Baker Street. Within months, Watson was assisting Holmes on his various investigations. In the mid-1880's, Watson married his first wife, about whom only limited facts are available. Although now wed, Watson often found time to assist in his friend's adventures. Following the death of his first wife in late 1887, Watson returned to 221b, where he lived until his second marriage to more well-known Mary Watson (née Morstan) in mid-1889. This volume covers this earlier period from soon after Holmes and Watson's first

*meeting through the early months of Watson's second marriage. During this time, Holmes was building his practice, and Watson did not publish any narratives of Holmes's cases until late 1887. Thus, Holmes was still somewhat unknown at this point. It was during this interval that the two first became friends, and then "brothers, not in blood, but in bond."**

**From the film Sherlock Holmes (2009)*

The Adventure of the Slipshod Charlady

by *John Hall*

You may well surmise that following that first case in which I was associated in some small way with Mr. Sherlock Holmes, and which I have called *A Study in Scarlet*, I followed Holmes's work with some considerable interest, and even ventured to hope that I might again at some point, and in some humble capacity, be able to join with him in the chase. I was, as you may recall, sharing rooms with Holmes at the time, and I had no real occupation or interests of my own, so I clutched eagerly at any opportunity for diversion. Holmes, however, was then, as always, somewhat reluctant to encourage confidences, and I had to wait several weeks after the conclusion of that first sensational problem before he allowed me to share in another investigation.

It was late spring, and the weather was showing every promise of improvement after what had been a very dreary fortnight. I had risen a little before my usual hour, and was somewhat surprised to find that Holmes, so often a late riser himself, had already breakfasted. Before I could remark upon this, or do more than wish him good morning, he said, "Well, Watson, and how does your writing progress?"

"Pretty much finished, Holmes. And if I do say so myself, a very promising little tale. I have great hopes for both its publication, and its reception by the reading public."

"It will, I trust, be instructive? Scotland Yard could well use a proper textbook of detective procedure!"

I laughed. "I fear it will hardly be that, Holmes, although you may be sure that I have given full attention to your remarkable methods. But the public taste is both fickle and demanding, insisting upon entertainment, diversion, some degree of imagination, as well as mere dry and dusty factual exposition."

He groaned, and lit a cigarette.

"But surely you would not deny the power, and utility, of imagination?" I protested. "Had you not been able to imagine what had taken place in that dreadful house, then –"

He raised a hand. "That was hardly imagination, Doctor," he said in that pedantic tone which he sometimes adopted. "A purely scientific reconstruction of events, as the French put it, based solely upon observation and deduction."

"H'mm," said I, not wishing to argue the point before I had finished my breakfast egg. Then, recognising an opportunity, I went on, "And have you any small problems in hand just now which might call for your unique talents? Having finished my own account of that horrid and most puzzling case, I confess that I am at somewhat of a loose end, and would welcome some mental stimulus, even vicariously."

He smiled ruefully, and shook his head. "There is nothing of similar moment just now. It is true that I have one or two insignificant matters in hand, but they are mainly pedestrian enough, scarcely likely to appeal to your Epicurean palate." He paused. "However –"

"Well?" said I, eagerly.

"Well, then, there is one small problem that I cannot immediately solve. Tell me, Watson, why would a manservant spend all day in the cellar of his master's house?"

"H'mm. To avoid being asked to do some uncongenial work?"

Holmes laughed. "Practical as ever, Doctor! But it can scarcely be that, for the master is absent from the house all day, and there is no wife who might bustle about the place and give the man unwelcome orders."

"Well, then. Rats? Or perhaps he is helping himself to the master's wine?"

"There is, as far as I am aware, no wine. And no rats – and if there were, there is a useful and practical body of men known as 'rat catchers' who will solve that particular problem cheaply and effectively." He thought for a moment in silence. "I confess, Watson, that Mrs. Bradley's little problem has given me much difficulty, though doubtless the real explanation will prove to be as prosaic as your own very practical suggestions."

"Mrs. Bradley? Do I –"

"You have never been formally introduced, but I fancy you will recollect the lady. Some sixty years of age, or perhaps a trifle more, of the working class, usually somewhat down at heel?"

"Ah, yes! I noted her appearance down when I was writing up the study in scarlet which began our association." I glanced at the old notebook which lay upon the table by my elbow. "Here we are –'a slipshod elderly woman' was my rather ungallant depiction. I recollect that my first thought was 'bunions!' I did wonder if my professional services might be called upon."

Holmes laughed. "It is true you might be helpful in that regard," said he. "But it was the wish to consult upon detective, and not medical, problems that originally brought Mrs. Bradley to Baker Street about a month ago, and I must confess that I have nothing in the way of advice to offer."

"Perhaps if you were to lay the facts before me, it might help you to arrange them in a way which would prove capable of explanation?" I suggested tentatively.

"You are right, it does sometimes help to lay out the problem methodically. Very well, then. Mrs. Bradley is what is politely called a 'daily' or 'domestic,' or more vulgarly a 'charlady,' that is, she makes a slender living by cleaning floors, polishing furniture, and similar unskilled but necessary household tasks."

"Not – and no offence to her, or to others of her profession – but not the sort of person to have a problem which would require your services?" I ventured to suggest.

"You would hardly think so, but you would be wrong, Watson. Indeed, I have asked her to call in here this very morning before she goes to work."

Rather surprised I pulled out my watch. "So late? Late, that is, to begin daily work of that sort."

"Mrs. Bradley informs me that she begins work at ten in the morning, and finishes at three in the afternoon. Her employer is, as I say, absent from the house all day on business, so there is no question of her interfering with his activities by mopping the floor whilst he is at his desk writing letters, or some such task."

"I see. That in itself makes sense, but is somewhat unusual."

Holmes nodded. "It is one odd aspect among several. A curious household, I gather. Ah!" he said, as there was a ring at the front door, "I believe that's the lady herself. Please remain, Doctor, for I should be pleased to have your views on the matter."

A moment later, Mrs. Bradley was shown into our little sitting-room, and I escorted her to a chair, into which she sank with an audible sigh of relief. I had already remarked upon her dilapidated shoes – indeed, slippers would be nearer the mark – but now I took the opportunity to cast her a surreptitious glance, and observe her general appearance more closely. She was perhaps some sixty years of age, stout, with a mop of untidy grey hair escaping from beneath the frayed brim of an unfashionable hat. Darned stockings, and an ancient coat with a slightly greasy collar of fur from some unidentifiable species, completed the picture. Altogether you could scarcely expect to find a more typical, if timeworn, example of the class to which she so clearly belonged.

"Now, Mrs. Bradley," said Holmes in his most soothing voice, "this gentleman is Doctor John Watson, and I have told him something of your worries, but perhaps you would be so kind as to begin at the beginning, for his benefit, and pray omit no detail."

"Well, sir," said Mrs. Bradley, "I hardly know what to tell you, it all seems something and nothing, like."

I may add by way of parenthesis that her speech was the purest Cockney, with many a dropped "h" and the like. I shall not endeavour to reproduce it at all accurately here, as the reader will doubtless be able to imagine it.

Holmes, with an obvious effort of will, prompted her, "Pray allow us to be the judges of that, madam. Now, you began your employment some six weeks ago, is that not correct?"

"That it is, Mr. Holmes, and I rue the day! What with that Naylor sneaking about the place, and telling outright lies into the bargain! Why –"

"You forget, Mrs. Bradley, that the good doctor here knows nothing of the matter," said Holmes, with just the merest hint of asperity.

"Oh, to be sure! Well then, Doctor, and you, Mr. Holmes, though you've heard this already – well, then, six weeks or so ago I applies for this job with the colonel – Colonel Fanshawe, that is, and such a nice gentleman, what I would call a real gentleman, if you follow me – anyway, I applies for the job, the hours being so good, and the colonel, him being away all day at his office, and making no trouble and all."

"You got the job," said Holmes, "and entered upon your duties at once. There were, I understand, no other servants kept, save only the manservant, this Naylor whom you mentioned?"

"That's right, sir. And a proper little sneak he is, at that!"

"In what way?" I asked, intrigued.

"Well, sir, you'd be doing your floors, and that, and you'd look up, and there 'e is, standing in the doorway, or wandering about the corridors."

"I see. I must confess I see nothing particularly objectionable in that," I said.

"No, sir. Not in itself, as you might say. But then, a week after I started, the colonel, he says to me, 'Mrs. B. –' and 'e always calls me that, nice and pleasant as you please, and no edge to 'im at all –'Mrs. B., there will be some workmen in for a few weeks or so, down in the cellar. Some small repairs to be done, nothing to worry about, so pray do not be alarmed if you hear them banging and crashing,' something to that effect."

"And they duly arrived," Holmes supplied.

"They did, sir. Or 'e did, for there was only one of 'em, a nice young fellow. I saw Naylor – Mr. Naylor, 'e likes to be called, I don't think! – anyway, Naylor let 'im in, showed him to the cellar. Now, I –"

"One moment," said I. "Have you ever been into the cellar yourself?"

"Very good, Watson!" Holmes exclaimed.

"No, sir, I 'aven't what you'd call been down there," said Mrs. Bradley. "But I did – not to be sneaky, or anything of that – but one day when I'd the 'ouse to myself I took a peep in."

"And?"

Mrs. Bradley shook her head. "Nothing, Doctor! Just an old brick cellar. Nothing down there at all, excepting some old bits and pieces of furniture, and them very much the worse for wear, all banged about and that."

"No wine rack? No sign of rats?" asked Holmes, with a sidelong glance at me.

"No wine rack, sir, certainly. As for rats – why, if I'd even suspected such a thing I'd 'ave given my notice at once!"

"To be sure," said Holmes. "But thus far, with the

exception of your dislike for the manservant Naylor, you have given the doctor no indication as to what it is which so perturbs you."

"Indeed I 'aven't, sir. Well, then, like I was saying, I seen the young fellow come, but I never seen 'im go, being s 'ow I'd left before 'e'd finished. Now, that's all well and good, but the next day, Naylor, 'e tells me the young chap is already down in the cellar, and wasn't to be disturbed. Well, as the day wore on, I could 'ear some banging and that down there, and so I knew the young chap, 'e was 'ard at work, so after an hour or so I looks for Naylor to ask if I should make a cup of tea for the young man, that being only right and proper and expected, 'im being a tradesman and that. But Naylor now, 'e was nowhere to be seen, so I knocks on the cellar door, and calls out, did I ought to make a cup of tea."

"Well?" I asked.

"You may well say, 'Well,' sir! Well, it was Naylor 'imself who called out from the cellar, "Thank you, Mrs. Bradley, that won't be necessary." Now, what d'you think of that?"

"Why, that Naylor was down there, perhaps making sure the job was properly done?" I said. "Or perhaps the young man had asked him for a hand with some heavy work?"

"'Eavy work!' Mrs. Bradley found the notion amusing. "Not 'im, sir! No. no, you mark my words, Doctor, 'e's up to no good. And I've noticed that there ain't no young tradesman – no, nor old one neither! – around the place. But yet there's still somebody – and it's Naylor, that I do know for a fact – messing about in that same cellar, day after day. And what I'd like to know, Mr. 'Olmes, is what you might be able to do about it? Only I'll be ever so grateful if you could set my mind at rest." And this was said with such an evident and honest sincerity that I leaned over and patted her arm.

"I confess," said Holmes, "that your problem is indeed a curious one. And I fear that I have little to offer in the way of advice from your last visit. Perhaps, Watson, you have some words of wisdom."

Put thus suddenly on the spot, as it were, I struggled for words. "Ah – is the matter then so distressing, Mrs. Bradley, that you really cannot see your way to remaining in the house? There are surely other openings for you?"

"Now, Doctor! Isn't that just what I've been thinking myself?" said Mrs. Bradley. "But you see, the hours is so good, and the pay is so good – it's only the nagging worry, as you might call it." She hesitated, obviously waning to say more.

"Well, Mrs. Bradley?" said Holmes.

"Well, sir, there's two things. First –" and again came that hesitation.

"Well?" asked Holmes a second time, with a little more impatience in his tone..

"Well, sir, you might just think that it's an old lady's fancy, but I'm sure that little sneak Naylor followed me 'ere. And if you was to go to the door with me, and keep an eye open, I can promise you that you'll see 'im."

"And why should he follow you, do you think?" asked Holmes, evidently puzzled.

"Why, bless you, sir! To see if I've been 'ere to talk to you, like." "H'mm, I see. You said there were two things?"

"Ah, yes. You see, sir, Naylor, 'e let on that 'e 'as some urgent business errands to do for the master, this very afternoon. Now, suppose you was to call round, I could let you 'ave a look in the cellar, easy as anything. That way you might be able to tell me what you think, even if it's to say there's nothing to worry about."

"I see." Holmes glanced at me. "What say you, Doctor?" "An excellent notion," said I.

"Very well then. I have a note of the address," said Holmes, "and we shall call at, say, two o'clock. Is that satisfactory?"

"That it is, sir, and it'll set my mind at rest," said out visitor, clambering to her feet.

I rose to see her out.

"By the way, Watson," said Holmes in his languid fashion, "you might just stand at the door a moment, and see if Mrs. Bradley is indeed being followed."

"Very well."

"Oh, and Mrs. Bradley – how did you come to hear of me? I do not believe you mentioned that to Watson."

"Well, sir, it was a friend of the colonel's, a young chap 'e was, came to call on the colonel one day, only 'e was out. The young man, proper gent, he looks very forlorn, says he's come a long way, and wouldn't mind a cup of tea and that. So I makes him one, and somehow we got to talking –'e 'ad no sort of edge to 'im, talked as nice as you like, and somehow – don't you never ask me just 'ow – he gets me to tell him wha's been bothering me, and then 'e says: "You should talk to Mr. Sherlock 'Olmes, he's the man to solve this problem," and 'e gives me your address, writes it down on a bit of paper. And so 'ere I came," she finished with a note of triumph.

"I see. Very well. Watson?"

"Ah, yes. This way, madam." I led the way to the street door, and saw Mrs. Bradley off, but I did not return at once. Instead, I partly closed the door, and looked keenly out through the slit which remained. To my surprise – for I had put Mrs. Bradley's suspicions down to mere fancy – I saw a man lurk from out of the shadows, for all the world like some villain of melodrama, and take the same direction as Mrs. Bradley. My first instinct was to accost him, or at the very least to follow him, but then it occurred to me that we already knew his, and Mrs. Bradley's, destination. To follow would perhaps spoil Holmes's plans, and so, albeit reluctantly, I made my way back up the stairs, and told Holmes what I had seen.

"Ah. It shows that Mrs. Bradley's suspicions were correct in at least one regard," said Holmes. "Let us see if her other concerns are equally well founded."

It was with some considerable impatience that I set

myself to wait until two o'clock in the afternoon. I tried one of Clark Russell's collections, In the Middle Watch, but could not concentrate on it as it deserved, and it was with great relief that I heard Holmes saying, "We have twenty minutes to keep our appointment, Watson."

We left our cab at a busy crossroads on the outskirts of the City, and headed eastwards. Our road did not take us into very fashionable surroundings, and I observed as much to Holmes.

"Indeed," said he, "a military man, with an important occupation, and – what did our client say? Ah, yes, 'a real gent,' I believe. Such a man might be expected to have a more elegant establishment. Ah, but here we are. Hum! The house seems as faded as the street."

In this, Holmes was quite correct. I looked somewhat askance at the slightly dusty windows, the faded green paint on the door, the general air of neglect. Holmes rang the bell, and the door was opened at one by Mrs. Bradley, who had evidently been expecting us, and was in a state of some excitement.

"Oh, Mr. 'Olmes," she began, "am I pleased that you've come! As I said, Naylor – the little rat –'e's just gone out, says he'll be an hour or two. Now, if you'll step this way, sir, and I'll show you the cellar."

She was as good as her word, taking us to a plain wooden door which gave onto a flight of stone steps. "I won't go down there, sir, if you don't mind," said Mrs. Bradley, "I'd be that frightened of what we might find."

"That is very well," said Holmes, "Watson and I will manage well enough. Do you have a candle, or – ah!" as Mrs. Bradley produced a lantern and matches. "Excellent! You are an ideal client! Now, Watson, let us proceed."

I followed Holmes into the cellar. It was, as Mrs. Bradley had told us, a perfectly ordinary cellar, with brick walls. A few bits of old furniture and the like stood about, or lay, rather, for the detritus was scattered all over the floor: and old chair, the remains of a kitchen table, much battered, a hammer, and the like, were among the useless items which I noticed.

Holmes had gone over to one wall, one which I knew was the innermost wall of the house. He held up the lantern. "Ah!"

I looked where he pointed, and saw that several of the bricks had been removed, as if someone were trying to break through the wall into the adjoining premises. The bricks themselves were stacked neatly on the floor.

"Not the common or garden attempt at robbery, surely, Holmes?" I protested, the disappointment in my voice plain enough even to my own ears. But then I was disappointed, I admit it frankly. The case which had seemed to be possessed of some interesting points was nothing more than a trite robbery, or attempt at a robbery! And I could see that Holmes, too, felt let down. Let down, and perhaps even puzzled.

Now that the thought occurred, there was something not quite right about all this. Oh, I do not mean the attempt at theft, or anything of that kind. No, it was something else that nagged at me, though I could not have put into words just what it was.

"There is nothing more to be seen here, Doctor," said Holmes abruptly. "Let us regain the outer air and see what may be on the other side of this wall."

We left Mrs. Bradley mumbling something about what a relief it was to have us looking into the matter, and went out into the street. The corner was at no great distance, and Holmes paced it out carefully before turning into the road, somewhat broader than the one we had just left, which backed onto the colonel's house. I could see Holmes count out the steps as he walked briskly along, before coming to a halt in front of a fairly ordinary looking shop. I glanced up, to see a sign reading: "T. Dudley – Curios and Objects d'Art."

"I had half expected a bank, at the very least!" said I,

Doctor, would you see to this – lady?" and there was a slight but perceptible pause. "In a right taking, she is, sir."

"Show her in," said I. Mrs. Hudson did so, and to my astonishment the visitor was none other than Mrs. Bradley, and all too clearly in that 'right taking' of which Mrs. Hudson had spoken.

"Come in, Mrs. Bradley," I said, endeavouring to emulate Holmes's suave manner. "Pray take a seat and tell me your troubles. Perhaps, Mrs. Hudson, a pot of your delicious strong tea?"

"Thank you, sir," said Mrs. Bradley, "but there's no time for that.

The fact is, sir, I've 'ad something of a shock, as you might say."

"Oh?"

"Yes, indeed. You may recall as 'ow I said I'd thought of giving in my notice? Yes, well, now I won't need to, for the colonel, 'e's 'ad me into 'is study this very afternoon, and given me my notice! Says as how he 'as to go away, and the place is to be shut up, or let out, or some such."

It took a while for me to realise the importance of this. Then, "You mean to say that the colonel is leaving the house? When is this to happen?"

"Next Tuesday, sir."

"Indeed? That seems a trifle abrupt, does it not?

"Came right out of the blue, sir. Mind you," said Mrs. Bradley, "the colonel has paid me – handsomely, too – for the short notice. But you see, sir, with things being as they are, I thought Mr. Holmes should know at once."

I thanked her, and, after some lengthy reiteration of her statement, Mrs. Bradley allowed herself to be escorted out by our landlady, and I settled down to a reconsideration of the problem with a lighter heart.

If the house were to be closed on Tuesday of next week, then it was obvious that the pretended robbery of the curio shop would be that day, or possibly on the Monday. We, that is the official forces and Holmes, would be watching the curio shop, whilst the gang were – what?

It was that last question which brought me to a halt. But then, I had already determined that the actual crime was not to be directed against a bank or shop, whether humble or grand, but against an individual. Now, there is little point robbing a poor man! The crime, then, would be against someone worth the robbing. I picked up the illustrated papers, which Holmes always took, though seldom read, and began to peruse the "society" columns.

After an hour or so, Holmes returned, the disappointment evident in his face. In answer to my unspoken question he shook his head. "The matter is as dark as ever," he said, throwing himself into a chair.

"Perhaps not," I answered, with perhaps just a touch of pardonable pride. I went on to tell him of Mrs. Bradley's surprising news, and of my own thoughts on the matter.

Holmes listened intently, and when I had almost done, he clapped his hands. "Upon my soul, Watson, you have analysed the matter remarkably!"

"Is there anything amiss with my reading of it?"

"None that I can see. Sadly, all your reasoning does not narrow it down sufficiently."

"I am in hopes that it may, Holmes," I answered, and threw the latest of my society papers across to him. "There are notes in there of three foreign visitors due to arrive in London on Tuesday. It is my guess – my opinion, that is to say – that one of them is the intended victim." "H'mm." Holmes did not look entirely convinced. "It is an interesting line, Doctor, but still it may be that none of these –"

"But what is there to lose? You yourself have said that the field is too wide for your own brand of analysis. Even if none of the three is correct, we have lost nothing by watching them, or asking Lestrade to watch them."

"You are right," said Holmes. He opened the paper at the page whose corner I had turned down. "Well, then, what are your selections?"

"A Russian prince –"

Holmes held up a hand. "His name is known to me. His family is a good one, but financially negligible."

"There is an American heiress, coming to England to marry an earl –"

The hand went up again. "Her father disapproves of the match, and will assuredly disinherit her should she follow her heart."

"Indeed? I had not heard as much, nor have the writers of that paper."

Holmes laughed. "It is not widely advertised. Next?"

"Next, and last, I fear. The South African diamond magnate, Barney Granato, is coming to London on business."

Holmes nodded. "He is a more likely candidate, I agree. But he has the reputation of carrying a couple of pearl-handled revolvers with him, and of travelling in company with his bodyguards, a half-dozen former prize-fighters."

"H'mm," I said ruefully. "A formidable army for any crook to face!" I reflected a moment. "And besides, I was reading just the other day that diamonds are transported not by Mr. Granato, but by very ordinary, perhaps rather drab, individuals, so as not to draw unwelcome attention to them. I –" And here I broke off, for Holmes was staring into space with that curiously abstracted expressing which he sometimes wore. "Holmes?"

"I beg your pardon, Watson. You know," he said, rising to his feet, "I think you may have hit the nail on the head. But I must make further enquiries." And before I could ask him anyone of the half-dozen questions which rose to my mind, off he went, and I did not see him again that night.

Nor did I see him at all the next day, which was Saturday. You may be sure that I pestered Mrs. Hudson for any word of him, but she knew as little as did I. I racked my brains, but could not see what it was that Holmes must have seen. The day passed in some frustration.

By Sunday, I was irritable, and when I saw Holmes, which was late in the day, he refused to say anything, beyond asking if I might be free to join him on Tuesday!

I shall not write of my state of mind on the Monday. Fortunately Holmes was absent most of the day, or Lestrade might have been obliged to arrest me for assault and battery.

By Tuesday, all my impatience was gone. I was merely eager to follow wherever Holmes led. And he led me first to Scotland Yard, where we collected Lestrade and a silent lady dressed in some sort of black uniform, after which we all four went to Victoria train station.

At the first opportunity I steered Lestrade to one side and indicated the black-clad lady. "Oh," said the official detective, "that's one of our police matrons. Useful in these cases, Doctor."

Before I could ask what "these cases" might be, Lestrade grabbed my arm and pulled me into the shadows. "This is our train," he hissed in my ear. "Or it is if Mr. Holmes has the matter right."

The train from France pulled in, and the usual throng disembarked. Lestrade indicated one man, a tall gentleman in heavy furs. The man stopped on the platform, looked round. A couple of men moved towards him, evidently expecting him. Behind them walked a middle-aged lady, well-dressed, handsome enough, but with something about her which seemed familiar to me. There were greetings and handshakes all round.

I was about to question Lestrade, when the little group on the platform moved towards the exit, and the cab rank. They made no attempt to join the queue waiting for a cab, though, but moved a little to one side, as if waiting for something. Then a carriage pulled up, and they all made to get into it.

It was then that Lestrade blew his police whistle. And then events moved so fast that I could scarcely follow them. A whole crowd of men seemed to appear from thin air, and seized the two men who had met the tall passenger from the train. The tall man himself seemed to be helping with the seizing business, while the police matron did a similar service for the middle-aged lady. And for good measure, the driver of the carriage had whipped up his horse and was trying to get away, while Lestrade, showing considerable courage, grabbed the reins and bridle and tried to stop him!

In less time than it takes to write, the whole thing was over. A couple of closed police vans appeared from the shadows, and the two men plus the lady and the driver of the carriage, were all driven away.

Lestrade, looking somewhat dishevelled but very proud of himself, accompanied Holmes and me back to Baker Street, where my first task was to address the brandy and soda. "I assume that was the Russian prince?" I asked, as nonchalantly as I could.

Holmes nodded. "Or, rather, one of Lestrade's men impersonating him, the real prince being detained for his own safety at Dover."

"But I thought you said he had nothing worth stealing?"

"Nothing of his own. But you gave me the clue, Watson, when you mentioned that diamond couriers are so often colourless individuals, not wishing to attract attention. The prince was acting on behalf of a Russian lady who wishes – discreetly – to dispose of some jewellery, without her husband being troubled in the matter. The prince was to have been met at the Savoy Hotel, but the gang turned up here, and said there was a change of plan."

"Ah!" Then I frowned. "You know, Holmes, that lady on the platform looked a bit like a younger Mrs. Bradley."

Holmes and Lestrade laughed out loud. Lestrade said, "She was, Doctor! That is, she was a lady known variously as Miss Skeffington, Miss Wells, Mrs. Lamont –"

"And Mrs. Bradley," Holmes finished.

"She started off as a lady's maid," said Lestrade reminiscently, "more years ago than I care to think. Joins the household, gets to know the house, and the family, then –

you name it, robbery, blackmail, anything. Oh, yes, a long record, your Mrs. Bradley."

"The scheme was not without merit," said Holmes. "And it does illustrate the advantages of being an accomplished artist in make-up and disguise, something I have already noted, and indeed used."

"So the whole story of noises in the cellar was a sham?" I asked. "And the story of the young man who suggested your involvement?"

Holmes nodded. "Designed merely to arouse our – my – interest, and set me on a false scent, as they feared I might somehow discover their scheme independently. Still, I think, Lestrade, you will not be too unhappy with the result?"

"Indeed not, Mr. Holmes! Thanks for the brandy, Doctor, but I must be on my way." And he rose to his feet. "It's all worked out very nice, and nothing too complicated about it, not like some of your theories, Mr. Holmes."

"True. Unless, Watson, there are any small points you would wish cleared up?"

"No, all very straightforward, Holmes. Although I do just wonder how the American heiress will get on with her English lord."

"Ah, for that you will have to consult next week's illustrated papers!" said Holmes. "No doubt it will be a case of omnia vincit amor. Though for me," and he waved a hand at the morning's post, which contained the usual appeals from puzzled clients, "for me it must, I fear, be always a matter of labor omnia vincit."

continent. This attempt, incidentally, proved to be fruitless, and the results of his researches never saw the light of day.

The rain was falling, and few cabs and even fewer pedestrians were on the street, as I stood in the window of our rooms in Baker Street observing the scene below. "Halloa!" exclaimed Holmes, who had laid down his pen with a gesture of impatience, and joined me at the window. "A client, if I am not mistaken."

The corpulent man approaching our house certainly seemed to bear all the distinguishing marks of those who sought the assistance of Sherlock Holmes. The vacillation in his movements, and the nervous glances at the numbers displayed on the front doors of the houses of Baker Street, had by now become almost as familiar to me as they were to Holmes.

As we watched, he glanced upwards, and caught sight of us standing in the window, as we in turn observed him. Hurriedly ducking his head downwards, he quickened his pace, half-running to the door, and within a matter of seconds we heard the pealing of the bell.

We returned to our seats as Mrs. Hudson announced the arrival of our visitor, presenting Holmes with his card.

"A somewhat uninspiring choice of name," he announced, after examining the card, briefly presenting it to his long aquiline nose, and presenting it to me, where I read simply the name "Henry Taylor" and the title "Merchant". "No matter," he continued, "the truth will eventually come out. Show him up, if you would, Mrs. Hudson."

The man who presented himself a few minutes later was clearly in the grip of a powerful emotion, in which fear appeared to be mingled with grief.

"Sit down, please, Mr. Taylor," Holmes invited him. "You have come far today, and no doubt you are tired."

"Why, yes, Mr. Holmes, indeed I am." The words were uttered in an accent that betrayed our visitor as hailing from one of our more northern counties. He seated himself in the armchair usually occupied by Holmes's clients, and I was able to observe him more closely.

Clad in a tweed suit, more fitted for the country than the town, his large frame was still heaving with the exertion of having climbed the seventeen steps to our rooms, and to my professional eye, this, combined with his over-ruddy complexion, indicated some problems with his health. His left hand gripped a stout blackthorn, and the corner of a sheaf of papers peeked out from beneath his coat. His eyes were reddened, as though he had been weeping.

"Forgive my impertinence," Holmes said to him after about a minute had passed in silence, "but is your visit here connected with your recent loss?"

I myself had, naturally, remarked the mourning band attached to his right sleeve.

For answer, Taylor raised his head, which had sunk to his breast, and answered in a lugubrious tone, "Yes, Mr. Holmes, that is indeed the case." Another silence ensued, broken only by the wheezing emanating from our visitor as he slowly regained his composure. At length, he spoke again, in a voice heavily charged with emotion. "Gone, Mr. Holmes. Gone. Struck down in the full flower of her beauty by a fell hand."

"Murder, you say?" exclaimed Holmes in a tone of some excitement. The news seemed to arouse him from his languor. "How very fortuitous – I mean to say that it is fortuitous that I have no other cases on hand, of course. The police...?"

"The police have their suspicions as to who may have committed this foul crime, but I believe them to be in error," replied the other. "This is why I have come to you. I wish to seek justice for my dear wife, Martha."

"Tell me more," Holmes invited him, leaning back in his chair and regarding our client with that curious hooded gaze of his. "Watson, take notes, if you would be so kind."

"I am a merchant of cloth and other such goods,"

began our visitor. "Some years ago, my first wife died of consumption, leaving me with two young children. As a busy man of business, I found I was unable to care for them as they deserved, and I thereupon lodged them with my sister in the town of Burton upon Trent, and made due financial provision for their support. Though my sister is a good woman, and took excellent care of them, I nonetheless felt that my children deserved to be with their father and his wife. In addition, living alone was irksome to me, and I therefore cast about for a wife. When I moved to the city where I currently reside, my eye was caught by Martha Lightfoot, the daughter of a neighbour, and after a brief courtship, we married, and my children, Stephen and Katie, returned to my home." He paused, and I took the opportunity to offer him a glass of water, which he accepted gratefully. "Well, sir, it seems I could not have made a better choice for a wife. Martha was devoted to my children as if they had been her own, and they, for their part, appeared to adore her in return."

"Excuse me," Holmes interrupted him. "May I ask the ages of the principals in this case?"

Our visitor smiled, for the first time since he had entered our room. "I suppose that some would term our marriage – our late marriage, that is – a December and May affair. When we married, some two years ago, I was fifty-three years of age, and Martha twenty-two. Stephen was at that time twelve years old, and Katie ten." He paused and mopped his brow with a none-too-clean handkerchief. "We were a happy family, in so far as my work would allow it."

"What do you mean by that?" Holmes asked him sharply.

"Well, Mr. Holmes, my work involves a good deal of travel, and obliges me to be away from home for considerable periods of time. I considered it to be somewhat of an imposition on Martha for her to care alone for two youngsters, but as I mentioned, she and the children appeared to have a harmonious life together. That is," he sighed, "until the events of a month ago."

"Pray continue," Holmes requested, as our visitor seemed to have sunk into some kind of reverie.

"I came back from an extended trip that had lasted for a week, and discovered my Stephen in an uncharacteristically sulky mood, and with what appeared to be a bruise upon his face. I assumed that he had received a blow while scuffling with his playfellows, as lads will, but on my questioning him, he informed me that the blow had been struck by my wife. He refused to give the reason for this event, simply referring me to Martha. When I questioned her, and confronted her with the accusation, she admitted to striking the child, but claimed it had not been a deliberate action."

"No doubt she was able to give reasons for this assertion?"

Taylor sighed. "Yes. She informed me that she had observed Stephen taking money from the maid's purse. A small sum, to be sure – a few pence only – but theft is theft, no matter what the amount, do you not agree, Mr. Holmes?"

"Indeed so," answered my friend, with a half-smile.

"She remonstrated with him, and an argument ensued, during the course of which she attempted to retrieve the money, and struck the lad in the face. She swore to me with tears in her eyes that it was an accident, and she had never had any intention of doing him harm. He, when I questioned him later, admitted that he had taken the money in order to purchase some trifle, but claimed that Martha had deliberately delivered the blow to his face."

"And which one did you believe?"

Taylor sighed. "I believed my wife, Martha. Much as I love my Stephen, he has proved himself to be less than truthful in the past, and I have had cause to admonish him. I fear that the sojourn at my sister's did nothing to improve his character. She is a woman whom some might term over-kind, and she indulged his whims while he was living there, at the expense of his character."

"I take it that relations between your wife and your son

deteriorated from that time?"

"Indeed so, Mr. Holmes. As I mentioned, I am often compelled to be away from home, and so it was for this past month. However, on recent occasions when I returned from my travels, it was painfully obvious to me that my wife and my son were on poor terms with each other. I confess that I was completely ignorant of any way in which this breach could be mended, and was forced to endure the spectacle of those whom I love in a state of mutual enmity. Mealtimes were a particular torment, where each seemed to find every opportunity to insult and belittle the other. If one could be banished from the table, peace would have prevailed, and as master of the house, I could remove one of the sources of conflict. But which one was to be removed, Mr. Holmes? I ask you, for I could not resolve that riddle." He paused, as if for effect. "And then, Mr. Holmes, we come to the events of yesterday."

"It was last night that your wife died?"

"Indeed it was only yesterday. I returned home to find Martha lifeless, stretched out in her own blood on the drawing-room floor. She had suffered a series of stab wounds to the body."

"And your son?"

"I discovered him in the scullery, with a bloody kitchen knife. He was cleaning bloodstains off his clothes in an almost frantic manner. The water in the basin in which he was washing his hands and garments was a scarlet mess, Mr. Holmes. I never want to see the like again."

"And his story?"

"He told me that he had discovered my Martha in the room, with the knife beside her. Despite his recent dislike of her, he is not at heart a bad lad. He believed that she was not dead, but severely wounded, and attempted to move her to make her more comfortable. It was during this operation that he determined that she was, in fact, dead, and it was at this time that his hands and clothing became covered in blood. He picked up the knife –"

"Why did he do that?" I asked. Taylor shrugged. "Who can tell?"

"The mind causes us to act strangely and without rational motive under unusual conditions," remarked Holmes. "I can think of several similar cases in my experience. Go on, Mr. Taylor."

"He picked up the knife, as I say, and carried it with him into the scullery, where he started to wash his hands and to clean the blood from his clothes. When I encountered him, I immediately ordered him to cease what he was doing, and to come into the street with me, where I gave him over to a passing constable. It gave me little pleasure to do so, but I felt that justice must be served."

"Quite so, quite so," murmured Holmes, but his words seemed to me to lack conviction.

"I felt in my heart that it was impossible that he had committed such a base deed, but what other explanation could be given?"

"You mentioned a maid," said Holmes. "Where was she while this was going on?"

"It was her afternoon off." "I see. And your daughter?"

"She was visiting a schoolfellow. My son and my wife were the only two people in the house when I returned."

"When you returned, was the house door to the street locked?"

"The police asked me the same question. Yes, it was. The door leading to the back yard was also locked."

"And there was no sign of entry through any other aperture? A window, for example?"

"To the best of my knowledge, there was no such sign."

"And the police?"

Taylor spread his hands."What can they do, but believe that my son is guilty? What other explanation could there possibly be for these events? They are confining him, and I fear he will hang."

"It is the work of a minute for me to be ready," I answered him. "Good. If I recall correctly, there is an express train from Euston at fifty-three minutes past the hour, which will bring us to the Trent Valley station before the day is too far advanced. Be so good as to confirm it in Bradshaw."

I did so, and reported this to Holmes. "I confess that I am confused regarding our client's motives," I said to Holmes. "On the one hand, he appears to love his son with true parental feeling by approaching you in an attempt to establish his innocence. On the other, he seems keen to blacken his name, as shown by his confession that the child is not always truthful. Also, by immediately giving his son in charge to the police, Taylor seems to have assumed that he was indeed the culprit, without bothering to make detailed enquiries."

"Indeed, there are several mysteries about this aspect of the matter, which I think we can only clear up by means of a visit to the scene. Come, Watson, let us make our way to the fair city of Lichfield."

We alighted from the train at Lichfield Trent Valley station, a mile or so from the centre of the city, and hailed a cab to take us to the market square. From there, we walked along Dam Street until we reached number 23, close to the Cathedral. A police constable was standing outside the door.

Holmes introduced himself to the constable, and requested permission to speak to the Inspector in charge of the case.

"I've read of you in the newspapers, sir," replied the policeman, "and I am sure that you will be welcome, but I have to talk to Inspector Upton first before I allow you inside, if you don't mind, sir." He went inside the house, and re-emerged a minute or so later, followed by a uniformed officer, who identified himself as the inspector.

"Mr. Holmes, sir, welcome to Lichfield. A pleasure to make your acquaintance, though I fear there will be not much for you to do here. We are pretty certain that the young 'un is the culprit."

"You received my telegram?" Holmes asked him.

"Why, yes sir, we did indeed, and Taylor has presented your card to me. You'll be happy to know that the room is not significantly changed from when Taylor entered it and discovered his wife there, though of course we have removed the body. As I say, there is really no doubt that the lad did it. Shocking case. I can't remember anything like this happening here in the past. This way, sir."

He led the way into the front room of the house, which had been furnished in a good, if provincial style. Holmes stood in the doorway, and surveyed the room's contents, which included a desk by the window, and a chair lying on its side beside it. Some dark stains marked the carpet and the bearskin rug beside the desk.

"The front and back doors of the house were both locked, Taylor told us," we were informed by Upton. "All the windows appeared to be shut, and there was no other means of entrance into the house."

"Unless the murderer came down the chimney, or through the coal-chute, assuming there to be such a thing in this house."

"True enough, Mr. Holmes, as regards the coal-chute, but no such apparatus exists here."

"The case against the boy certainly seems strong, then."

"Strong enough, Mr. Holmes. It's a pity, as he seems like a nice lad.

Just a sudden flash of temper, and –" The inspector shrugged. "Where was the body located?" Holmes asked.

By way of answer, the police officer started to step forward to point out the spot, but was restrained by Holmes. "Please, Inspector," he implored the other, "let us not disturb any further the remaining evidence that will help us determine the murderer, faint as it may be by now."

"Very well, then," replied Upton. "Mrs. Taylor was discovered by Taylor lying on her back, over there by the desk, with her head nearest the chair."

"And yet she had been sitting at the desk, had she not, and the chair was overturned in the struggle with her murderer," mused Holmes to himself. "Strange. Taylor told me that the son, Stephen, had moved the body, but did not provide any details," addressing the policeman once more. "Do you know more?"

"According to the son's statement, he discovered his mother – rather, his step-mother – lying on her side, and merely moved her onto her back, and at that time determined that she was dead."

"I see," said Holmes. "And where was the knife discovered, according to this statement?"

"Beside the body, on the floor."

Holmes said nothing, but stood in silence for a moment before dropping to his hands and knees, and pulling out a lens from his pocket, with which he proceeded to examine the floor, crawling forward towards the desk as he did so. At one point he paused, and appeared to be about to retrieve something from the rug, but checked his movements and continued his appraisal of the carpet. The policeman and I watched him from the doorway for the space of about five minutes.

At length he stood up, and dusted his garments, before turning to the desk and using his lens to scrutinise its surface, and the inkwell which still stood open, as well as the pen and the blotter and other objects that lay upon it. "Your men have been busy," he said to Upton, "and have almost, but not completely, destroyed the traces of the events that took place. Nonetheless, many points of interest still remain. May we view the body of Mrs. Taylor?"

"She is at a local Inn, the Earl of Lichfield Arms, in Conduit Street by the market square," replied the inspector. "Though I fail to see that there is much to be learned from a further examination."

"There may well be more than you imagine," answered

my friend. "May I advise you that no-one is to enter this room until I have finished my investigation?"

I could see that the police officer resented this usurpation of his authority, but he assented to Holmes's request, and instructed the constable at the door to prevent any entrance to the chamber.

The inspector accompanied Holmes and myself on the short walk to the inn, where we were shown to an upstairs room, which had been cleared of all furniture save a deal table on which lay the body, covered by a sheet.

"There has as yet been no autopsy, of course?" Holmes enquired.

On receiving the information that this was the case, he requested and received permission to draw down the sheet and examine the body. There were several wounds to the abdomen, obviously inflicted with a sharp instrument.

"In my opinion," I said to Holmes, in answer to a query of his, "this wound here could well have reached the heart. Of course, without a post-mortem examination, it will be impossible to say with certainty that this is the case, but my experience with bayonet wounds leads me to this belief. Even without the other wounds, this alone could be the cause of death. Shock and loss of blood would also be a factor in the cause of death."

"Thank you, Watson," Holmes said. "As you rightly point out, this cannot be confirmed until an autopsy is performed, and it would be premature to certify this as the cause of death. But, dear me, this murder was committed in a frenzy of passion, was it not? I count at least five major wounds, and several grazes where the weapon has almost, but not completely, missed its mark." He bent to examine the ghastly wounds more closely. "Watson. Your opinion on the nature of these? Specifically, how they were delivered."

I, in my turn, bent to the cadaver. "Delivered to the front of the body, with the blade entering from the right and above for the most part." "That was also my conclusion," said Holmes. "Mrs. Taylor appears

to have been quite a tall woman, Inspector. Can you confirm that?"

"I believe she was some five feet and seven inches in height." Holmes made some notes in his pocket note-book.

"And the boy?"

"He is somewhat small for his age. I would put him at a little under five feet."

"And it would take considerable strength, would it not, Watson, to cause these wounds?"

"Indeed so," I confirmed. Holmes bent to the body once more, and eventually stood straight and addressed Upton again.

"What was the state of the boy's mind when the constable took him in charge, Inspector?"

"According to the constable's report, he was shaking. The constable judged him to be in a state of fear."

"That is hardly surprising," Holmes commented. "And he has not confessed to the murder?"

"He continues to insist that he entered the room and discovered his step-mother lying in her own blood. As to the knife, he says that he has no idea why he picked it up and carried it with him to the scullery where he washed his hands and clothing."

"Those in such a condition often are unaware of their actions," answered Holmes. "I think we may attach little importance to this. You are satisfied, of course, that the knife discovered with the boy is indeed the murder weapon?"

"Why, what else could it be?" asked Upton in surprise. "You may see it for yourself at the station. I take it you will wish to interview the boy?"

"If that is permitted."

"Surely," replied the inspector. "Though I fear you will be wasting your breath if you are attempting to establish his innocence."

"We shall see," answered Holmes. "By the by, where is

Taylor now? He did not seem to be in evidence at the house."

"He has left the city for the day. He told me that he had urgent business in Birmingham to which he must attend, and I allowed him to go there."

"I have a feeling that you may never again set eyes on Mr. Henry Taylor," Holmes told him.

"Why, what can you possibly mean?" asked Upton in surprise and dismay. "Do you mean that he means to do away with himself in despair? Have I let him go to his self-inflicted death?"

"By no means," smiled Holmes. "The truth will prove to be at once simpler and more complex than that."

"You have me scratching my head," said Upton in puzzlement, and led the way to the police station, where he produced for our inspection the knife that had been discovered by the body.

Holmes produced his lens, and examined the blade, covered with now-dried blood, closely. "It is impossible to say with any certainty without knowing the exact position and location of the knife when it was found," he announced at length, "but it seems to me that this knife was not the murder weapon. Has it been identified, by the way?"

"Yes, Taylor recognised it as one of the knives used in the kitchen for preparing food. The maid, Anne Hilton, likewise identified it, as indeed does the boy, Stephen. But why do you say that it is not the murder weapon. Surely it is obvious?"

"Too obvious," retorted Holmes. "Two factors lead me to this conclusion, which, as I said, must remain tentative for now. Firstly, the blade, as you will observe, is almost triangular in shape, with a narrow point, and widening towards the hilt."

"That is a common design," answered Upton, "and I fail to see how you can make anything of that."

"Ah, but the wounds on the body were performed using a narrower blade. Either that, or this knife was not inserted you there once Staunton, whoever he may transpire to be, arrives here."

"Come, Watson," Holmes said to me, and we passed through the pleasant streets of this old city to the George, where we secured a most comfortable room, and bespoke an early dinner, anticipating the arrival of Staunton.

Over the course of our meal, I attempted to interrogate Holmes regarding what he had discovered, and the conclusions he had drawn, but much to my chagrin, he refused to be drawn, and discoursed instead on the life of Doctor Samuel Johnson, a native of the city that we were currently visiting. I could follow his reasoning with regard to the knife, and was forced to agree that the knife that had been discovered by the body was in all probability not the murder weapon. It also seemed to me that the boy was unable to have inflicted the wounds that had caused the death of Mrs. Taylor, by reason of his under-developed physique.

We had just finished our meal when a uniformed constable entered the dining-room, much to the consternation of the hotel waiters, and informed us, with a strange smile, that Mr. Henry Staunton from Sutton Coldfield was now at Lichfield police station.

"Inspector Upton's compliments to you, Mr. Holmes," he added with a broad grin. "He thanks you for your discovery of Mr. Staunton, sir."

We followed the countable to the police station, where we encountered the inspector who wore the same smile as his constables. "Mr. Staunton is in the next room," he told us, and opened the door – to reveal Mr. Henry Taylor!

"What is the meaning of this?" I asked. "Are Henry Staunton and Henry Taylor one and the same person?"

"Indeed so."

Our client's face had turned red with anger. "How the devil did you discover all this?" he demanded of Holmes.

"You thought that by removing and destroying the

letter that your second wife had written to your first wife, informing her of Mrs. Taylor's new-found knowledge of Mrs. Staunton, you had removed any possible evidence of a motive, did you not? But you failed to notice that she had blotted the envelope. Your true name and address were clearly visible on the blotter, reversed, naturally."

"My God!" Staunton sank back in his chair.

"Bigamy, eh?" said Upton. "Well, my lad, we can have you for that."

"And add to that the murder of Martha Taylor, as I suppose we must call her," said Holmes, "though I fear her actual marital status must be in some doubt."

"I never meant to kill her –" cried Staunton, and bit off the words as they came out of his mouth.

"Oh, but I think you did indeed kill her, and then worse," said Holmes. "In my whole career, I have hardly ever encountered such a cold-hearted diabolical piece of treachery."

"Your proof?" taunted the other.

"It would be easy to prove to a jury that the blows that killed Martha Taylor were not inflicted by the knife found beside her body. The blows that killed her could only have been inflicted by a stiletto blade, as any wide blade would have been stopped by the ribs. Once that doubt had been established, your son would walk free. No other possible weapon was discovered in the house. You may have thought you were being clever by killing with one weapon and leaving another, more plausible instrument to implicate an innocent party – your very son – but you ignored elementary anatomy."

"That might prove my son's innocence, but it hardly establishes my guilt," protested Staunton defiantly.

"True," agreed Holmes. "However, there is the matter of the missing seal from your watch chain, the empty clasp of which I noticed when you visited us in Baker Street." Staunton looked aghast and grabbed at the chain in question with a look of horror on his countenance. "No, it did not fall off somewhere else. It is currently pressed into the bearskin rug in the front room of the house in Dam Street. Did your men overlook this, Inspector? Pressed in there by the weight of a body lying on it, and covered with blood. It is impossible that in that state it was ever there before Martha Taylor was struck down.

"Let me reconstruct the events for you, gentlemen. Mr. Staunton took a fancy to have more than one name, and more than one family. It happens to some men. I am myself not that way inclined, but I regard this aberration with an amused tolerance. As Mr. Taylor, he was widowed, and he removed himself to Lichfield, where he cast about for a new partner. Mrs. Staunton is obviously not suited as the ideal sole helpmeet and companion of his life –"

"Leave her out of this, damn you!" exclaimed Staunton, angrily. "By all means," answered Holmes with an equable air. "In any event, Miss Martha Lightfoot fitted the bill, and she appears to have been a good match, and an excellent parent to the two children of the first Mrs. Taylor."

"The best," sighed Staunton, with what seemed to be genuine regret. "But she became suspicious of her husband's frequent absences, which were not always as concerned with his supposed business as she had first thought. Somehow, perhaps by means of a private detective, or some other method, she discovered that her supposed beloved husband was maintaining another establishment in neighbouring Sutton Coldfield, and she decided to confront her husband with the knowledge. At this time, a coolness developed between her and Staunton's son.

"She told Staunton that she was about to reveal his double life, and confront his other wife with the knowledge of her existence. Frightened that he was about to be ruined, and quite possibly be prosecuted, for his duplicity, he returned home and saw his wife writing at the desk. He immediately guessed what she was about. He quietly let himself into the house and went to the kitchen for a knife. Entering the drawing-room, he confronted his wife, who was indeed writing the fatal missive. A violent argument ensued, during which he produced the kitchen knife, and in defence, she snatched up the long paperknife that lay in its holder on the desk. You really should have taken better note of that empty knife-holder, Inspector."

"Since we believed the murder weapon had already been discovered, it seemed to be of no importance," answered the abashed police agent.

"Well, well. Be that as it may. In the ensuing struggle, which took place in near-silence, the kitchen knife was dropped, and the stiletto paperknife passed from Martha Taylor to Henry Staunton, who in his blind fury used it to kill the unfortunate woman. It was at about this time that the seal was ripped from the watch-chain. The fastening is twisted on both the chain, and the seal itself, and I have no doubt that you will easily find a perfect match there, Inspector.

"You will remember Doctor Watson's characterisation of the fatal wounds, and also note the fact that Staunton here is left-handed. His son is right-handed, as I ascertained when I asked him to sketch the scene of the murder. The wounds could only have been inflicted either by standing behind the victim and stabbing her by reaching over her shoulder, stabbing downwards – a most awkward way of delivering the blows, and one which is contradicted by the position of the body's head relative to the chair – or alternatively if the victim was standing, by stabbing with the murderer facing his victim, using an overhand grip – less effective, perhaps, than the underhand grip, but ultimately fatal. Am I correct so far, Staunton?" He received no answer, other than a silent, grim-faced nod, and continued.

"Being faced with the undisputed fact that he was now the killer of the woman with whom he shared his house, his principal object now was to avoid detection. He quickly snatched up the fatal letter in its envelope, which had only just been addressed and blotted before he entered the room. He knew his son was in the house, and his twisted mind instantly conceived a way in which he could escape blame, and transfer it to his own flesh and blood."

"A foul and heinous act," growled Upton.

"He secreted the stiletto, and smeared the kitchen knife with blood before letting the chair fall with a crash, to alert the boy and to draw his attention, before letting himself out of the front door and silently re-locking it. He disposed of the murder weapon, and I have no doubt that if you drag the Minster Pool at the end where Dam Street runs close by, you will discover it there. The rest you know."

"I never meant to kill her!" wailed the unfortunate Staunton. "It was my intention only to prevent her from sending the letter."

"That's as may be," replied Inspector Upton in stony tones. "But instead of confessing to your guilt like a man, you attempted to fasten the crime on a poor defenceless young man – your own flesh and blood at that."

"I never meant him to go to the gallows," cried Staunton, in an agony of distress.

"Maybe you did not," answered the police agent. "But I will make every effort to ensure that you make that trip yourself. Thank you, Mr. Holmes. You have saved a young man's life, and prevented a grave miscarriage of justice."

"All I ask," replied Holmes, "is that my name not be mentioned in connection with this case. Inspector Upton shall take all the credit for the observations and deductions, and the bringing to justice of Mr. Henry Staunton. Come, Watson, our task is done, and I think that we shall sleep well tonight at the George before our return to London on the morrow."

"But why in heaven's name," I could not refrain from asking Holmes as we made our way from the police station, "did Staunton ask you to clear the boy's name, given that this inevitably would lead to the proof of his own guilt?"

Holmes shook his head. "He believed that he had committed the perfect crime, and that suspicion would never fall on him," he said. "We may see his retaining me as an act of bravado and cocking a snook at the police. After all, who would believe that a man who had hired the foremost man in his field to clear his son's name would himself be guilty of any wrongdoing? Unfortunately for Mr. Henry Staunton, he underestimated my abilities, as have so many others in the past. It is their loss."

"And the world's gain," I added.

Holmes's only answer was his familiar sardonic smile.

The Kingdom of the Blind

by Adrian Middleton

It was during the late autumn of our first year together that my relationship with Sherlock Holmes, the celebrated detective, took on the semblance of a routine. He had, for some months, continued to conduct his affairs without my assistance, mentioning only a handful of his cases and excusing his often lengthy disappearances with little or no explanation. On several occasions I had stumbled upon him coming and going in a number of rudimentary disguises. Each of these, he later explained to me, was put to use in different parts of the city.

"The secret to good intelligence," he had said upon his return to our apartment in the early hours of the morning, "is establishing a long and unremarkable presence in those parts of the city where crime, and potential clients, frequent. If I can pick up the rudiments of the different trades at the same time well, that improves the accuracy of my deductive reasoning."

"And the bruises?" I enquired, noting that many of his forays resulted in personal injury which he was, invariably, loathe to discuss.

"Rough and tumble is a way of life on the streets, Watson. The giving and taking of beatings is a matter of note that fixes my characters in the memories of those from whom I obtain my information; and it is a safer alternative to thievery and intemperance."

"I have no need to practice my medical skills, Holmes," I retorted. "You should take better care of yourself."

"I can assure you that it is only superficial – the London criminal relies more on reputation than skill, and as long as he thinks he has the upper hand there is little danger. I avoid the hardened sloggers for the best part."

"Except when your hubris gets the better of you."

"And have you seen that happen?" He challenged. "Control and discipline are bywords for professionalism. I know my limits."

"Indeed," I harrumphed, unconvinced. "You can at least rely on me to attend when you exceed them."

"Do you know, I believe that I can," he said, shaking away the traces of Fuller's Earth that had greyed the hair of his latest disguise, before making a fresh pot of coffee as I set about collecting the morning papers.

Upon my return, Holmes had changed into his dressing gown and was standing at our window, observing the beginning of the day's intercourse while I settled into my armchair to read the Illustrated London News. While my attention was focused on news of troops returning from Afghanistan, Holmes's continued to observe, occasionally glancing at his fob as if noting the time of those events which transpired on the streets beneath.

"We have a visitor, Watson," he said, gesturing towards the street below. "A friar of the Dominican Order – possibly Dutch – recently returned from Rome."

Joining Holmes at the window, I glanced across the street where the man who had attracted his attention paused, waiting to cross as a hansom passed him by. He was a young and portly man, with a great black overcoat and a wide brimmed hat, which I conceded gave him the air of a clergyman.

"Are you sure he's for us, Holmes?"

"His gaze was directed upon this very window, Watson, and his choice of crossing place is similarly specific. See? He crosses now so that he will arrive at our door."

"How can you be sure he is a friar?" I asked.

"I am occasionally called upon to carry out interventions on behalf of the Vatican. In doing so I have had the opportunity to study certain aspects of ecclesiastical society. For example, the weather is fine, and the cassock is the usual form of street dress. That our visitor wears a capello romano hat shows he has no fear of being identified as a Catholic, so the heavy coat may only suggest that he does not wish his order to be identified. While the hat is without distinguishing features, suggesting a deacon or a seminarian, the hairstyle suggests that it covers a tonsure. Hence a friar."

"That still doesn't explain why he might be Dominican, or Dutch," said I.

"He carries beneath his arm two rare books of Dutch origin, and the Blackfriars are the most studious, the most surreptitious, and the most well-travelled of the Catholic orders."

"And Rome?"

Holmes merely smiled, asking if I would be so kind as to attend to the door. Returning to his chair, he was perfectly composed by the time we heard the knocking that announced our guest.

"Come," said Holmes loudly as I opened the door.

The friar entered the room silently, his piercing blue gaze scouring it as he removed his hat, revealing, as Holmes had predicted, that the top of his head had been shaved.

"Mister Holmes?" he said, with an unmistakably Dutch accent, "I am Brother Pius Augustus of the Order of Preachers, rector pro tempore to the Catholic University in Kensington."

"A Dominican?" Holmes smiled at me, making no effort to conceal his triumph. "This is my associate, Doctor Watson."

Acknowledging the man, who placed his hat and the two volumes he carried upon a side table while I closed the door and withdrew to take a comfortable spot by the window.

"Please," Holmes continued, "be seated, and tell me what matter brings you directly from the Apostolic Palace?"

The young friar took the seat opposite Holmes, pausing to look in my direction. For a moment our eyes locked and it felt as if he was looking directly into my soul. I withered, breaking away as the friar turned his gaze towards my friend, who met it with an equally steely look of his own. It was suddenly as if I were not present, and that these two powerful minds were locked in some invisible test of strength from which, I had no doubt, Holmes would emerge victorious.

"How could you tell from whence I came?"

"While both of those books were recently bound in the ecclesiastical province of Utrecht in the Netherlands, they have since been returned to Rome."

"How could you possibly know this?"

"The uppermost volume bears a seal. Archivum Secretum Apostolicum Vaticanu. Stamped on a new binding, it confirms you were in the Vatican compound quite recently. Furthermore, your coat has been weathered by your journey, suggesting you are presently returned to these shores."

"I am impressed," said the friar. "You have been to the Holy See yourself?"

"On several occasions," my friend confirmed. "While there I gained some understanding of Catholic binderies – I had intended to turn my notes into a monograph, but the subject was so specialised that I dismissed its usefulness. It seems the knowledge found a purpose after all."

"Then you are, indeed, the man to consult." "Indeed? Then you had best state your case."

"It is a matter of the gravest importance, Mr. Holmes. The fates of the Roman Church and of all forms of Christian worship, rest upon it."

"Hmm." Holmes sunk into his chair, his fingers steepled. "I must have the truth, and all of it, sir. It seems unusual that you would visit me at this time of the morning."

"Why do you say this?"

"I presume that you are a devout follower of the Liturgy of the Hours, and therefore you do not conduct meetings without careful timing. A planned appointment would have to take place between early and mid-morning prayer, and yet here you are, in my office, at the very time you should be observing terce. Your visit is therefore an unscheduled one."

"That is so," said Pius, slumping a little at Holmes's deduction. "I will tell you all. You have heard of the philosopher Empedocles?"

Holmes nodded. "Not just a philosopher. A political activist and a fraudster."

"Fraudster? Why do you say that?"

"As I recall, Empedocles was meant to have certain... powers.

Similar to those of Jesus Christ, if I am not mistaken."

"So the histories would tell us, but why would that make him a fraudster?"

"I hardly think the Catholic Church would be interested in canonizing him. He claimed to be a god."

"I can assure you that his miracles were genuine. It was Empedocles who established that the four elements of earth, air, fire and water make up the structures in the world. His powers were derived from an understanding of the divine, and they directly inspired the works of Saint Albertus Magnus."

"Albertus the Dominican?"

"Quite so, Mr. Holmes. The works of Empedocles were recorded in the Index Librorum Prohibitorum, and held in the Vatican Secret Archive until the sixteenth century, when they disappeared."

"So they are both sacred texts and banned?"

"The Church has been attempting to recover them

ever since. Imagine, Mr. Holmes, such secrets falling into the wrong hands. Miracles performed by heathens would undermine the very foundations of the church."

"You seriously think this book can enable the performance of miracles?" I asked. "Are we talking about medical miracles like making the blind see and the lame walk, or those of the biblical variety, like summoning plagues or walking on water? It's preposterous."

"No more preposterous than our own saints performing such miracles, Doctor?" said Holmes, gently chiding my interference.

"Well..." I realised I was on tricky ground, not wanting to offend the church.

"We are talking about real power, gentlemen, and we believe that power may fall into the wrong hands. Whilst travelling through Europe I learned that certain...terms, first used by Empedocles and later Albertus Magnus, have started to emerge here in London. These terms could only have come from the lost papyri, and I can only conclude that these heretics have access to them."

"Who are these heretics?"

"They are Freemasons, of the Rosicrucian Society of England. Dr. William Westcott and Dr. William Woodman. Woodman is the Supreme Magus of his Order, and they are expanding quickly into all of England and Europe."

"I know of them," said I. "Woodman is a retired police surgeon, and Westcott is a Deputy Coroner in the East End."

"So he is," said Holmes, "and you are sure these men are a danger?

Surely a formal approach –"

"Out of the question. The Catholic Church must have nothing to do with them. The Holy Father has been quite specific on the matter. It is his belief that the sect of the Freemasons are determined to bring the Holy Church into ruin."

"And what would you have me do? Expose the Order in

some fashion, or simply retrieve the lost texts?"

"Retrieve the texts, if you can. I am told that Woodman has a translation, and that a German Countess, Frau Sprengel, holds the originals."

"Told by whom?"

"A fellow priest that I met upon my travels. As you can see from what I carry, my interest in books is notable."

"I see. I am sure you will understand that burglary is not a service that I provide. All that I can offer is to negotiate on your behalf. Anonymously, of course. Is there, perhaps, a sum that the Church would be willing to pay for the retrieval of such documents?"

"Absolutely not! I ask only that you confirm the existence and whereabouts of these papers. This will enable...further action to be taken."

"Very well, Brother Pius, I shall look into these Freemasons to determine true origin of this manuscript. If it exists, I shall confirm its location to you."

"That seems a most acceptable arrangement, Mr. Holmes. If you need me, I shall be at Abingdon House."

With that the friar rose, retrieved his hat and books, and left.

"Well, Watson?" said Holmes once our guest had departed. "What say you?"

"Clerical mumbo-jumbo if you ask me," said I. "Miracles indeed." "It is not what we believe that makes this case of interest, but what the friar believes."

"The friar? Surely he is just a messenger."

"Hardly. Upon closer examination, I observed a number of characteristics that disturbed me. The books, for example. There is a reason that he keeps them close. No volume bearing the seal of the secret archive may be removed. They are considered to be the Pope's personal property."

"Are you suggesting that he stole it?"

"That may be a strict interpretation, but I suspect he believes his actions are both legitimate and justified. Did you observe the title of the uppermost book?"

"I did not," said I. "I do recall the second had a word upon its spine. Empto. Probably Emptor, or buyer. A catalogue or index of book for sale?"

"Well spotted, Watson, but the title of the uppermost book was Logicae Seu Philosophiae Rationalis Elementa."

"The elements of logical or rational philosophy?"

"I have no doubt that his story was otherwise true, but on whose behalf is he pursuing miraculous powers? Brother Pius is following a most personal agenda."

"To become a miracle worker? There is little chance of – Holmes, his eyes!" I said, recalling the piercing gaze. "There was something about his eyes."

"Indeed. He is a student of mesmerism. I am pleased that you noticed."

"Don't be quite so surprised," said I. "I'm not a complete bumbler." "Of course you aren't. One day you might even learn the trick that turns observed fact into logical deduction."

The Georgian town house that William Woodman kept in Stoke Newington was a grand affair, far beyond the meagre salary of a retired police surgeon. According to Holmes, diligence and a good inheritance had left him with the means to keep both his London home and a country garden in Exeter. Even before we reached the main door there was evidence of his horticultural prowess, with tall exotic plants obscuring its frontage with a display of variety and colour that would not have gone amiss at Kew.

The butler – a short and stocky man, with a thick grey beard and scarcely any hair – was so poorly blessed that his features brought to mind the philosopher Socrates, renowned for his ugliness. Perhaps the talk of Empedocles had brought this thought to mind, or perhaps it was the stark atrium that greeted us, alternately lined with exotic succulents and the marble busts of diverse philosophers in the manner of a public building rather than a private home.

"Impressive," said Holmes as we were escorted up the grand staircase that led us to the doctor's private rooms. "It would seem that Dr. Woodman receives a good number of guests here, and on a regular basis."

The butler remained silent at Holmes's observation, but the implication was clear – that Woodman conducted masonic rites at his home. Atop the stair, we were guided past a portrait of Woodman himself, dressed in full masonic regalia – something which drew an irritated tut from my companion. He looked quite regal adorned by the signs and symbols of his office, made more so by the splendid bifurcated beard that dominated his face.

Moments later, with our presence announced and the servant withdrawn, we stood at the heart of an impressive library. Its walls were lined with mahogany shelves that stretched from the floor to the ornate alabaster coving that skirted the ceiling. On the floor was spread a plush Turkish carpet, its chequered pattern broken up by a variety of motifs – compasses, levels, skulls, stars, and crosses – reflecting its owner's passions. The shelves were well-ordered, with travelogues separated from historical and religious volumes. On the far wall I saw an impressive selection of Latin and Greek volumes – mostly esoterica and books of philosophy. Enough to momentarily draw my attention away from our host, with whom Holmes seemed to be making firm friends. Woodman was much like his painting, but portlier and thinner of hair, with bold white flecks peppering his beard. He dressed plainly, but well, and carried beside him an ornate cane which, somewhat garishly, was carved from ivory and topped with a silver skull and crossed bones.

Their handshake lingered, just enough for me to note its purpose, and I wondered if I would be aware had I not already been told of the doctor's interests.

"Mr. Sherlock Holmes," the doctor greeted us warmly. "I have heard good things about you. Are you here to –"

"I shall not dwell on niceties, Dr. Woodman," said

Holmes. "We are here on a delicate matter, concerning a rare text believed to be in your possession."

"Oh?" Woodman's jaw dropped, clearly shaken by the statement. Composing himself, he stepped away from us, gesturing toward the shelves of his impressive collection. "As you can see, I own many books. Perhaps you can pick out the volume concerned."

"This particular volume is not here," said Holmes, perusing its contents. "Not in this room at least. Perhaps next door...."

"Next door? There is no adjoining room."

"On the contrary, Doctor. While there are no visible doors, you appear to have chosen to adapt one of your shelves so that it may function as the entrance to the study that lies beyond. The shelf containing philosophy, I'll venture."

"How can you know that, Holmes?"

"Pile direction, Watson. A simple enough deduction." "I'm sorry?" I did not follow.

"The carpet. When one is cleaning carpets it is usual for dirt to be brushed in a single direction – towards the door, where it can be easily swept and collected. In this room, with but a single door, the direction of the carpet pile moves away, and one can see the cleaning strokes have created a unique pile direction, showing that dirt was swept towards a single point on the opposite side of the room – towards the door concealed behind 'philosophy'."

"Forgive me, Mr. Holmes," said Woodman, his pleasant demeanour giving way to irritation. "While I commend your powers of observation, I fail to see how such impertinence can be excused. I welcome you as a guest, and in return you request – no, you demand – to be shown into a private part of my house. It is unbecoming of a brother –"

"Or of a gentleman. Indeed, Doctor, I must apologise. It is natural for a man of my profession to assert himself when he is being misdirected, and no offence was intended. If the text concerned is not available for examination or, indeed, for acquisition, then a polite refusal would suffice. I had assumed you would be more interested in negotiation."

"Of course. I, too, apologise. I believe I know the text of which you speak, and I should indeed have declined your request."

"Might I ask the name of the text?" Holmes asked. "I'm sorry."

"My client failed to name it. I was given such information as to confirm its identity on sight, but he neglected to reveal its title."

"The black friar. Well, he is a persistent fellow, though I am surprised that compensation might be offered. His last attempt to obtain it involved harsh demands and the threat of eternal damnation."

"No, I am not negotiating on behalf of the clergy." That was news to me. Assuming it to be some subterfuge on Holmes's behalf, I held my counsel. "My client merely wishes to keep the original safe. I take it that Frau Sprengel is a fiction, and that you own both the original document and its translation?"

"The Countess? Ha, I see. She is real enough. I was in her company when the friar last approached me. It was she who had the text translated."

"On the Continent?"

"She operates out of Nuremberg," Woodman confirmed, "but before we talk further, I must ask who it is you represent, Mr. Holmes?"

"I am not at liberty to say, other than that my client has held certain records since the dissolution of the monasteries during the time of Henry VIII."

"So," Woodman's mood lightened, "am I to understand that you wish to acquire the book, but not for the friar?"

"You keep mentioning this friar," said Holmes, bald-faced, "but who is he?"

"A client of Frau Sprengel, like myself." "A regular client?" Holmes pressed.

"Regular enough that I've seen him twice – once abroad and once here, in London."

"Excuse me," said I, desperate to catch up. "Why would a Latin-speaking friar need an English translation?"

"He seeks either edition," said Woodman. "The Frau is a businesswoman with many clients. Her services are highly sought after, especially since –"

" – since the Italian Unification?"

"Quite so, Mr. Holmes," said Woodman, turning his attention to the bookshelf and activating a concealed catch. "Please observe my rules. This is my private collection, and many items are of great personal value. I trust you have no interest in my translation?"

"It is yours to keep, Doctor, although I suggest you make another copy at the soonest opportunity. I suspect your friar will not give up its pursuit so easily."

Swinging away from us, the concealed door opened onto a near identical room to the first, with equally full shelves. The singular difference was the floor. In place of carpet was polished parquet, and in the centre of the room sat a large table surrounded by chairs, suggesting that the chamber doubled as a private meeting room. A pile of books rested on the table, and it was to these that Woodman gravitated. Among them, wrapped within a velvet cloth, sat a hefty volume. Sliding it carefully across the table, the doctor gingerly eased back the covering to expose a large weathered binding, heavily dog-eared, with its spine barely holding it together.

"This," said Woodman, "is the Ars Philosophica of Empedocles, itself a Latin translation from lost papyri."

Holmes drew a magnifying glass from within the folds of his coat, leaning forward to examine the cover in more detail.

"There is an Index mark," he said, "barely visible and of great age, but it confirms from whence the book came. Might I see the translation?" Woodman gestured towards a second volume, and Holmes and I could see that it was a freshly bound copy of the original. Not just a documented translation, but a facsimile in which the Latin had been replaced with English."

"So, Frau Sprengel is herself a bookbinder?" "Of the highest quality. You did not know this?"

"I had my suspicions," said Holmes. "Now, let us discuss terms on the original."

Our hansom journey back to Baker Street was one filled with questions. Having held my tongue throughout our visit to Stoke Newington, I could barely contain my curiosity.

"Well played, Holmes," said I, congratulating my friend on his acquisition, "but why did you purchase the book when the friar asked only for its whereabouts? And what was all that about another client?"

"It was no deception, Watson." Holmes smiled thinly, patting his velvet-wrapped prize as he spoke. "I do indeed have a second client. Two in fact."

"So Brother Pius Augustus –"

"Shall be told the whereabouts of the translation in due course, but he shall not know that we have the original document. We shall visit him presently."

"How did you know Woodman had both copies?"

"I didn't, but it follows that if you pay for a document to be translated you may have acquired that document first. When I realised that our friar had attempted to secure the book whilst in Europe, several of my suspicions were confirmed. What I can be certain of is that Brother Pius Augustus has no Papal approval."

"How –"

"My work for the Vatican has been most discrete and, more importantly, could only be surmised from the various enquiries I have made in and around the secret archive. The Holy Father and I have a...personal understanding."

"Great Scott, Holmes. You're saying that the Pope himself is your client?"

"He is a client. Several years ago I travelled in Europe, and paid a visit to Rome. It was a difficult time. Tensions between Italy and the prisoner in the Vatican were strained, and my request to receive access to the Index Prohibitorum was unusual. Nevertheless, I was received by Cardinal Pecci, the Camerlengo of the Holy Roman Church, and we discussed my requirements at length. It turned out that he had been something of a detective himself. During his time as provincial governor of Benevento, he had rooted out an entire criminal conspiracy. Quite the policeman; and so he already had knowledge of me when my name crossed his desk.

"We struck up quite a friendship, and after three weeks we struck a bargain. I would receive an entry card to the secret archive, along with a retainer from the Cardinal, in exchange for certain services. These I perform sporadically, and in due course Cardinal Pecci became Pope Leo XIII."

"So you acquired the book on his behalf?"

"After a fashion. The service I render is one of detection and retrieval, but – as I explained to Dr. Woodman – the book is not to be returned to the Vatican. Not yet, at least. Books have been disappearing from the archive for many years, but in 1870 the seizure of the Papal States saw many documents and works of art disappear, and Cardinal Pecci believed that an underground trade was in operation, and that the Vatican was no longer safe. A détente has been negotiated between the Anglican and Roman churches. Britain, as the dominant world power, is better placed to protect the world from those forces that might otherwise challenge the status quo, and has agreed to the secure storage of whatever papal treasures I uncover."

"And the Freemasons?

"I have no view on the matter. It is true that Pope Leo has spoken out against them, but that is not my concern. I shall fulfil my obligation to the friar, and also my duty to the Pope. For now, Frau Sprengel of Nuremberg beckons, and I suspect I shall be gone for a number of weeks. If Woodman's information is correct, she lies at the heart of the smuggling conspiracy, and I may enjoy some success in my continuing service to Rome."

Upon our return to Baker Street, Holmes and I carefully packaged his prize, arranging for its delivery to a private establishment in Westminster. At the time, I attached no significance to the gentlemen's club with which I would become acquainted in the years to come. Holmes then turned his attentions to some research and other correspondence, asking that I turn my own attentions to an account of our day thus far. It was not until after we had taken tea that, with the evening drawing close, we summoned a cab and paid a visit to Brother Pius Augustus.

"Why so late in the day?" I had asked.

"The Liturgy of the Hours, Watson. The habits of the clergy are quite strict, and I have timed our arrival to coincide with the commencement of Evening Prayers. That should give us a good half hour."

We arrived at what appeared to be an abandoned premises in the heart of South Kensington. Abingdon House, the former Catholic University College. It had been bought up some years ago, having become an ivy-covered ruin, but the new owner, Monsignor Thomas Capel, had great plans, convincing the Archbishop of Westminster that it could provide a fee-paying education to those seminarians of wealthy families whose entry into Oxford and Cambridge had been forbidden by papal decree. Staffed by an eclectic mix of lay tutors ranging from the eccentric genius to the ethically corrupt, the experiment was a dismal failure. Beset by financial irregularities and scandals concerning the moral values of his students, Capel was removed as Rector in '78. Its tarnished reputation saw the College emptied of its remaining students. Whatever purpose it had since been put to, the building again looked sad and derelict, the ivy overgrown and a strange miasma infused the air around it.

"What is that awful smell?" said I as we passed through

"Explain to me why all the books I have seen are banned volumes listed as missing from the Index Prohibitorum?"

The boy's face fell, and he withdrew with haste.

Rather than await our host, Holmes rose from his seat, gesturing for me to follow. Christopher moved quickly through the empty house, and we were careful to make as little sound as we could. The faint drone of distant evensong aided our stealthy pursuit of the boy, but on more than one occasion he paused to listen out for us. Each time we froze, holding our breath steady and awaiting his continued movement.

Passing through the kitchen, Christopher stepped out into the overgrown gardens, carefully picking his way along a well-trodden path that led us to the sound of the singing voices. As we closed upon a small chapel hidden well within the grounds, Holmes steadied me, allowing Christopher to put some distance between us.

"Do you hear those words?" whispered Holmes. "A musical chant in Latin. A psalm?"

"I distinctly heard them sing the praises of something other than God. Where Deum should have been, I heard Satanam!"

"Surely not," said I, aghast at the implications.

"With me, Watson!"

Holmes sprinted forwards, catching up to the cautious Christopher and dashing past him. Close behind, I paused to stop the boy, who called out as I ran on, following in my friend's footsteps.

I was at Holmes's heel, passing through the great oak door that led us into the chapel where the Satanic Vespers was in full sway. At first it looked no different from a Christian ceremony, but there were symbolic differences. The smoke that drifted from censers didn't bear the rich smell of incense, but something more...exotic. Holmes would later refer me to the rituals of the Wixárica Indians of Mexico, and the heads of wild cacti that they cultivate and use to dull pain and encourage hallucinations. Sure enough, their very presence was to affect my judgement in the coming hours.

As the seminarians knelt in prayer, Brother Pius Augustus stood at the head of the chapel, his robes a parody of the Catholic faith. Embroidered golden pentacles adorned the cope that he wore over his cassock. Over these was draped a great chain of office, at the centre of which was mounted an inverted pectoral cross. Behind him, set over the altar, was a decidedly unchristian carving, replacing the traditional crucifix. Instead, it was a tree in the form of a tau cross, from which a dying man – decapitated and suspended upside down – hung. I was uncertain of the meaning, but it quickened my resolve. Drawing my service revolver from my coat pocket, I held it aloft and discharged a round, its booming echo bringing an end to the sound of corrupted voices praising the depths of spiritual evil. As I did so, the dozen youths knelt in prayer lifted their faces upwards, their blind eyes seeing only the twisted visions induced by the foul stench that filled the chamber.

"Brother Pius Augustus!" Holmes barked, "I believe you may have overstepped your authority in this matter."

The priest's hate-filled eyes looked coldly upon us, with no acknowledgement of shock or surprise whatsoever.

"By what authority do you enter these premises, Mr. Holmes?" he snapped.

"You invited me to report at my convenience. I did come to share my discoveries, but I can see that you are otherwise engaged in the corruption of innocent souls."

"On the contrary, Mr. Holmes, I draw my power from them. Behold!"

For the second time I witnessed the friar's mesmeric gaze, but this time in a different context, and a chill swept through my bones as I could feel my own resolve begin to weaken. Sherlock Holmes, however, simply tilted back his head and laughed, and as he did so, the penetrating gaze subsided, and the friar's shoulders slumped.

My friend, meanwhile, reached into his coat and withdrew a leaf of carbon-printed paper. "This," he explained, "is a copy of the missive I dispatched to his Holiness in Rome this afternoon."

Holding it forth for Brother Pius Augustus to snatch from his hands, Holmes continued. "It outlines your activities, smuggling books from Rome under the pretext of binding, and of how you trade some books on the black market in return for books more appropriate to your needs. I shall be travelling to Nuremberg presently, where I hope to confront Frau Sprengel to obtain her testimony. It was unwise of you to try and use me to deal with your rivals."

"How did you know this?" Pius Augustus demanded.

"The second book you carried into my rooms. The word Empto was imprinted upon its spine. This can surely only be Liber officiorum spirituum, seu liber dictus Empto Salomonis, de principibus et regibus demonorium. A legendary book of spirits thought lost in the sixteenth century. A treasure to those who pursue the dark arts, and it was enough for me to construct an argument convincing enough to see you excommunicated."

"Boys..." Holmes called upon the dozen blind seminarians, "you should consider yourselves lucky that my letter was posted before I learned you were complicit in this abhorrence. We shall return to the House, whereupon you shall prepare yourselves for a visit from the Archbishop of Westminster, whom I believe has jurisdiction in this matter."

With those words, he turned upon his heel and we marched from the chapel, a column of blind seminarians marching in our wake. As we headed towards the house, I paused for a breath of air, quite giddy from the heady infusion that had filled my lungs. As I did so, glancing up, I saw something – a sign – I hope never to see again.

"Holmes!" I cried. "The Moon! See how large it is, and see how it is bleeding."

"I see it, Watson," he replied, "and I see that you are

much better at administering strong drugs than you are at inhaling them."

The Adventure of the Pawnbroker's Daughter

by David Marcum

"I appreciate the gesture," said my friend, Sherlock Holmes, that spring morning, "but I do not foresee a happy conclusion. Still," he continued, reaching for his pipe on the mantel, "if you persist in going forward with this plan, perhaps you would allow me to suggest a title?"

I turned from my desk, where I had been pursuing my labors in solitude for quite some time. As was often the case when some pressing matter did not result in his rising early, Holmes had slept late, and had just entered the sitting room from his adjacent bedroom. Without a glance toward the coffee pot on the table, he made his way toward the fireplace, where he proceeded to pack his pipe with all of the plugs and dottles accumulated and dried from the previous day. A disgusting habit, to be sure, but by this time, after having shared rooms with Holmes for a little over a year, an unsurprising one.

"A title?" I asked. "How on earth do you know that my work here needs a title? Perhaps I am simply constructing a list of items to purchase when I go out for a walk."

"Clearly you are not working on such a list," he said, teeth clenched around the stem of his pipe, working to get the tobacco scraps burning. "The journal you have open before you would not be used for that sort of thing. Rather, you are certainly constructing something of greater importance than the list that you have suggested. Obviously, you have been referring to some of the documents that are also arrayed on your desk. I will not insult you by referring to the other indications that point in the same direction. Therefore, the probabilities are that you will need a title.

"Perhaps," he continued, dropping into his chair, "you already have one in mind, but I truly fear as to what it might be. Might I suggest, instead, something along the lines of 'Some Notes Upon the Tracing of Homicidal American Cab Drivers Residing Within the Capital, as Related to Particularly Vicious Revenge Crimes and Long-Standing Mormon-Associated Feuds, with Associated Documentation Concerning the Use of Chance When Selecting Obscure Water-Soluble Poisons.' "

He was nearly out of breath by the time he finished this recital, but there was a twinkle in his eye and a trace of a smile upon his lips, and I realized that, even though he obviously knew about the subject of my morning's work, he was not seriously advising that I denominate it as he had suggested.

"In what way did you ever – ?" I started to ask how he had guessed, before I remembered that Holmes never did that.

Seeing that I was aware of my near-error, he replied, "Last night, before you went up to your room, you appeared to be giving thought to some matter or other, with regular glances toward your desk, and your journals kept therein. Finally, upon standing up, you walked to the mantelpiece, where you took a moment to finger the wedding ring, still lying there over a year after the fact, that was found with the body in that house in the Brixton Road. Clearly you were considering adding to the work that you threatened a year ago to write and publish, recounting our first investigation together. When I entered this morning and found you writing, the confirmation was complete."

I nodded. I had been trying to progress toward a published version of that occasion when I had first been privileged to observe Holmes's methods, involving the capture of Jefferson Hope. I have long kept journals, and my lack of the need for a surfeit of sleep, especially after the events of the Afghan campaign, had often let me write deep into the night. I regularly made extensive notes of Holmes's cases. But this matter, referred to by Holmes as involving "the scarlet thread of murder" and "the finest study I ever came across: a study in scarlet," was different, in that I wanted it to be polished for presentation to the public. It had been something over a year since the events had occurred, and I had felt the stirrings once again to have the thing published. And yet, I was still having difficulties in determining how to write the larger portion of Jefferson Hope's own tale, which explained those events of so long ago that had served as the motivation for the crimes. Perhaps something would suggest itself at some time in the future. Looking down at what I had already accomplished that morning, I decided that my labors were sufficient unto the day, and stood, whereupon I moved to my chair to the left of the fireplace, across from Holmes in his.

In those days, Holmes still tried to maintain the idea that he was capable of, for the most part, conducting his practice from his armchair. He had described for me, on the day when he first explained his profession, that he was consulted by a great number of people, and that he was generally able, simply from hearing their description of the facts, to set them on the right scent. Sometimes, however, he was forced to rise and go forth to examine things first hand. "Now and again," he had said, "a case turns up which is a little more complex. Then I have to bustle about and see things with my own eyes."

I did not realize it then, in the spring of 1882, that when Holmes was attempting, as often as possible, to reach his solutions from his armchair, he was no doubt trying to emulate his older brother, Mycroft, who functioned in much the same way for the government from his regular haunts within Whitehall and Pall Mall. In those early days, I did not yet know of Mycroft's existence, and simply thought that Holmes was trying to perfect his methods in order to show that, with the correct information, and also by drawing educated and experienced conclusions, an armchair reasoner could do better than any Scotland Yarder who was physically on the scene of a crime. Little did I realize that I would soon see a demonstration.

Having recently been rewriting the portion of my manuscript dealing with this very aspect of Holmes's practice, I led with a question regarding some of his more recent clients, most of whom had required a certain amount of investigation in the field. From there, Holmes and I had settled into a discussion of other facts related to the Jefferson Hope case, and I suddenly realized with a mixture of amusement and concern that Holmes did not seem inclined to notify Mrs. Hudson that he was up and about. His pipe would apparently be serving as his breakfast this day, as it had on so many other mornings.

I was considering whether to ring for more hot coffee for my own benefit when we perceived the bell at the front door. In a moment, we heard the sound of movement coming up the steps.

"Lestrade," said Holmes. "Unmistakable. And he has someone with him. A girl, I think, from the lighter tread. Young enough to take the steps quickly, as compared to the inspector's more seasoned and steady gait. Do you hear how she takes three steps to his two, and then waits for just a moment as he catches up, the scuff on the stairs from his boots as regular as clockwork? And of course that inward twist of his foot is the same as if he had called out his presence."

A knock on the door proved that Holmes was correct. It was our friend, the inspector, with a girl of no more than twenty, and possibly younger. She was dainty, a pretty thing, and looking quite small, even next to the short, wiry policeman. Her blonde hair was pulled back rather severely and pinned beneath a small hat, but that fact could not hide either its luster or curls, and only served to accentuate the fresh healthy color of her complexion.

Lestrade showed the girl forward toward the basket chair, before comfortably making himself at home in front of the settee. As we stood, he introduced her as Miss Letitia Porter. "Of Limehouse," he added.

"How do you do?" said Miss Porter.

Holmes turned his head and gave a speculative glance. "Surely not originally from Limehouse?" he said. "I fancy somewhere more to the east."

She looked startled for a moment, and then said, "I grew up with my mother in Clacton-on-Sea. I only returned to live here with my father two years ago."

Holmes nodded. He gestured for her to sit. When she had done so, the rest of us followed.

"How did you know?" she asked. "Where I grew up?"

Holmes crossed his legs and said, "I have made something of a study of various accents. It is a little specialty of mine to identify most of the manners of speech in the different London districts, although I have not yet carried my researches to the point where I can identify specific streets. On a larger scale, I can delineate a number of regional dialects. Yours, from the eastern coast, was mere child's play."

As the girl glanced toward Lestrade, who looked as surprised as she, Holmes said, "How may we help you today?"

The girl dropped her eyes, and then twisted slightly to defer to Lestrade, who was leaning forward with his arms resting on his knees, hat grasped in one hand. He cleared his throat, sat back, and placed the hat beside him. "Miss Porter dropped in today at the Yard seeking our assistance. She fears that her father, who owns a pawn shop in Limehouse, is in some sort of danger, although she cannot precisely define its nature. After hearing her story, I thought that this matter might be of interest to you, Mr. Holmes, and we wasted no time in coming around."

Holmes's eyes cut toward the Lestrade, and the two shared a knowledgeable look which went over my head. Holmes then turned his attention back to the girl, who had not seemed to notice the quick exchange between the consulting detective and the Inspector. Holmes made a small come-along gesture to her as he wished for her to commence her explanation.

Clearing her throat, she twined her small hands and began to speak. "I was born here in London, an only child. My father owns a small pawnbroker's shop in Limehouse, at the southwest corner of Commercial Road where it meets Bekesbourne Street. It was where we lived when I was very small, in the rooms upstairs. When I was but two years old, my mother, who had never been comfortable here in the rough life of London, returned to her people by the sea, taking me with her. My parents remained legally married, but had no further contact with one another, except by way of the occasional letter.

"My father continued to reside above his shop, making a living, and seemingly content to get by, year after year. I grew up with my mother's family, aware of my father, but never communicating with him, in respect of my mother's wishes. Two years ago, when I was sixteen, my mother passed away from a short illness. My grandparents, with whom we had lived since moving back to Clacton-on-Sea, had died a few years earlier, and I was left living in the house where I grew up, but with it now under the ownership of my uncle and his wife.

"I may say that my aunt-by-marriage and I did not get along very well, and I began to feel that I must seek a life elsewhere. While disposing of my mother's possessions,

I came across many of her old letters from my father, written both when they were courting, and later, after their separation. While they had never seen each other again after we left London, it seemed that that they may have, in truth, had some lasting feelings for one another. Father had expressed a genuine interest in my progress and well-being, and it occurred to me that it might be a good thing if I were to return to London, the idea of which had never seemed unpleasant to me, as it had to my mother.

"To relate the matter in as short a manner as possible, I wrote to my father, expressing my interest in joining him, and he was very amenable to the plan. I left the house by the seaside where I grew up, moved back to the capital, and soon settled into the routine of being a pawnbroker's daughter."

"And that was two years ago, you say?" interrupted Holmes. "Nearly," the girl replied.

"Go on."

"I must admit that I seem to have some skills in the working of the business. My father and I quickly became the best of friends, and he had no compunction regarding me learning the trade. I am rather proud to admit that I have an eye for spotting little treasures here and there, and in the time since I've returned, I've become adept at dealing with the public as well. Quite frankly, my father's business has more than doubled since I have started assisting him.

"About three months ago, we had become so busy that we found it necessary to hire an assistant. I was involved in the selection, and we were fortunate enough to employ a man named Floyd Willis. He is tall and strong, quite handsome actually, and as willing to take orders from a woman as he is my father, which is an important aspect to our arrangement. It should come as no surprise, then, that the two of us, thrown together so frequently, should fall in love. We are to be married later in the spring." She held out her hand, showing a modest engagement ring.

We murmured our congratulations, although Holmes's

best wishes were more perfunctory, as he obviously desired for the story to continue, the scene now having been set. However, to the girl's surprise, he leaned in for a closer look at the ring. "May I?" he said, surprising her as he took her hand and proceeded to turn it this way and that, studying it for a moment before releasing her and leaning back in his chair. "Please go on," he said.

She took a breath and said, "We now come to the matter which led me to seek assistance, in spite of my father's wishes that the entire affair should be ignored. A couple of months ago, not long after the new year began, Father and I went downstairs one morning to discover a sheet of paper lying in plain sight on the countertop in the main shop. The front door was still locked, and there was no indication of how anyone could have gained entrance to our building. We were both certain that there was no sheet of paper there when we had closed up and gone upstairs the night before. Even before unlocking the shop that morning, we made sure that the building was still secure, and that no one had remained hidden inside from the night before. I insisted upon it."

"And this note?" asked Holmes. "What did it say? Do you still have it?"

"No, Mr. Holmes. After reading it, my father burned it. But I still remember quite vividly what it said: 'Your days are numbered, as are the grains of sand within the glass. You shall pay for your sins.' "

"What sort of writing was it? What of the paper?"

"It was quarto sized," she said, looking to her right, over Holmes's head, as she seemed to visualize it. "It was yellowish, and peculiarly thick."

"Was the writing small, or did it fill the page?" "Oh, it filled it from top to bottom and side to side."

"And the writing itself? Was is practiced, or crude?"

"Crude, I should say. The letters were quite square, and the ink had bled into the paper."

"Black ink?"

"Yes, I believe that it was. I only saw it for a moment before Father dashed it into the fireplace."

"Did your father have any explanation of the matter?"

"He gave none. I was obviously concerned, due to both the threatening nature of the words, and the fact that the note had been placed into our shop, which was securely locked."

"And what of his reaction?" asked Holmes. "Was he concerned as well?"

"He did not seem to be. Rather, he seemed angry, although he did not lose his temper." She glanced to the side, frowning. "He did say something along the lines of 'So that's his game, is it?' or something to that effect." She returned her gaze to Holmes. "I cannot quite recall."

"And there have been other warning letters as well?"

"Yes, two that I know about, but I was unable to read them, as Father destroyed them as soon as he found them. I believe that he started rising earlier than usual to make sure that he entered the shop first."

"So there could have been other letters in addition to the ones that you have seen?"

"Yes," she said.

"How was it that you saw the other two, and yet you were unable to read them?"

"On those occasions, I heard Father rise early and make his way downstairs. I slipped down behind him and saw him retrieve the letters from the counter. They seemed to be the same type of paper, and were lying in the same place. As soon as he read them, he threw them in the fire."

"And there was already a fire going in the shop on those mornings?" "We have a stove there that we leave banked from the night before. The remaining coals were enough to burn the letters."

"Why did you not go down early on your own on some mornings to get a look at one of the letters?"

"Quite honestly, Mr. Holmes, I was afraid. I did not

"Why did your mother leave him? Did she have any knowledge that you have gleaned through conversations or correspondence that might give any hint of unsavory activities in your father's background?"

"Nothing, Mr. Holmes. Their letters were simply news about each other's lives, and about me. And my mother was never open to discussing my father with me while she was alive."

Holmes was silent for a moment, and then said, "Your visit to Scotland Yard this morning. What did you hope to accomplish?"

She seemed at a loss for just a moment. "To be frank, I am not certain. The situation has become increasingly intolerable, due to the tension within the shop. It was worse this morning, between my father and Mr. Willis. Finally, I resolved that I could stand it no longer, and I set out to seek help. Without telling either of them, I quietly left and walked to Scotland Yard."

Holmes raised his eyebrows. "You walked? Surely not! That was quite a distance to traverse, from Limehouse to Whitehall."

"Not nearly as far as you would think, Mr. Holmes," said Miss Porter. "In truth, I wanted to use some of the time to think. I need help, but I also did not want to do something which might cause more trouble. In all honesty, I was afraid that I might inadvertently expose some secret of my father's, or of Mr. Willis's. But at the same time, if Mr. Willis is in fact the kind of man that is threatening my father, then I wish to know the truth before our betrothal progresses any further."

"Quite," said Holmes. "As I'm sure Inspector Lestrade would tell you, the situation as you have so far described it does not fall within the purview of the police. No actionable crime has been committed, and the victim of whatever persecution that is occurring, your father, has made no effort to secure any assistance, official or otherwise."

Miss Porter opened her mouth to object. Before she

could speak, Holmes continued. "However," he said, "I do see some points of interest, and I would be happy to look further into the matter." He stood abruptly. "May I see you into a cab? Limehouse is simply too far to return by foot."

The girl looked confused, glancing from Holmes to Lestrade and back. Lestrade stood, more slowly, and said, "You will be in good hands with Mr. Holmes, miss. Let me see you down to that cab." He glanced at Holmes, and then back to her. "I need to stay and discuss another matter with these gentlemen, but I will look in on you in a day or so, if that will be all right."

"Yes, yes, that will be fine, I suppose." She nodded good morning to Holmes and me, and then let Lestrade guide her downstairs.

As I heard the front door opening, I started to ask Holmes a question, but he simply raised a finger and stepped over to his scrapbooks, held on the shelves to the left of the fireplace. At that time, Holmes's scrapbooks were not nearly as extensive as they would grow to be over the years. Yet, even in those days, they were formidable. They were not so much actual books as albums, filled with loose sheets and newspaper clippings, some carefully glued into their well-ordered places, while others were arranged in a cabalistic pattern that only Holmes could identify. And then there were the leaves of paper that were simply stuffed in between pages, threatening to flutter to the floor, or – heaven forbid! – into the nearby fireplace if each volume were not opened with great care.

When Holmes and I first agreed to share the Baker Street rooms in early January '81, I had obviously had no idea what I was getting myself into. I had moved my things around from my hotel the very evening we entered into the agreement, and Holmes had arrived the next morning from his former lodgings in Montague Street, depositing a number of boxes and portmanteaus into the center of the sitting room. For a day or two, we busied ourselves in the unpacking and arranging of our possessions. I quickly noted that Holmes had a great deal more than I, and also that he needed more space in which to lay it out. This was understandable, as I had only been back in England for a little over a month, following my return from overseas service. I did not begrudge the extra space needed for Holmes's various possessions, except in one instance.

I had spotted early on that set of shelves to the left of the fireplace. I thought it would be just the place for the few volumes that I had acquired and wished to show off to their best advantage – some Clark Russell sea stories, a set of Dickens books that I had found very cheap in Charing Cross Road. However, before I could claim the shelves for my own, Holmes dragged over several boxes, opened the first he came to, and started loading down the shelves with his scrapbooks.

I had simply sighed and changed my plans. My health was still quite fragile in those days, and I objected to rows of any sort. It was not worth the trouble to ask him to share even a little of the shelf space. Now, many months later, I couldn't imagine anything in that spot but the scrapbooks. Time and again, they had proved their usefulness when Holmes needed to refer to some note that he had made, or to verify an obscure fact that might make all the difference in one of his investigations.

As I watched, Holmes walked to the middle of the room, flipping from page to page and humming tunelessly to himself. Lestrade returned to the sitting room and stopped inside the door. Seeing what Holmes was doing, he laughed, bent, and slapped his knee. "There's no getting past you, is there, Mr. Holmes?" he cried. Holmes glanced up, a twinkle in his eye.

"Is this the matter that you wished to stay behind and discuss?" he asked, raising the book.

"The very same," replied the inspector.

I cleared my throat. "I find myself at a loss," I said.

"It is simple, Doctor," said Lestrade, dropping into the basket chair before the fire, so recently vacated by our new client. "The lady's father, Lyton Porter, is one of the biggest criminals still unprosecuted."

"Tut, tut, Lestrade," said Holmes. "Innocent until proven guilty. You do not want to slander the man."

"Then tell me what you think, Mr. Holmes," said Lestrade. "Tell me what libelous statements you have in your magical book, there."

Holmes glanced up with a smile and said, "In spite of the risk of committing myself in front of witnesses, I will tell you. I have noted here, in my very own handwriting, that Mr. Porter is, in fact, quite notable for being one of the most notorious fences currently operating in the East End."

"Exactly," said Lestrade. "That's partly why I wanted to bring the girl to you, when she showed up this morning with her story." He turned to me. "I wanted to find out what Mr. Holmes's notes on the man said." Twisting in his chair so that he could see Holmes, he said, "Those books have been useful once or twice in the past. Why, I remember back when you lived in Montague Street, I stopped by one night. The City and County had just been robbed, and I –"

"Water under the bridge," said Holmes moving to his own chair and sitting. "What is your own knowledge of Mr. Lyton Porter?"

"As you said, the man is a fence. We know it, but so far we have left him to his own devices. He's useful in his own way right now, and it's just a matter of time until he stumbles. Perhaps this affair with the threats, ostensibly from the fiancé, is just the thing to start chipping away at him."

"It may interest you to know," said Holmes, "that I have recorded that Lyton's meteoric rise to his position as king of the Limehouse fencers only began two years ago." He paused knowingly, and Lestrade simply looked puzzled, but I thought that I dimly understood.

Finally, Lestrade said, "I fail to see the significance of

that, except that the man's daughter returned to live with him two years ago. Are you saying that he increased his criminal activity in order to obtain more income, now that he needed to maintain a larger household? Or did the arrival of his daughter somehow make him more careless, so that we became aware of him for the first time, when in fact he had been operating for much longer than that? And did this man Willis move in on him, and is now trying for a piece of the business?"

"I'm not saying anything yet," replied Holmes. "It is simply a fact to be documented and considered."

Lestrade wondered if there were any other relevant notes concerning Lyton Porter. Without comment, Holmes turned the book toward Lestrade, who leaned in for a look. I stood in order to see as well. There was one word, written in the margins in Holmes's careful fist: Manipulated.

Lestrade glanced at me with his eyebrows raised questioningly. He turned the same glance back towards my friend, who had closed the book and was in the process of replacing it on the shelf. When Holmes offered nothing else, the inspector appeared to be disappointed, and soon thanked us and departed, promising to return soon to discuss any new developments in the case.

"So much for that," said Holmes, dropping into his chair. "I must smoke a pipe or three to decide how to proceed in this matter."

"You apparently saw more in our client's story than I did," I said. "Not so much in her story, but rather in her appearance and her actions."

"Her actions? She did nothing but sit on that chair and relate her story to you."

"Ah, Watson, there were so many other cues, if only you had known how to interpret them. Alone, they might mean nothing. Together, they told me a completely different story from what her mouth was saying. That was what interested me enough to take further interest in the case."

He reached for his pipe, intending to think in silence, but I wanted to know more. "Tell me, then. Tell me this different story that you heard from what Lestrade and I heard."

"It was not anything that could be heard, Watson. It had to be seen, and once seen, it had to be understood." He packed some fresh shag into the pipe – the clay, I was happy to see, and not the disputatious cherrywood – and said, "She was lying, Watson. Although it certainly wouldn't be the first time that a client has done that. The question is, why?" And he lapsed into silence.

I went about my own business for the next hour or so. I had planned to take a walk, but decided to remain, in case something of interest were soon to present itself.

It was approaching eleven o'clock when a ringing of the bell startled me. Holmes glanced up and met my gaze. "Are you expecting another visitor?" I asked.

He laughed. "Indeed, Watson. I am expecting a visitor later today, a rather important one, but not yet, and I doubt that Lord Carlington will ring the bell with such fervor when he arrives. No, this is undoubtedly something unexpected."

This proved to be the case. A heavy tread climbed the stairs, and in a moment our door was opened to reveal a constable, bearing a missive. "From Inspector Lestrade," the man rumbled. Holmes quickly read the note, and then moved to his desk, where he retrieved a sheet of his stationery from the drawer and proceeded to write a series of short sentences. Then, folding his reply, he handed it to the constable, with instructions to relay it to the inspector with all possible speed. With a touch to his helmet, the constable turned and departed, as solid as when he had arrived.

Only then, noticing my curiosity, did Holmes say, "It is murder, Watson. I must admit, that I did not expect anything to happen quite so soon."

"Murder?" I repeated, half rising from my chair. "Who has been murdered? Should we have accompanied the constable?"

telegram. While he was in the midst of this activity, Mrs. Hudson climbed the stairs and entered, drying her hands on her apron, and wearing a barely concealed look of peeved irritation.

Holmes finished, and turned with a charming smile. As usual, Mrs. Hudson could not stay upset with him for very long, and she graciously took the telegram, promising that the boy in buttons would dispatch it immediately. Expressing thanks, Holmes followed her to the door, closing it behind her and then returning to his chair, where he picked up his pipe and resumed his silent considerations.

Lunch came and went, but I ate alone as my friend pondered. Finally, long after Mrs. Hudson had cleared the table, and much later in the afternoon, Holmes stood and began tidying, something that he did only irregularly, and usually when he expected a visitor.

He glanced at the clock on the mantel and said, "We still have a few minutes before our visitor arrives. Do you have any questions regarding the case?"

"All that I have are questions. Do you mean the matter of the murder and the suicide, or about those letters for Lord Carlington there beside you?"

"Oh, the deaths in Limehouse, of course. The affair of the letters must simply take its course. I can see that you are puzzled about my refusal to join Lestrade at the scene."

"I am. You seem as if you already know what happened."

"I fancy that I do, although I have asked Lestrade to obtain a few confirmatory facts before absolutely establishing the truth."

"Speaking of truth," I said, "I meant to ask earlier about when you said that Miss Porter had lied, but you clearly did not want to discuss it then. How did you know that?"

"Ha!" said Holmes with a grin and a slap on the arm of his chair. "Good old Watson! You have put your finger on the very heart of the matter!" He leaned forward, with his elbows on his knees. "Tell me a story, Watson," he said, suddenly making no sense at all. "Tell me about the first time you were ever on a train!"

I looked at him in surprise, but he wiggled a finger and urged me to comply. I closed my eyes for a moment, casting back for the memory. Then, I opened them and looked up above the fireplace as the details emerged before me. "It was on a trip from my parents' home to that of my grandmother. I was only a wee lad –"

"That's enough," he said, interrupting me. "And now, tell me what you would do if you found a wallet on the street containing a thousand pounds?"

I thought to question these mad and random instructions, but I knew by now that Holmes had a purpose for this, although I could not fathom at all how it related to the deaths of the poor girl's father and fiancé. I ordered my thoughts before replying, "I suppose that I would attempt to find the owner. Perhaps the wallet would contain some sort of –"

"That's enough, Watson," Holmes said, interrupting me once again. "Did you realize what you were doing?" he asked.

I laughed. "No," was my simple reply, instead of elaborating on the fact that his requests had made no sense whatsoever. "I suppose you'll explain to me how these questions are somehow relevant to the matter."

"Quite." He settled back in his chair, and – with another glance at the clock – said, "Years ago, I happened to notice a curious behavior in myself. Once aware of it, I could not ignore it. To explain it simply, whenever I thought about something that had happened before, an actual event that I had witnessed, I would cast my eyes up and to the left as I visualized it in my head. Even being aware of this trait did not stop me from doing it whenever I would consider a memory. Conversely, when I would picture something that was completely imaginary, such as what I would do if I found a wallet with a great deal of money inside, I would glance up and to the right.

"I found that something similar happened when thinking of sounds. Remembered sounds would make my eyes glance in a more lateral direction to the left, and if I were to construct or imagine a conversation, for instance, I would find that my eyes were resting in a lateral direction toward the right.

"Having noticed this trait in myself, I began to study if it was present in my fellow man. To my amazement, it was. Time and again, during a conversation, people would frequently glance up to the right or left while they told me something or other. Less rarely did I observe the lateral glances indicating remembered or fabricated sounds, but that happened as well.

"Oh, it doesn't always work, mind you, and if a person is left-handed, it sometimes works in reverse. But on the whole I have found it quite reliable. Before long, I was able to tell with a fair degree of accuracy who was telling the truth and who was lying. I can assure you, such a skill, properly cultivated, is quite useful in my profession."

I was amazed, and with a laugh, I replied, "I should think so."

He smiled. "I suppose that, like a magician, I should not easily explain what is in my bag of tricks. When I asked you to recall our first train ride, you glanced without thought to your left, up toward the mantel. I asked about an imaginary situation, and you glanced to the right, above our dining table. As an indicator, it has proved itself useful time and again. It is not absolute, you understand, but as an overall compass needle, it is quite effective."

"And you determined that today, based upon her reactions while telling her story, Miss Porter was lying about something."

"More specifically, about nearly everything of importance," said my friend. "When she was telling about her parents' separation and the move to the seashore with her mother, she either made direct eye contact, or glanced up and to the left, indicating that she was seeing real memories. The same was true when describing her success at learning the pawnbroking business, and when and why Mr. Willis came to work at the shop. But I believe from her actions while describing it that her engagement to Mr. Willis was a fiction."

A light dawned. "You made a point of looking at her ring."

"I did. And her finger underneath it showed no signs whatsoever of long-term wear, as evidenced by a person who wears a ring daily for extensive periods. I suspect she simply picked up a ring from a tray in the shop to add credence to her story.

"Of course, when she reached the part of her tale regarding the threatening notes and the subsequent argument between her father and his assistant, she was – without fail – fabricating the entire business. I am certain of it."

"But to what purpose?" I asked. "And how does that relate to the events in the pawnshop?"

"Ah, the knowledge that she was lying, as well as one or two other trifling observations made while she was here in our sitting room, made me suspicious of her. Although I suspected that something was going to happen at some point in the future, I had no idea that the crime would reveal itself so soon. The fact that the murders did happen almost immediately makes the whole thing quite clear to me."

I felt some exasperation, as I did not yet see the greater picture that he was slowly revealing. But before I could ask any further questions, the bell rang, and within a few moments, Lord Carlington was shown into our presence.

There is no need to relate here the extensive and seamy details of the precise and final deconstruction of that man's threadbare character on that day. The story has since played out in the press, to the great embarrassment of his father, the unfortunate Duke, and further picking at that wrecked man's reputation will serve no useful purpose. Suffice it to say, the situation could have been much worse, especially for the Duke, and Holmes's handling of the situation was masterful. When he showed Lord Carlington the documents that he possessed, the others that he had been hired to retrieve were quickly placed into his possession. At the conclusion of the matter, Lord Carlington rose to his feet, looking even more gaunt than when he had arrived, tottering on his feet as if he were being stretched too thin. He didn't seem to notice the bell when it rang from the street, and he made no acknowledgement to either Lestrade, Miss Porter, or the accompanying constable when he passed them coming in as he bolted for the steps. Sadly, the man would be dead within a fortnight.

Lestrade and Miss Porter found the same seats as before, while the stolid constable placed himself with his back to the door. Almost immediately, however, a knock behind him caused him to step aside, revealing Mrs. Hudson, with a telegram in hand. She passed it to Holmes, glanced around at the room's assembly, and departed. The constable resumed his post. Lestrade had arrived with a Gladstone bag, and he carefully placed it by his feet.

"Excellent," murmured Holmes as he read the telegram, and then placed it without comment on the octagonal side table beside his chair, where the packet of letters had so recently rested. Looking at Lestrade, he asked, "Did you find it?"

Lestrade nodded, and Holmes glanced toward Miss Porter who appeared puzzled.

"This telegram," he said, "is a reply to an inquiry that I set in motion not long ago. I had not expected an answer quite so soon, but sometimes things work out. I have an associate in Clacton-on-Sea, a man named Garren that I once helped out of a pesky little problem. I had thought that my question for him might need some extra time, in order for him to complete a more thorough investigation, but it seems

was a lie.

"When word came of the two murders, I instantly realized what your plan must have been, and I sent a wire to my agent in Clacton-on-Sea, and instructions to Lestrade." He turned to the inspector. "You say that you found it?"

"I did. It was pushed down in some other dirty clothes."

He opened the Gladstone bag by his feet and pulled out a yellow dress, spattered with blood.

The girl gasped, the first sign that I had seen of any sort of reaction.

I think it was only then that she realized she was well and truly caught. "As you wrote in your note, she must have been spattered when she killed Willis – it was a very messy murder – and then after she killed her father, she went back upstairs and changed to her current dress before going to the Yard."

Holmes gestured with a finger toward the dress in Lestrade's hand. "It must have been very messy indeed. You verified that she never went back into the shop after opening the door, finding the bodies, and fainting, as observed by the cabbie and other passers-by?"

"That is correct," said Lestrade.

"Then," Holmes said, shifting his finger to now point at the hemline of the girl's current dress, the same that she had worn during her morning visit, "she probably obtained that small spot of blood along the hemline there when she passed through the shop after changing clothes," said Holmes. "She was certainly careful, but not careful enough. I had noticed the spot on her dress when she was here the first time, at the same time that I was observing she had not walked to Whitehall as claimed. If she had truly walked, there was always the chance she could have received the spot on some street. But we know she did not walk. At the time I noticed that stain, I simply filed it away. Later it gained a great deal more importance."

"That it did," agreed Lestrade, raising his head from

where he had bent to see the bloodstain. Then he stood up, and the constable moved forward, sensing what was going to happen next. "Miss Letitia Porter, I place you under arrest for the murder of your father and Floyd Willis." He continued the formalities, but she did not seem to hear. She was physically turned toward Holmes, but her face was staring up at the mantel to her left.

"Do you see, Watson?" Holmes asked. "Do you see it? She is remembering what she did this morning, trying to think if she could have done anything differently."

Her eyes then cut sharply to Holmes, and then, after a long moment while Lestrade continued to speak, they drifted up to the right, just for a second. "And now," Holmes added, "she's imagining the various possibilities of how to escape this predicament."

She looked back at Holmes again, and then with an unexpected shriek, she lunged at him. But before she could sink her nails into Holmes's face, Lestrade had her arm, spinning her around and into the approaching constable. Within moments she had been bundled out of the sitting room and downstairs.

"They are never to be trusted, Watson," said Holmes softly. "Not the best of them, and certainly not this pawnbroker's daughter."

Later that evening, Lestrade returned to let us know that the girl had made a full confession. He inquired how Holmes had known that she was lying, but Holmes did not choose to explain his knowledge regarding the way that people behaved when visualizing real or constructed memories. Instead, he gave a vague answer concerning his deductions about the girl's engagement ring, the dress and its slight bloodstain, and his determination that she had ridden in a cab when she said that she had walked, resulting in his questioning all of her statements. This seemed to satisfy our friend the inspector, and he departed soon after.

"After all, Watson," said Holmes when the man had

gone, "my ideas about this sort of involuntary action are not thoroughly researched or proven. It would not be a good idea – in fact it might be dangerous in the wrong hands – to present it as otherwise until more data has been established. Should you ever publish a monograph about these little cases of mine, you must be sure not to mention this trick."

I laughed. "As a matter of fact, you simply don't want to give an advantage to the criminals. Or to your rivals at the Yard, I'd wager."

Holmes smiled in agreement. "Perhaps you are right. Possibly someday. But right now, a poor consultant needs every advantage that he can get."

"Then I thank you, Holmes," I said, "for letting me in on one of your many secrets."

"Ah, Watson," he replied, "you are an equal partner in this agency now, and as such you need to be fully equipped with every tool in your toolbox. Yet, I despair, as you still so often see but do not observe. While you did not yet know the method that I used to read the girl's glances during her story today, you should have seen that her dress was far too fresh to have walked so great a distance across London. Surely, there were seven different indicators –"

He could see my reaction to that statement, so he quickly changed the subject and suggested a dinner at Simpson's, which was a rare treat indeed in those days, as a way to celebrate the recent fee from the Duke. We both knew that his two-month's share of the rent that he had just earned would be somewhat depleted from such a meal, and that a new case would be necessary in order to replace the spent funds, but that night, with the memory in both our minds of the trapped girl's suddenly vulpine face as she was led away by the constable, seemed to require some sort of special reward to counter the unpleasantness of it all.

By way of an epilogue, I would like to mention the small encounter that led me to recall these events. Just the other day, I was down by the south end of the new Tower Bridge, standing where Jacobson's Yard used to be located. It had all been torn down when the bridge was built a few years ago. I still remembered that night, not quite seven years earlier, when the signal had come, in the form of a waved white handkerchief, letting us know that Mordecai Smith's boat, The Aurora, was departing from its hiding place at Jacobson's to begin that mad and dangerous dash down the river, pursuing Jonathan Small, the last of the Four. Holmes, Athelney Jones, and I were waiting on a similar steam launch across the river, hugging the shore by the Tower, little realizing what the rest of the night would bring.

Now, I was pretending to look over toward the Tower itself, shining in the morning sun on the far side of the Thames. The tide was in, and the wind was raising a gray chop on the water's surface. I say that I was pretending to look at that old historic pile, but in reality, I was glancing to my right, towards the bridge, to see for sure that a certain man carried out his instructions and exchanged one package for another. This went as planned, and I then gave the signal, a touch to the brim of my hat with my left hand, to a small, dirty lad sitting on a nearby barrel, eating an apple. Without acknowledgement, he jumped down and scampered toward the bridge. He was, of course, one of Holmes's Irregulars, and he was carrying word that the next phase of the complicated investigation had commenced.

It was then that I saw an expensive carriage stop nearby. While the horse skittishly took a step or two forward and back, the door opened, and a woman stepped down. She was clearly one of those impoverished unfortunates who prey and are preyed upon throughout the East End. The attention that the area had received back in '88 had done very little to alleviate their terrible circumstances.

As the woman found her footing, she turned back to the carriage, and a man's arm, covered in a sleeve of very rich-looking fabric indeed, flipped her a coin, which she tried to catch, but dropped. The carriage door slammed shut, and I heard the sound of a stick knocking inside. The driver, thus alerted, gigged the horse into a trot and departed into the first advances of an impending fog.

I glanced across the river to see that the Irregular was now to the west of the Tower, and conversing with another very similar-looking lad. The second one nodded, and took off running toward the north, into the City, while the first put his hands on his knees to catch his breath. Looking away from them, I found my gaze wandering back to the unfortunate woman as she unbent from retrieving the coin.

As she straightened, her eyes locked with mine, and I was shocked to realize that I knew her. It had been thirteen years since her arrest and conviction, and except for her eyes, I do not think that I could have identified her. She was only in her early thirties now, but time in prison had wasted her. Gone was the pretty girl with the lustrous curls. In spite of Holmes's testimony and her own confession, she had escaped a life sentence, due to somehow charming the jury, and had instead served only ten hard years. But what years they must have been.

I could see that she recognized me as well. Miss Letitia Porter, if miss she still was, glared at me with a raw hatred. It lasted only a second, before her gaze drifted off to the right. Then, with a grim smile, she shifted her eyes back to mine, and making an abrupt turn, she walked away from the river, into a rat's warren of streets.

It was an unsettling experience, and I can only imagine what she was thinking when she smiled. It cannot have been a good thing, whatever she was picturing then, either for Holmes or myself....

from my sleep. I hurriedly threw on my dressing gown, pocketed my bullpup and rushed downstairs to find Holmes similarly dressed and armed.

"What happened?" I enquired, my voice barely a whisper.

"From the sound, I can only tell you that a .476 calibre Enfield Mk I revolver has been fired within twenty yards of our abode, Watson," Holmes replied grimly. "I intend to step out to investigate further."

"I should like to keep you company, if you do not object," I offered. "Thank you, Doctor. Your assistance may be invaluable. I suspect we shall have an injured person at hand shortly."

We passed an anxious Mrs. Hudson in the hallway. Insistent knocking, growing increasingly desperate with each passing moment, beckoned us to the front door. Holmes waved Mrs. Hudson away to safety, and gestured at me to take up a discreet position, so I could assist him if our late-night guest bore intentions of assault. The detective threw open the door.

A raggedly-dressed young man stood outside, one hand still raised towards the knocker and the other clutching his abdomen.

"Mr. Holmes?" he whispered hoarsely.

To my surprise, Holmes pulled him in immediately and closed the door. The boy leaned against the wall, breathing heavily. His dark eyes were wide as he stared at Holmes.

"Oh, but you are more beautiful than I was told to expect, Mr. Holmes," the boy sighed dreamily. "May I paint you?"

I was rendered speechless. Holmes appeared embarrassed and flabbergasted in equal measures. Then the boy collapsed and I noticed the dark blood coating his fingers, realising he had been delirious with pain.

"Get your medical kit ready, Watson," Holmes said urgently. "I will bring up our visitor."

I rushed upstairs and grabbed my bag and some clean linen. We might not have the antiseptic environment of a hospital, but I would not let an infection take my patient. But where could I perform the required surgery? Our living room did not offer a surface large enough.

"My bed should suffice," Holmes said, walking in with the boy in his arms.

Wordlessly, I followed him to his bedroom and spread the clean linen on his bed. With as much care as a mother would display for her injured child, Holmes laid our visitor on the bed. He proceeded to turn up all the lights.

In the well-lit room, I could see the beauty of that young, smooth, golden face and felt a wave of fury sweep through me. The boy could not have been more than fourteen. How dare a ruffian harm a child?

Holmes's soft voice broke through my anger. "How may I assist you, Watson?"

"Cut away his clothes, if you would, Holmes. I need to see the bullet wound," I told him, pouring alcohol on both our hands.

Holmes nodded and carefully removed a strip of the boy's blood-stained shirt.

"It might be better if you removed the shirt completely," I suggested.

Twin spots of colour appeared on my friend's pale cheeks. "I am afraid that may not be prudent, Doctor," he said. "Our client is a lady."

I could only stare at him in shock. However, as I turned my eyes back to my patient, I realised he was right. The figure under those ragged-boy clothes could only belong to a woman.

As it turned out, she was a rather fortunate young lady. Once I had cleaned the blood, it appeared that the bullet had passed cleanly through her side without touching any vital organ, and there was nothing for me to do except clean up the wound and bandage it. She would be fine. Holmes heaved a sigh of relief when I informed him. He laid a set of spare clothes on the chair and we left the girl to rest. We would get her story when she awoke. I was quite exhausted myself, but curiosity gnawed at me.

"A foreign lady," I said to Holmes.

He nodded. "Indeed, Watson. I was not able to deduce much, but it appears she is from our Indian colonies, belongs to a royal family – or at least a very affluent one, studies at the University of London, is a voracious reader, dabbles in art and the violin, seems to be good at horse-riding, fencing and shooting – and is presently caught in a web of international politics. She was abducted recently, but either escaped or was rescued soon."

"How could you possibly know that?" I asked, amazed. "She asked if she could paint you, so I can understand her affinity for art, but how could you know the rest?"

Holmes gave me a small smile. "Look at her boots and jewellery, Watson – custom made, extremely expensive. Also, the soil is clearly from Gower Street. From the dents on her nose, she regularly uses eye glasses, even at this young age – clearly reads a lot. So, a young, studious and rich foreigner in Gower Street – could it be anyone other than a student at the University College London?"

I nodded, following his observations. "You mentioned she plays the violin, rides, fences and shoots."

"Riding boots, calluses and gun-powder residue," he replied. "And if I am not mistaken, that is an 1874 Chamelot-Delvigne in her pocket."

"Abduction? Did you deduce that from the rope-burns on her wrists and ankles?"

"Bravo, Doctor."

"But why on earth is she dressed as a man, Holmes?"

"I suspect it was to foil an assassination attempt," he remarked. "I shall know more upon an investigation of the contents of her coat pocket and satchel."

My face must have betrayed my thoughts, for Holmes laughed. "Do not worry, my good doctor, I assure you that I have our client's permission." He regarded me thoughtfully.

"I suggest you rest while you can, Watson – I shall wake you if your patient has any need of you."

I was too tired to argue, so I took his advice. As it turned out, our visitor did not wake until Mrs. Hudson was sent to help her out of bed. One look at the apparel Holmes had laid out for the young woman and our landlady was kind enough to bring up some of her own laundered clothes. Finally seeing the girl dressed in feminine attire, I realised what an utterly beautiful woman she would be in a few years. Even though the dress was plain and ill-fitting, I could easily believe Holmes's conjecture that she was a princess.

"Good morning, your Highness," Holmes greeted her, and almost simultaneously, I asked, "How do you feel?" when Mrs. Hudson and my patient appeared at the breakfast table. I noted absently that Holmes seemed to be observing the princess rather intensely.

"Much better, thank you, Doctor Watson, Mr. Holmes," she replied softly. "You have all been very kind. And please, you must call me Ada – everyone does. I am afraid my Indian name is not conducive to the British tongue, but 'Ada' is quite close to the shortened version."

I was surprised to note she spoke with an upper-class British accent.

She smiled at my surprise.

"I have mostly been educated in Europe," she said. "My father is uncharacteristically modern, and I have been rather fortunate for it."

Mrs. Hudson had thoughtfully set up a third place for breakfast, and Holmes invited our client to join us. She took up the chair gratefully and we ate together in silence.

The Princess was the first to speak when we took up chairs near the fireplace.

"Did you have a chance to look through my papers, Mr. Holmes?" she asked quietly.

"Indeed," Holmes replied.

"And what do you make of it?" she enquired.

"I prefer not to hypothesise until I have adequate facts, your Highness," Holmes told her. "I must confess myself stupefied, though, at the absence of any symptoms of poisoning."

Ada laughed. "Oh, you are right, Mr. Holmes, I have been poisoned. However, in my family, we are inured to most varieties of venom, and for anything more potent, we have a vaidya – I suppose you could say doctor – at hand. I have not been seriously harmed."

Holmes nodded, but did not look very convinced. "It might be best for you to give us the facts first," he said instead.

Ada smiled ruefully. "Of course, Mr. Holmes, I shall do as you say. I suppose I was hoping to see your skills of deduction first-hand. Victor was always rather verbose about your talents. And when your...." She paused and glanced at me. "Well, M suggested that I consult you at the earliest."

Holmes frowned and the Princess smiled again. She really did have a rather fetching smile. The M she had spoken of, I learnt several years later, was none other than Mycroft Holmes.

"I apologise, Mr. Holmes, Doctor Watson – my brains are still rather addled. Let me narrate the events that have led me here in chronological order." She paused again. "I am afraid it is a rather long tale, but I shall endeavour to make it as brief as possible."

"My father is the King of Terai, a small Indian territory. Incidentally, Mr. Holmes, your friend Victor has lived in our kingdom for several years now, and I have been friends with him since I was a child. It was he who first spoke of you." She smiled fondly. "But I digress. My father is a great believer in education, gentlemen, and at his insistence, all his children – there are six of us – have been thoroughly educated in various parts of the world. This has also helped us further our international relations. Consequently, our little kingdom has prospered even more. Lately, however, my father has not been keeping very well and desires to see all his children married. My brothers and sisters are significantly older, and therefore, already well-settled. While I would prefer to complete my graduation before I wed, my father's plight does not allow for such delay. As it is, I am sixteen, which makes for a rather old bride in traditional families. It was initially believed that there would be a dearth of suitors for my hand...now, however, it appears that the problem is quite the reverse." She paused and smiled sardonically. "I do have a rather significant dowry to my name."

"Currently, I have four perfectly fine men willing to take me for a wife. One has been chosen by my father and our mutual acquaintance M, and the rest by my siblings. The first, Sir Norbert, is a British nobleman of impeccable heredity, tragically impoverished. The second, Rajkumar Vikramaditya, is an Indian prince from a neighbouring eastern state. The third, Prince Pierre, is the heir to the throne of an African kingdom. The fourth, Dokter Diederik, is also a European gentleman of Dutch origin, not titled, but immensely rich. I have met each one, Mr. Holmes, and they are all wonderful gentlemen...and I am unable to choose. Ordinarily, I would blindly follow my father's advice, Mr. Holmes – he is the wisest man I have ever known, but recent events have made me wary. The warning letters in my bag started pouring in a fortnight ago. There have been three assaults on my person and two break-ins at my London residence in the last week. I am reluctant to bother my father with this, so I have consulted with M, who has been akin to a guardian to me since I arrived in this country. I intended to visit you at a decent hour last evening, but I was cornered in my apartment by a gang of ruffians. My guards fought them off bravely, allowing me to escape in disguise, while my maid dressed herself in my clothes and fled in another direction as a decoy. The man who followed and shot me on Baker Street must have taken me for a messenger sent to seek your assistance."

"You were abducted two days ago," Holmes said. She nodded.

"Did you know your captor? How did you escape?" I asked. "Faithless man," she said quietly. "It was one of my friends from the university. Fortunately, my men caught up with the carriage I was in."

"Where was he supposed to take you?" Holmes asked.

"I do not know, Mr. Holmes. He killed himself before we could take him to the police."

"Are you quite certain you do not have any lingering effects of poisoning? Watson may be able to help."

"Thank you. That is very kind of you."

"May I enquire if any your suitors or their assistants bear the initials K.O.?" Holmes asked.

The Princess stared at him in shock. "None," she said eventually. "But you are – or were – close to someone with those initials," Holmes said, watching her keenly.

"Yes. Kaarle Olivier is my best friend," she replied defiantly. "Why did you not go to the police?" Holmes asked.

"M advised against it." "Does he have any ideas?"

She looked away. Holmes frowned, but before he could question the princess further, Mrs. Hudson appeared with the newspapers. It was unusual for her to bring them up herself; obviously she desired to check up on Ada, whom she now considered to be under her wing.

Holmes pounced upon the papers. The front page declared, "Defenestration in London!" Holmes quickly passed the paper to me and I read out loud:

> *Late last night, a young woman was thrown out of her third-floor apartment window at Gower Street. The girl, who was killed upon impact, has been identified as Her Royal Highness, Princess Advyaitavadini, youngest daughter of the Indian King Abhayananda of Terai. Her entire entourage, consisting of six trained guards, three male servants and three female servants, has also been*

> *found to be killed in a violent fight while defending the princess. The deceased, known to her friends as Ada, was well-liked amongst her fellow students at the University. Her friends have confessed that the princess had been threatened and attacked previously as well, but had refused police assistance. This brutal massacre of thirteen people, however, is being investigated by Scotland Yard, under the able leadership of Inspector G. Lestrade, whom the public may remember from the Jefferson Hope case.*

Ada had lost all colour and tears poured down her cheeks. Her hands shook, portraying her distress, and I was reminded that she was still barely more than a child.

"I must go to the university at once, Mr. Holmes," she cried, pushing herself off the chair with some effort. "This news must not travel to my father at any cost."

She staggered towards the door but faltered halfway. Fortunately, Mrs. Hudson caught her.

"Now you listen here, young lady," Mrs. Hudson scolded. "You are to stay here and rest. Mr. Holmes and Dr. Watson will take care of your troubles."

"But...."

"No buts. Look at the state of you, all pale and trembling! What you need is a cup of good, strong tea," our landlady said firmly, and proceeded to press a cup into the girl's hands.

Holmes took a seat next to the traumatised girl and said gently, "I shall attempt to contain the news, barring which, I shall ensure that news of your survival accompanies any notification from the university. However, you must stay hidden here until I return. Watson and Mrs. Hudson will look after you. Do you understand?"

She nodded tearfully.

Holmes turned to me. "Watson, no one must see her. If we have any visitors not accompanied by myself, escort her to my room. I expect Lestrade shall come by at some point.

Be ready."

"Certainly, Holmes," I promised, understanding his warning to be armed and prepared.

"Mr. Holmes," Ada called softly. "My people...they have to be cremated, and their ashes sent home to be scattered in the holy river. I do not know who the thirteenth person is, but if she is Christian, she ought to be buried here. If you require me to identify my people, I shall accompany you."

Holmes's grey eyes glittered like diamonds as he turned back to the girl.

"Who knew the specific number of people in your entourage?" he asked.

She frowned. "I am not sure. It was not exactly a secret."

"Do you have any idea who the unknown woman might be?"

"It could be the milkmaid, the charwoman or the laundry girl – they were friendly with my staff and often visited socially. In fact, Jane – the laundry girl, and Satyanand – one of my guards, were hoping to marry when we returned to Terai." Ada pursed her lips, eyes bright with unshed tears. "You will find out who did this, won't you, Mr. Holmes?"

"I shall certainly endeavour to do so," Holmes replied.

Ada nodded, visibly assured. "Please spare no expense. No price is too dear to me to avenge the murder of my people!"

Holmes nodded his assent. "How many of your suitors are presently in London?"

"All of them."

"One last question, before I leave," Holmes said quietly. "Could you describe Sir Norbert and Dokter Diederik?"

Ada smiled. "I can do better. I can give you their pictures." She fetched a small album from her dress pocket and handed it to Holmes, pointing out each of her suitors.

Holmes appeared pleased. "Thank you," he said. "I shall be back soon."

Holmes was away for several hours. I changed the

dressing on Ada's wound, and then looked through the papers Holmes had spent the night poring over. There were fifteen envelopes, several of which bore stamps from exotic cities. Each contained an insult, scrawled on a torn piece of foolscap in an untidy hand with scarlet ink:

> *Vile worm, thou wast o'erlook'd even in thy birth. (London)*
>
> *You are not worth another word, else I'd call you knave (London)*
>
> *I wonder that you will still be talking. Nobody marks you. (Madrid)*
>
> *Here, thou incestuous, murderous, damned Dane, Drink off this potion! (Helsinki)*
>
> *Dissembling harlot, thou art false in all! (London)*
>
> *I shall laugh myself to death at this puppy-headed monster! (London)*
>
> *Thou unfit for any* **place** *but hell. (London)*
>
> *Away! Thou'rt poison to my blood. (Calcutta)*
>
> *More of your conversation would infect my brain. (Cairo)*
>
> ***Away,*** *you mouldy rogue, away! I am meat for your master. (Havana)*
>
> *O faithless coward! O dishonest wretch! Wilt thou be made a man out of my vice? (Milan)*
>
> *Take her away: for she hath lived too long, To fill the world*

> ***with** vicious qualities. (Hamburg)*
>
> ***I** shall cut out your tongue. 'Tis no matter, I shall speak as much wit as thou afterwards. (London)*
>
> *O you beast! I'll so maul you and your toasting-iron, That you shall think the devil is come from hell. (Krakow)*
>
> *Heaven truly knows that thou art false as hell. (Odessa)*

I stared at the scraps in disbelief. When I looked up at Ada, she was smiling sadly.

"Shakespeare. I thought the first few were a joke," she said, her voice quiet.

There was also a small diary filled with neat, feminine handwriting, meticulously noting down the date and time of receipt of each letter, and the Shakespearean play each message was taken from – *The Merry Wives of Windsor, All's Well that Ends Well, Much Ado about Nothing, Hamlet, The Comedy of Errors, The Tempest, Richard III, Cymbeline, Coriolanus, Henry IV, Measure for Measure, Henry VI, Troilus and Cressida, King John,* and *Othello.* Ada had also noted down the bold and underlined words separately.

The underlined words read: "*worm word Nobody Drink potion false death poison infect meat faithless man take her away speak afterwards beast devil art false*" and the bold words read "*call place Away with I*". Even I could see the barely concealed warning in the papers and the missive to call India. I wondered what else Holmes had deduced from these. How was it even possible to deliver these letters so regularly from such different locations?

Ada had also made a list of her staff members, including the local hires and their contact details. Similarly, she had also listed the London addresses of her suitors.

I recognised the English nobleman immediately. He was at least thirty years older than our young princess! When I made a remark, Ada simply smiled and said, "They all are; at forty seven, your bachelor Englishman is in the younger half. The Indian is the youngest at thirty five – and I am to be his fifth wife. The African is fifty two, and I shall be the second wife; the first died recently. The Dutch is seventy, a famed misogynist until now."

"Would you not prefer to wed someone close to your own age?" I enquired, curious.

She smiled sadly, her bright eyes dimmed. "I have a duty to my kingdom, Dr. Watson; I do not have the luxury of love."

I had a sudden thought. Could it be that the warning disguised as threats were the work of a rejected admirer from a failed love-affair? I did not realise I had spoken out loud until I saw the stricken expression on her face.

"M thinks so, too – in fact, I made the notes under his instructions," she said unhappily. "But I know Kaarle would never do so!"

"I am glad you think so, *ma mie*," came a soft voice from the door. Ada jumped out of her seat with a cry of "Kaarle!"

Monsieur Olivier strode in and engulfed her in his arms. She sobbed quietly on his shoulder.

I took a moment to regard the rather striking blue-eyed, dark-haired young man before Holmes, who had followed the young man in, cleared his throat delicately.

The young pair sprang apart immediately.

"Je suis désolée, mon trésor," Ada said quietly. She turned to Holmes. "How did you find him, Mr. Holmes?"

"From the letters," Holmes replied. "You had, rather helpfully, written down the Shakespearean references. All foreign places started with the same letter as the play's title, and the bold words were followed by such letters of the alphabet. 'Call MH. Place CCH. Away for MH. I KO.' I paid a visit to the Charing Cross Hospital and found him in the morgue, looking for you. Child's play."

The princess directed her flashing dark eyes at the young

Frenchman. "It was you," she spat. "You sent those letters! You killed my people!"

Monsieur Olivier winced. "*Non, ma mie, non,*" he pleaded. "I merely attempted to warn you. There is a great conspiracy afoot. You are in grave danger, ma mie."

Ada glared.

"He was with M," Holmes said gently.

Ada turned her furious gaze back to the boy. "How do you know M?" she demanded.

"That ought to be a story for another time," Holmes interrupted impatiently. "We have more pressing concerns."

Ada stepped back, gathered herself and reclaimed her seat. "You are right, of course, Mr. Holmes. My apologies."

Holmes gestured for the young man to take a seat as well. He lit his pipe and I offered cigarettes to the boy.

"Cremation and transit of the ashes have been arranged," Holmes said, his voice quiet and soft. "Notice of your safety is also en route to your family."

"Thank you," Ada whispered. Her eyes shone with grateful tears. "The additional victim appears to be Jane Miller, your laundry girl,"

Holmes continued. "She is the only person unaccounted for. Requisite funeral arrangements have been made."

Ada nodded.

"News of your survival has been contained so far. I would like to keep it thus until we are able to locate the perpetrator." Holmes blew out a long spiral of smoke. "Monsieur Olivier has been trying to warn you of imminent danger for the last two weeks. M and I agree with him."

"But why would anyone want to kill me? No one stands to gain anything from my death. Once I am married, my death would undoubtedly benefit my husband, but till then, I am pretty useless." Ada frowned and glared at her young friend. "How do you know?"

Kaarle winced. "After we parted in Geneva, I went to meet my father. I accidentally stumbled upon a conspiracy involving Terai. Your father is not on his deathbed. Each of your suitors is a political plant. The British, Dutch and Indian represent their own, and the African is a French agent."

"But Terai is neutral!" Ada exclaimed. "We have always been peaceful."

Kaarle shook his head. "Terai is rich, independent, and possesses a powerful military force. It is strategically located and impossible to avoid for any trade route through Asia. You are surrounded by British, French and Dutch colonies, as well as rebellious Indian states. It is no secret that you are the favourite daughter of your father, and unlike most kingdoms where the crown automatically passes down to the eldest son, your family has been known to be eccentric enough to choose a successor deemed worthy. Your father himself was the fourth son, was he not? And your grandfather the second son-in-law?"

Ada nodded, her eyes wide.

"Your husband would be in the race for the crown of Terai, a most desirable object for each of your neighbours. The French and the Dutch would gain a strong foothold in the east, and will be able to wrest control of several states from the British. The British would become invincible if they won Terai. Any Indian state that has your unconditional support would gain not only a great army, but also a political advantage against European intruders. Also, even though your father is non-aligned, some of your siblings are very involved in the Indian independence movement. You have been known to sympathise."

The Princess lifted her chin defiantly. "I advocate peace, like my father before me. However, if you saw the brutalities heaped upon my countrymen, you would feel the need to rebel, too. Terai is only safe because we are powerful enough."

"Nonetheless," I interjected. "This does not explain why anyone would wish to harm Ada. Surely it is in the interest of these men to keep her alive and happy with them, so they could win her hand?"

Holmes smiled. "You have cut straight to the heart of the matter, my dear doctor," he said. "While the British, French, Dutch and Indians stand to win, others stand to lose. As such, eliminating the princess is a good way of reducing the risk. One less contender to the throne."

Ada sprang from her seat. "Are you implying my relatives are involved, Mr. Holmes?"

"I do not theorise without adequate data," Holmes replied calmly. "But you suspect?"

"It is only logical."

"No," Ada declared. "Please cease your investigations. I shall return to my homeland immediately."

"Are you out of your mind?" Kaarle cried. "You will be killed on the way!"

The princess remained stubbornly silent.

Holmes turned his raptor gaze upon the young woman. "There is no dignity in death by betrayal," he said quietly. "If a member of your family is indeed responsible for this assault, would their next move not be to eliminate your father and other dissenting members of your family?"

She staggered. Holmes caught her gently and led her back to her chair. I had always known Holmes to be chivalrous, but he usually disliked women. In this instance, however, I could see genuine concern for the girl in his eyes. Was it because she was barely more than a child, or could it be that Holmes's projection of machine-like imperturbability was false?

"Do not exert yourself, Ada," Holmes said softly. "You have been poisoned, abducted and shot at; you require rest."

Kaarle's eyes widened in shock. "But I warned you! Did you not heed my words?"

"I did," Ada said softly. "I was prepared for the wormwood in the wine and hemlock in the quail."

"Correct me if I'm wrong, your Highness, but were you with one of your suitors each time you were attacked?"

Holmes asked.

She nodded. "I had wine with the African prince; it was one of his special vintages from his vineyard in Bordeaux. Quail was served for dinner with your British peer. I was taken from the street right outside the Indian prince's hotel, and the attack last night happened just after I returned from dinner with the Dutch gentleman."

"What happens to your dowry if you die?" I asked.

She shrugged. "I suppose it reverts to my father's treasury." She looked straight at Holmes. "My relatives would not care about that. It is not a significant sum of money for my family."

Holmes nodded.

I turned to the boy and asked, "Who is beast devil?"

"I am unsure," Kaarle replied. "As I said, I overheard two men talking of Terai. I sent out whatever information I had through mail to warn Ada – in parts, so that they would not be intercepted, and *prima facie* nonsensical, so that they would be dismissed as innocuous. I had the two agents arrested and made my way to London immediately. I arrived at Charing Cross last evening."

The bell rang.

Holmes quickly sent our young guests to his bedroom with strict instructions to stay out of sight.

"I have been expecting you, Lestrade," Holmes said, greeting our visitor.

Inspector Lestrade shook his head sombrely. "It's an unholy mess, I tell you, Mr. Holmes. Some foreign princess got herself killed, and the Prime Minister descended upon us." He smiled. "We know who did it, but we need your help to find the fellow."

Holmes arched an eyebrow.

"The princess left everything in her will to a Kaarle Olivier; she was sweet on him in Switzerland, her friends say. We know Olivier arrived in London yesterday. Probably wanted to marry the girl, but she was to wed someone of her own class – must have killed her in a jealous fit."

"And her entourage?" Holmes asked. "Died protecting her, didn't they?"

"Do you honestly think one man could have killed thirteen people single-handed?" I interjected hotly.

"Accomplices."

"Tell me, Inspector, are you familiar with the brothers Zvíře and Ďábel?" Holmes enquired.

"Beast and devil!" Lestrade exclaimed. "Are they involved?"

"It is likely." Holmes took in my befuddled expression. "Mercenaries, my dear doctor, named for their looks. These two make a most vicious pair of criminals. Their origins are unknown, and they are fluent enough in at least six languages to disguise themselves as natives. I believe they are wanted by several nations."

Lestrade groaned.

"I believe we may be able to capture them," Holmes told the policeman. "However, I shall need full cooperation of Scotland Yard."

"By all means, Mr. Holmes." Lestrade's beady eyes glinted with excitement. "What do you need?"

A devious smile appeared on Holmes's thin face, and, for a moment, I was reminded of a bloodhound catching a scent. "We shall lay a trap, my dear Inspector, and I need bait."

"What bait?"

"I believe you are aware of the shooting here last night?" Lestrade nodded.

"I would like Scotland Yard to publicly state that valuable information on the perpetrators has been found at Baker Street, and an eye-witness has survived. The police have a solid lead and shall arrest the culprits soon."

"Now, look here, Mr. Holmes, I can't put out false information."

"It is true."

"What?"

Holmes smiled. "We have an eye-witness who was shot by Zvíře last night, presently under the care of Dr. Watson."

"I need to see him," Lestrade said stubbornly. Holmes glanced at me.

"I'm afraid my patient is not in a state for visitors at the moment, Inspector," I replied. "However, we may be able to set up a meeting later today."

"Rest assured, Inspector, once we have the thugs, your eye-witness will testify if required. Also, as always, I would like you to keep my name out of it." Holmes's demeanour was sombre. Even at that young age, he was quite masterful. Lestrade agreed reluctantly and departed.

"Now we wait, Watson," Holmes sighed.

Lestrade kept his word. The evening papers carried the bait.

Barely an hour later, Sir Norbert, Ada's British suitor, appeared at our doorstep. He looked much younger than his forty-seven years, and was unusually handsome. His long fingers clutched the evening Times.

"Mr. Holmes," he said softly. "You must find my Ada; I know in my heart that she is alive."

"What makes you so sure?" Holmes asked sharply.

"This." The nobleman held up the newspaper. "I knew each man and woman that looked after Ada, Mr. Holmes. If only one person survived, it is she. These Indians – *Rajput*, they are called – would protect their charge at any cost. If Ada perished, the rest would commit suicide."

"Interesting," Holmes remarked.

Sir Norbert's response was cut off by the entry of a rather large elderly gentleman.

"Where is *het meisje*?" he demanded.

"Interesting," Holmes repeated. "Dokter Diederik, I assume?"

"*Ja*. Where is she? We will go to Maastricht and be safe."

"Why do you assume she is alive?" I asked.

"I believe it is more surprise than assumption, my dear

Watson," Holmes drawled. "After all, our guest here is an excellent shot."

Instantly, in a coordinated move, Diederik grabbed me and held a gun to my head, while Sir Norbert drew a sword from his cane and rested the tip on Holmes's throat.

Holmes appeared indifferent. "It is a .476 calibre Enfield Mk I. I was right after all, Watson. I can confess to a monograph on the subject." "Clever, aren't you, Holmes?" the Englishman spat. "Now, where is the girl?"

Holmes shrugged nonchalantly. "How would I know?"

The sword pressed in. I could see droplets of blood beading on Holmes's pale neck.

"Would you like me to shoot your friend?" Diederik growled. Holmes's eyes flashed silver with contained rage. "If you harm Watson, Zvíře, I promise you and Ďábel shall not leave this room alive."

I finally understood. Zvíře and Ďábel had been posing as Ada's suitors!

Ďábel laughed. "You are hardly in a position to threaten," he mocked. "Now tell me where she is and I might let you live." He jabbed the blade further.

Holmes ignored him.

A door opened. "Stop," Ada commanded. "Let them go." "Do not come out!" Holmes shouted.

The princess stepped out of Holmes's bedroom. Her hand was steady as she aimed her pistol at the scoundrels.

"Now, Watson!" Holmes cried.

Pandemonium ensued. Two shots rang out, followed by a cry of pain and the sound of shattering glass. Holmes knocked the sword off Ďábel and delivered a swift left hook. Simultaneously, I brought up my good leg in a brutal kick and Zvíře staggered, giving me ample time to pistol-whip him. Kaarle dived at Ada and both hit the floor. Kaarle moved quickly to shield her. Lestrade and a dozen policemen burst in.

Holmes and I stepped back, allowing the policemen to

handcuff the two rogues. Zvíře was hit in the arm by Ada's shot and his bullet had shattered the framed painting behind her head. Kaarle had saved her life.

"Now, gentlemen, would you care to enlighten us regarding the identity of your employer?" Holmes asked cheerfully, holding his handkerchief to the cut on his neck.

"Go to hell," Zvíře growled.

"What are you willing to offer us in return?" Ďábel asked at the same time.

"That would depend on how valuable your information is," Holmes replied. "If it is good enough, we may forget that you assaulted and attempted to murder the princess."

Lestrade protested, but Holmes held up a hand to silence him.

"The money came from India. We heard references to a Ranjit Singh."

Ada paled. "The royal counsel. We must inform my father." Holmes nodded. "And who is your British contact?"

"We do not know the principal. He is simply referred to as the professor. We only met with one of his agents, a university student named Horace Bloomington."

Holmes turned to Ada. "Your abductor?" "Yes," she said softly.

"Very well," Holmes said. "Assault and attempted murder charges will be dropped."

The criminals smirked.

"However," Holmes continued, "You will be charged with the murders of the real Sir Norbert and Dokter Diederik as well as thirteen innocent men and women."

"You cheat!" Ďábel cried, lunging at Holmes. He was restrained by two able-bodied policemen.

"Congratulations, Lestrade, on a case well-solved," Holmes told the shocked policeman. "You will find the murder weapons on your prisoners, and bodies of the two gentlemen at the Highgate cemetery, close to a birch tree, judging from the mud on their shoes. Also, the charred end of Zvíře's sleeve and the soot on Ďábel's trousers betray their presence at the crime scene last evening. I have no doubt that you will be able to extract the names of their accomplices hired for the act."

Lestrade thanked Holmes effusively and departed.

"Thank you, Mr. Holmes," Ada whispered. "You have brought peace to the souls of my fallen compatriots."

"How did you know?" Kaarle enquired.

"It was elementary," Holmes replied. "Zvíře and Ďábel had to be in close proximity to the princess, which indicated the suitors. Fortunately, I recognised them from their pictures. They may not remember, but we have crossed paths before." He looked up at our curious faces. "It had best be discussed over dinner."

After Holmes regaled us with his tales over a lavish dinner at Simpson's, I asked Ada about her future.

"I suppose I shall have to marry either Vikram or Pierre," she said sadly.

I noticed the stricken expression on Kaarle's face. Before I could say anything, though, Holmes announced that he had an errand to run and requested Kaarle to accompany him. Ada and I returned to Baker Street.

Unable to bear the aura of misery surrounding my companion, I finally asked her the question which had been plaguing me. "Is there no way you could escape this unwanted marriage? Your father is not ill, you may be able to buy some time."

"It does not matter, Dr. Watson," she wept. "I would never be permitted to marry Kaarle, even if I renounced my husband's claim to contend for the throne of Terai. We need the political support. If I did not have a duty to my kingdom, I would have happily taken this chance to be presumed dead."

I could only offer her a warm beverage in consolation. Exhaustion crept in upon her, and I sent her to bed. I waited up for Holmes, but at the stroke of midnight, I found myself too drowsy to sit and retired to my chambers.

Holmes and Kaarle finally appeared at breakfast. It was obvious that they had been up all night. Kaarle's cerulean eyes were red-rimmed, as were Ada's. A wave of sympathy coursed through me at the plight of the young couple.

Holmes rested a hand on the boy's shoulder. "Ada," he called gently. "Kaarle would like to have a few words."

Ada looked up apprehensively.

Kaarle winced. "I may not have been entirely truthful about my origins in the past," he began, eyes downcast. "I am not French, though my mother was. I am the crown prince of a small island nation off the coast of Nice. I have been in exile for several years, but I have now been reinstated – and finally in a position to ask for your hand in marriage." He knelt before her and held out a solitaire ring. "Advyaitavadini," he pronounced carefully. *"Ma belle, ma petite, ma bichette, ma mie-je t'aime, veux-tu m'epouser?* Would you do me the honour of being my wife? *Kya aap hamari ardhangini banengi?"*

Ada stared at him. "When did you learn Hindi?" she whispered. "You learnt my language for me, the least I could do was to learn yours," the crown prince muttered, his cheeks aflame. "I should also tell you that I have M's blessing, and I have sought your father's approval through him, which, I am assured will be forthcoming. My father sends his regards as well." He looked up at her hopefully. "So...will you?"

A beatific smile spread across our young princess' visage. "Yes," she whispered shyly. *"Oui. Haan."*

The ring was slipped on. The euphoric groom-to-be picked her up and twirled about the room, both of them giggling like schoolchildren.

Holmes and I exchanged an amused glance.

"Mr. Holmes, Dr. Watson," Ada said breathlessly, as Kaarle finally released her. "Would you be our witnesses?"

Kaarle nodded enthusiastically. "Without you, we would

be dead. Without you, we would have been torn apart. We owe you our life and our happiness. The traditional ceremonies in our respective kingdoms would be arduous, but we would like to have a small church wedding in London before we depart, and we would be very honoured if you would be our witnesses."

Holmes had a strange look on his face. For an instant, I was afraid he would reply in the negative. He glanced at me and I nodded slightly.

"It would give us great pleasure," Holmes said quietly.

Much to our embarrassment, the young couple flung themselves at us. I patted the boy's back awkwardly while Holmes turned an alarming shade of red in the girl's arms. Then Ada embraced me and Kaarle enveloped Holmes. When we were finally released, the prince laughed.

"*Désolé,*" he said, smiling. "We forget how reserved the British are." He took his fiancée's hand. "We shall be in touch, gentlemen. *Au revoir.*"

The young royals departed with a spring in their steps.

I could not contain my curiosity any longer. "Holmes, did you mete out romantic advice to the boy last night? Did you take him to this M you all keep talking about?"

Holmes nodded and refused to meet my eyes. I smiled to myself, preparing to tease my friend.

"Not a word, Watson!" he shook his head. "It was only logical."

He turned dramatically, his greatcoat bellowing behind him like a cape, and, for the want of a better word, *fled* – quite possibly to delete all traces of sentimentality from his brain-attic!

The Adventure of the Inn on the Marsh

by Denis O. Smith

In glancing over the records I kept during the time I shared chambers with my eminent friend, the renowned detective, Mr. Sherlock Holmes, I am struck by the many occasions on which what appeared at the outset to be but a trivial affair became, in the end, a deadly serious investigation. Not infrequently, too, a case which began in London would oblige us to travel far beyond the capital and deep into the countryside in search of a solution. The case associated with The Wild Goose of Welborne, which I shall now recount, provides a good illustration of both of these points.

It was a pleasant, breezy day during the first week of September, 1883, the sort of weather that seems to freshen the air after the heat of the summer, and freshen, too, one's own energies and aspirations. Holmes and I had both spent the morning endeavouring to tidy and bring order to the sheaves of papers and documents which had built up on every surface during the previous months. We were about to take lunch, satisfied with our morning's work, when a ring at the doorbell announced a visitor. A moment later, our landlady ushered a young couple into our sitting-room, announced as Mr. and Mrs. Philip Whittle.

"I am sorry to intrude if you are eating," the young man said in an apologetic tone, "but this was the only time I could get away from work to see you."

"Not at all," returned Holmes affably, putting down his knife and fork and standing up from the table. "One can eat at any time. I had much rather hear what it is that has brought you here to see us."

"We have had a very odd experience," said the young man, as he and his wife seated themselves on the chairs I brought forward. "We cannot think what to make of it."

"The details, if you please," said Holmes.

"It is soon enough told. We stayed recently for a few days at an old inn, The Wild Goose, which lies in the marshland near the north Norfolk coast. It is the second time we have stayed there. The first time was at the beginning of June, when we stayed there for a week."

"Upon the occasion of your honeymoon, no doubt."

The young man looked surprised. "Yes, it was, as a matter of fact," said he, "but how did you know?"

Sherlock Holmes chuckled in that odd, noiseless fashion which was peculiar to him. "Since your wife removed her gloves, she has been displaying two very fine rings upon the third finger of her left hand. One is undoubtedly a wedding ring, and the other, with a sparkling stone in it, is no doubt an engagement ring. They both appear relatively new and shiny, and, moreover, the wedding ring is still a little loose, as is apparent when your wife touches it with the fingers of her other hand, which she has done several times already. It demands no great leap of logic to surmise that your wedding took place not very long ago, and that your week's holiday in Norfolk constituted your honeymoon."

The young lady flushed to the roots of her hair.

"I apologize for alluding to your personal circumstances," said Holmes quickly in an urbane tone. "It is a little hobby of mine – trifling and no doubt silly – to deduce facts about people from their personal appearance."

"That is perfectly all right," said Mrs. Whittle with a little smile. "Such a hobby may prove useful in this case, if it helps you get to the bottom of the matter," remarked Whittle. "We were married at the very end of May, and immediately took a week's holiday in Norfolk, as you surmised. One or two of my married friends had spent their honeymoons at the seaside, at Margate, Brighton and places like that, but my fancy was for somewhere a little quieter, and Prudence agreed. When we heard from a cousin of mine of The Wild Goose, on the Welborne Marsh in Norfolk, it sounded ideal. It is a wild and beautiful spot, very popular with bird-watchers, I understand, as it is a haven for birds of all kinds. We spent most of the week there, in walks over the countryside or by the sea, and when we moved to Cromer, for the last two days of our holiday – even though Cromer itself is a quiet, charming and select sort of seaside town – it seemed to us very noisy and bustling compared with where we had been staying.

"We had enjoyed our stay at The Wild Goose so much that when the opportunity arose recently to take another brief holiday, both Prudence and I at once thought of returning there. We therefore travelled down to Norfolk last Friday, and stayed until Monday morning. However, the pleasure of being there, which we had been looking forward to so much, was marred by one odd little circumstance. As I was entering our details in the register, I turned the pages back to see the entries for the beginning of June, with Prudence looking over my shoulder. You will appreciate, no doubt, that the occasion of our honeymoon meant a lot to us both, and the urge to see 'Mr. and Mrs. Whittle' written somewhere for the first time was irresistible. Imagine our astonishment and dismay, then, to see that on the week in question there was no trace of our names whatsoever!

Of course, I looked on the page before and the page after, but we were not there. Our names had simply vanished from the book completely, as if our visit to The Wild Goose had never taken place!"

Holmes rubbed his hands together in delight, a look of

interest on his face.

"Did it appear to you that a page had been removed from the book?" he asked.

Whittle shook his head. "Perhaps it had, but if so, it must have been done very neatly, for I didn't notice anything of the sort. Besides, there were other names written in on the dates we had stayed there. It was not that everyone's name had disappeared from that week, just ours."

"Did you recognize any of these other names?"

"No, but I scarcely knew the name of anyone else that was staying there. We rather kept ourselves to ourselves, if you know what I mean, when we were there in June. As a matter of fact, it was very quiet then, anyway; there were very few other people staying there. I understand it gets much busier during the wild-fowling season. But the register now shows that a Miss Stebbing, a Mr. and Mrs. Williams, and a Mr. and Mrs. Myers were staying there at the same time as we were, and I don't remember any of those people."

"Did you mention the matter to anyone at the inn?"

"I certainly did. I mentioned it to the girl who was attending us as we signed in. But she said she had only worked there for a month and didn't know anything about it. 'If you've got any questions,' she said, 'you'll have to ask Mr. Trunch.'"

"He being the landlord?"

"Exactly. I raised the matter with him that evening. He said he couldn't remember as far back as June. 'I have lots of visitors coming and going all the time,' he said. 'You can't expect me to remember everyone.' I pointed out to him that his memory was not the issue. Rather, it was the disappearance of our names from his register. He then suggested that we must be mistaken. 'I don't think you were ever here at all,' he said, and suggested that we had, rather, stayed at The Old Duck, which lies about three miles distant, across the marsh. Of course, it is ridiculous to suppose that a man could forget in three months where he had spent the very first holiday with his wife, but when I pointed that out to him, he became very irritable and almost abusive, and I had to let the matter drop. I must say his manner quite spoiled our memory of our previous visit there."

"It is certainly an odd experience," remarked Sherlock Holmes after a moment, "but there may be some rational explanation for it. Perhaps, for instance, a jug of water was accidentally spilled onto the register, rendering some of the pages illegible, including the one on which your names were written. Then, perhaps in attempting to rewrite the page from memory, someone has simply failed to recall your name. It may be that the 'Mr. and Mrs. Williams' which is now written in the book was someone's attempt to remember your name. Of course, that would not explain the landlord's unpleasant manner towards you. One would imagine that if such an explanation were the case, he would simply have informed you of the fact. But perhaps he has an unusually poor memory, and is embarrassed about it. Perhaps he drinks heavily. If so, he wouldn't be the first landlord of a remote country pub to consume all the profits in liquid measures, and I understand that excessive drinking has a very detrimental effect on the memory. Or is there something else?" he enquired, eyeing the young man closely.

Whittle nodded. "There has been a further development, which we have both found very upsetting, and for which such simple explanations cannot account."

"Very well. Pray proceed."

"We returned to London on Monday, having enjoyed our few days away despite the inauspicious beginning. Yesterday morning, however, this letter arrived by the first post." As he spoke, the young man took an envelope from his inside pocket and passed it to Holmes, who took from it a single sheet of paper which he unfolded upon his knee and studied intently for a few moments.

"What do you make of it, Watson?" said he, as he passed the letter to me and turned his attention to the envelope. The note, which was not signed, was a brief one, written in black ink in the centre of an oddly square-shaped sheet of paper, and ran as follows:

> *Asking many questions can be a dangerous course. Keep out of matters that do not concern you, and mind your business. This is a warning to you.*

"What a very unpleasant and menacing letter!" I remarked to Whittle. "I am not surprised it has upset you both."

"It was posted in central London," said Holmes, "so it is unlikely to have come directly from the landlord of The Wild Goose himself. But the information that you have been 'asking questions' must surely have come from him, so he is evidently in communication with someone in London. The paper is unusually thick and heavy, but is an odd size. I wonder –"

He took his lens from the shelf and examined the letter closely through it. "Something has been cut off the top of the sheet," he said, "probably a printed heading which included an address. It has been carelessly done, though: there are a couple of tiny black marks at the top edge, where the scissors have clipped the bottom of a row of printed letters. There seems something familiar about it. Let me see –"

He sprang from his chair and began rummaging through the piles of old letters on his desk, which he had spent the morning putting in order. Presently he selected one and held it up beside the letter Whittle had received. "This is a letter of thanks I received from a client to whom I had been of service a few months ago," he said. "I think it is the same. Yes, undoubtedly it is the same. See," he continued, passing the sheets to our visitors. "The type of paper is a precise match, and the little traces of a line of printing that the scissors have left correspond exactly to this line on the other sheet."

"But that letter is from the German embassy!" I cried in

astonishment, as I leaned over to verify his observations. "I cannot believe the German embassy would send such a crude threatening letter to Mr. and Mrs. Whittle! And why should they, anyway?"

Holmes nodded. "The Germans may be a forceful people, but – in my experience, at least – they like things to be done in a legal and proper manner. There is evidently nothing official about this letter. I imagine that someone employed at the embassy, acting on his own initiative, and without official sanction, has simply used a sheet of official notepaper as it was to hand, having cut the top couple of inches off to preserve, as he hoped, his anonymity."

"Then it is of no help to us in solving the problem."

"I should not say that, Watson. It confirms, after all, our suspicions that the writer of the note is probably a foreigner, as suggested by his incorrect rendering of the common idiom, 'mind your own business'. Can you recall, Mr. Whittle, if there were any foreigners staying at The Wild Goose at the time of your first visit there?"

"Yes," replied Whittle. "Now you mention it, I do recollect that there were two men there who I thought were probably foreign. One was middle-aged, with close-cropped sandy hair and a very large moustache, the other was a young fellow, about my own age, a little on the plump side. They kept very much to themselves and never spoke to us, but I overheard them talking once or twice. Sometimes they spoke in English, but with very strong accents, and sometimes in a foreign language. It may have been German for all I know – I am not familiar with that language, so I can't say."

"We thought they were probably keen bird-watchers," added Mrs. Whittle. "The landlord had told us that people come from all over Europe to study the birds on the Welborne Marsh."

"One evening when we were eating," Whittle continued, "a third man arrived and joined them at their table, a tall man with a bald head, and they all talked together very

not deny it. If a national championship in time-wasting were to be held, I should probably set a new all-comers record. But that is when I have no case to engage my brain. When I am on a case, it is a different matter, and it is infuriating not to be able to get on as quickly as I would wish."

"You could go down to Norwich this evening, anyway," I suggested after a moment. "You could lodge for the night somewhere in the city centre, and make an early start in the morning."

"Of course, you are quite right, old man. That is the sensible course of action. It is only tiredness and irritation that prevented my seeing it. I will take your advice, Watson, on one condition."

"What is that?"

"That you accompany me."

"I should be delighted to do so. I was thinking only the other day that it would be pleasant to get away from London for a day or two before the nights start closing in."

"Then it is settled," said he, putting his pipe down and springing from his chair with a renewed vigour, "although I can't promise that you will find our expedition the holiday you have been looking forward to, Watson." He pulled open the top drawer of his desk, and, taking out his revolver, began to examine the chambers, then he glanced my way. "Pack a bag, then, old fellow, and let us be off!"

We caught the early evening train, reached Norwich just before nine o'clock, and put up at a small hotel near the station. In the morning we rose early, took breakfast at the hotel, and were in the office of the local newspaper, the *Eastern Daily Press*, soon after it opened. There we learned that as well as the daily newspaper, several weekly papers were also published, containing news specific to particular parts of the county. Holmes selected the daily papers of late May and early June, while I looked through the weeklies. Most of the news was trivial, or of purely local interest, and I was beginning to doubt we should find anything even remotely relevant, when my companion abruptly stopped his rapid page-turning.

"Hello!" said he. "Here is something, Watson!"

I leaned over to see what had caught his eye, and read the following:

CROWN PRINCE VISITS SHOE FACTORY

Prince Otto von Stamm, crown prince of Waldenstein, has this week visited a shoe factory in Norwich, where he was conducted round the premises in the company of the Lord Mayor, and was said to be greatly impressed by the modernity and efficiency he saw displayed there. Waldenstein has long been a notable producer of hides, but most are simply exported, and Prince Otto is keen to establish a leather-working industry within the principality to help alleviate the problem of unemployment.

"That sounds harmless and banal enough," I remarked.

"Yes, Watson, but it gives us, if not a German, then a German-speaker at least, in the county of Norfolk at the relevant time. Do you know anything of Prince Otto von Stamm?"

"He appears in the Society pages of the Morning Post fairly regularly," I replied. "I have frequently read such references as 'Prince Otto seems to prefer London to his homeland', and 'We hear that Prince Otto has got himself into trouble again'. It is the usual sort of thing: a young foreign nobleman with more in his pockets than in his head. For some reason, London seems to act like a magnet to such people. I think he leads a fairly harum-scarum existence: visiting a shoe factory is the first sensible thing I've ever heard that he's done."

"Anything else?"

"Not really. I know he's fairly young – perhaps eight-and-twenty – but I know nothing else about him – and I know nothing whatever about Waldenstein, wherever that is."

"Waldenstein is one of those curiosities of European history," said Holmes. "It is one of the very few central European principalities which has not been swept up into the German Empire. It is very small – the population is probably not much greater than that of the town we are now in – and of no significance in itself. But its geographical position is a strategic one, lying adjacent as it does to both Germany and Austria. Its very existence creates a rivalry between the two great powers, both of which attempt to exercise an influence over it, and both of which would probably like to subsume it into their respective empires. Let us see if we can find anything else in these papers about Prince Otto's visit to Norfolk."

Our search for further reports on the young nobleman proved fruitless, but just as we were about to put the papers back in order, something caught my eye in one of the weeklies from the second week of June.

"This is a remarkable coincidence," I said. "More on Prince Otto?"

"No, but a fellow-countryman of his, surprisingly enough." I folded the page over and read aloud the following report:

FOREIGN VISITOR PRESUMED LOST AT SEA

Franz Krankl, a visitor to Norfolk from the principality of Waldenstein, is missing, feared drowned, after a boat in which he had rowed out to sea on an angling expedition was found washed up on a beach near Sheringham. The owner of the boat, inn-keeper and part-time fisherman, Albert Trunch of Welborne, says he had warned Krankl of the dangerous currents off the north coast of Norfolk, but Krankl had insisted he was very experienced in small boats. Herr Krankl holds a senior position in the government of Waldenstein, but was apparently here alone on a private holiday, and had been out of touch with his relatives for some time. A statement issued by the coast guard makes the point that all visitors must be made aware that there is a very great difference between conditions on inland waters and those encountered at sea.

"That is it!" cried Holmes. "It must be! Whittle informed us that the landlord of The Wild Goose was called Trunch, and now here is Trunch again, connected to a mysterious disappearance."

"It is certainly a striking coincidence."

Holmes shook his head. "It cannot simply be coincidence, Watson. The odds against it are enormous. Rather, these separate events are all links in a long chain of cause and effect, which will lead us to the truth. Trunch is clearly a link, so is this man Krankl, and so, I believe, is Prince Otto von Stamm, for I feel certain that he was the younger of the two men that the Whittles saw at the inn. It is to conceal his presence there, I believe, that the register has been altered."

"But if you are right," I said as we left the newspaper offices, "and it is Prince Otto's presence at The Wild Goose that someone is trying to conceal, why should the warning note to the Whittles have come from the German embassy?"

"As I understand it," Holmes replied, "Waldenstein does not have its own diplomatic representation in London. I believe that the German embassy acts on Waldenstein's behalf when necessary, in an informal sort of way. But someone at the German embassy may also, of course, have his own reasons for keeping the truth concealed. Don't look now, old fellow, but I think we are being followed."

"Is it the same man you saw in London?"

"I believe so. Anyhow, I observed this one – a man with a large moustache – outside our hotel this morning, and now he is outside the newspaper office. Evidently he – or a confederate – followed us to the railway station in London yesterday evening."

"What shall we do?"

"Nothing – or, at least, nothing other than what we were going to do anyway, which is to catch a train to Cromer, and make our way along the coast to the Welborne Marsh. It will be interesting to see if he comes with us."

The short branch train was already standing at the platform when we entered the station. We took seats in the compartment nearest to the front of the train, and Holmes positioned himself by the window, so that he could see anyone that came onto the platform. For almost ten minutes, he had nothing to report, then, just as the guard walked past our carriage after a consultation with the engine driver, and it was evident he was returning to his position at the rear of the train to give the signal to start, Holmes gave the "view-holloa".

"There he is!" cried he. "He has just broken cover, run onto the platform carrying a large leather bag, and climbed into the last compartment! He is following us to the coast!"

We reached Cromer in a little over fifty minutes, and hurried from the train to make sure we secured the station fly. Of the man apparently following us, there was no sign.

"He is lying low in his compartment," said Holmes under his breath, as we rattled off along the road by the station. "I saw the crown of his hat through the window. He evidently has no idea we have seen him."

Our journey took us at first through undulating countryside, but presently descended to low-lying, marshy terrain, where the narrow road meandered like a snake past rivulets and creeks, never far from the mud-flats and the sea. From time to time we heard the sound of distant gunshots, and saw the little puffs of smoke rising up from the hollows where the wild-fowlers crouched, waiting for the birds to fly their way. At length, after about half-an-hour, we reached a small, isolated village, which I saw from a sign was Welborne. The wind was blowing sharply off the sea now, the clouds overhead were dark grey, and there were a few spots of rain in the air. Our driver did not pause, but passed right through the village and on towards the sea. Half-a-mile further on, we at last reached The Wild Goose. It was a low, spreading building, with grimy lime-washed walls and a weathered-looking thatched roof, and appeared as ancient as the ground upon which it stood.

"We don't yet have all the threads in our hands," said Holmes to me, when we had paid off our driver and stood before the weather-beaten front door of the inn, above which a painted sign depicting a flying goose swung and creaked in the wind. "We shall therefore have to approach the matter in an oblique way. If in doubt, just follow my lead."

He pushed open the door, and I followed him into the dark interior. After a moment, a young woman in an apron appeared through a doorway, but when Holmes asked if we might speak to the landlord, she informed us that he was out, and would not be back for another hour. We decided then to leave our bags at the inn and take a walk across the marsh towards the sea.

It was a wild, tempestuous day now, and the nearer we approached the sea, the stronger the wind became, and the more the gusts seemed to veer and shift about us. At length we surmounted a steep shingle bank, and there before us lay the broad, heaving expanse of ocean, the breakers pounding the shore with a boom and a crash, sending mountains of spray into the air which the sharp wind whipped into our faces. I opened my mouth to speak, but abandoned the attempt almost at once: the thunderous noise of the sea blotted out all other sounds. After we had stood shivering for a few minutes by this deafening maelstrom, Holmes plucked my sleeve and indicated that we should retire behind the shelter of the shingle bank.

"The sea is very rough today," said he as we crouched down in the lee of the bank. "I suppose you were reflecting on the conditions the unfortunate Herr Krankl may have encountered."

"Among other things, yes."

"I should not trouble yourself with that thought, Watson. As I read the matter, Krankl was never in a boat at all. I strongly suspect he lost his life at The Wild Goose, on the evening the Whittles heard a quarrel there."

"You believe he was the third man, the tall man who arrived one evening, but was nowhere to be seen the following morning?"

"That does seem to me the likeliest explanation. But, come, let us get back to the inn, and see if Trunch has returned yet."

At The Wild Goose, in answer to our query, Trunch himself appeared after a moment from some back room. He was an absolute giant of a man, a good six-foot-four if he was an inch, with a chest like an ox. For a moment he stood looking down upon us with an expression of disdain.

"Well?" said he at length.

"A friend of mine stayed here not long ago," Holmes began.

"What of it?"

"When he came again more recently, he found that his name had been removed from the register."

"Oh, him! A snivelling trouble-maker from London! If you're on the same errand, you can sling your hook!"

He made to turn away, but Holmes persisted:

"It is, of course, a criminal offence to fraudulently alter books used for accounting purposes. The authorities take a dim view of that sort of thing."

"Oh, do they? What is that to you, Mr. Know-all? Are you one of those blood-sucking tax-collectors yourself? No? Then listen, friend, and I'll tell you what my father told me when I was a young man. 'Mark my words, son,' he said to me: 'there's always some swine wanting money, and the best way of dealing with them is to tell them to go to Hell.'"

Sherlock Holmes remained unmoved. "Something else you may not be aware of is that to attempt to conceal something criminal is itself a crime. In attempting such concealment you also lay yourself open to being charged as an accessory to the original crime, even if you had nothing directly to do with it."

"Just what are you saying?" demanded Trunch. His voice was still loud and scornful, but there was a note in it now, too, of apprehension, and it was clear that Holmes's remarks had had an effect. Holmes himself evidently perceived this, for he quickly pressed home his advantage.

"We know that Prince Otto von Stamm was here, and the other men."

"What if they were?" said Trunch defiantly, but the tone of bluster in his voice was rapidly ebbing away, and it was clear he was on the defensive.

"Whatever occurred here, you, as landlord, will be held responsible –"

"What humbug!"

" – especially as you helped conceal the truth by fraudulently altering the register."

"Someone else pulled out the page. I had to re-write it from memory. There's no crime in that. What else could I do?"

"But you didn't put all the names in again, did you? You deliberately omitted some."

Trunch's bullying manner had quite disappeared now. It is difficult to say what might have happened next, but we were interrupted by the re-appearance of the young serving-woman. She whispered something to the landlord and he nodded his head. "Come this way," he said to us, "and I'll tell you what happened."

We followed him through the doorway, along a corridor and into a back room. As we entered, I saw a large leather bag lying open on a side-table. Holmes evidently saw it, too, for I saw him glance that way and stop. But it was too late, the door slammed shut behind us. We turned, to see a man with a large, straggling moustache, who had been concealed behind the open door. In his hands was a large double-barrelled shotgun, which he pointed at us.

"Leave them to me, Trunch," he said in a strong, guttural accent. "I'll deal with them." He yanked open a back door and indicated we should go out that way.

"Now," said he, when we were outside in a small backyard, the cold wind whistling about our ears, "start walking." All about us as we left the yard, the Welborne Marsh stretched away as far as the eye could see.

"Don't be a fool," said Holmes over his shoulder, as we followed a muddy, winding track. "If it's your intention to murder us here on the marsh, you'll never get away with it."

"You forget, Mr. Busybody, that the wild-fowling season has now begun," returned our captor from behind me. Even as he spoke there came the sound of gunshots – one, two, three – from all about us on the marsh. "Your deaths will be ascribed to an unfortunate sporting accident. Sadly, such things do happen."

"You murdering swine," I cried. "Don't think we don't know about Krankl! Soon everyone will know the truth!"

For an instant he was silent, but it was only for an instant. "So," he cried, in a voice full of venom. "If you're so interested in Krankl, I can show you where he is lying, and then you can join him there! Keep walking!" he snarled, thrusting the shotgun sharply into my back. My mind reeled. There must be something we could do – we could not simply walk quietly to our deaths – but panic had seized me, and I could think of nothing.

Ahead of me, Holmes walked on steadily, his shoulders hunched against the cold wind, his hands thrust into his coat pockets, as we made our way deeper into the wilderness of the marsh. "Slippery path, this one, Watson," said he over his shoulder. "Mind you don't lose your footing!"

For a brief moment, I confess I was surprised that, in our desperate situation, Holmes should make such a banal remark. Next moment, I realized that he was telling me he wished me to slip and fall to the ground, perhaps as a distraction. How that would help us, I could not imagine, but if that was what he wanted me to do, then that is what I would do.

A short distance further on, as the path breasted a small rise and dropped away into a shallow dip, I saw my opportunity. I deliberately let my left foot slide away in the mud, and, with a loud cry, tumbled to the ground. At once our captor lowered his shotgun and pointed it at me, but in the same instant there came the sharp crack of a pistol-shot. Holmes's hands were still in his pockets, and I realized he had turned and fired his revolver through the fabric of his overcoat. There came a cry of pain from our captor, as the shot caught him on the left arm, and he raised the shotgun towards Holmes. With every ounce of energy in my body, I sprang up and threw myself upon him, forcing the barrels of his gun upwards and to the side. The movement evidently jerked his finger against the triggers, and both barrels discharged with a deafening roar into the open sky above us, then, with a force I would not have believed myself capable of, I swung my fist up and struck him on the chin with the most perfect uppercut I have ever delivered, sending him sprawling backwards into the mud. I quickly picked up the gun which he had dropped as he fell, as Holmes covered him, his revolver held rock-steady in his hand.

"Good man," said my friend to me. "Your swift action saved us all. Are you all right?"

"I think I may have depressed the knuckle of my third finger," I remarked as I examined my right hand, wincing with pain as I touched the spot. "It will probably need setting. I am not much used to fisticuffs."

There came a cry from behind us. I turned, to see a young man hurrying towards us down the path from The Wild Goose. "Stop! Stop!" he cried, waving his arms in the air. As he came nearer I recognized him from pictures I had seen in the illustrated London papers as Prince Otto himself. "Stop at once!" he cried as he came up to us, breathing heavily, his cheeks flushed with effort. "I want no more violence on my account, Schnabel. I have decided to make a clean breast of everything. After all, it was an accident."

"Be quiet, you fool!" said the other man in a harsh tone, as he struggled unsteadily to his feet. "How did you get here?"

"I learned late last night in London where you had gone, and caught the first train I could this morning."

"Tell us about the accident you referred to," said Holmes, covering both of them with his pistol. "It is, I take it, to do with Krankl, and Waldenstein's foreign policy."

"Don't tell them anything," said Schnabel quickly, but Stamm ignored him.

"You appear well-informed already," said he to us, "so you may be aware that my country has recently been in discussion with Austria, with a view to linking our future to theirs. This is the course long favoured by my father and his chief minister, Franz Krankl. However, Herr Schnabel here has been arguing on behalf of the German Empire that the better course is for us to favour his country. My father is frail and may not have much longer to live. When he dies and I succeed him, the decision will of course be mine, so it is something I must think about now.

"I was in this part of the country anyway, for some duty I had to perform, so Herr Schnabel and I arranged to meet for secret discussions at the most remote spot we could find, The Wild Goose. Unfortunately, Herr Krankl, who was also in England, got wind of what we had planned, and hurried here to try to dissuade me from this course of action. He arrived one evening and we quarrelled. I had had too much to drink, I admit, and was quite drunk. In the heat of the quarrel, I am ashamed to say, I lost my temper and struck out at him, he fell from his chair and hit his head so hard on the corner of the hearth that it killed him. Herr Schnabel here ushered me from the room – I was in no fit state to do anything sensible – and said he would deal with the matter. He disposed of the body somewhere on the marsh, and later bribed the inn-keeper, Trunch, to say that we had never been here, and that Krankl had hired his boat, put out to sea alone in it, and appeared to have been lost overboard."

"You have made a serious mistake," said Holmes.

"I know," returned Stamm. "I am ashamed of myself, both for being drunk, and for losing my temper with Krankl."

"That was not my meaning," said Holmes. "Your mistake was in permitting Schnabel to dispose of the body. Don't you see that that places you completely in his power? At any time in the future he could, by threatening to expose the truth, blackmail you into doing precisely what he wished you to do."

"Don't listen to him, your Highness," cried Schnabel.

"I imagine that that has been his intention all along," continued Holmes, ignoring the other man's outburst, "to have this hold over you, so that he could force you to do his bidding, as a puppet-master controls his puppets. On the night Krankl was here, he saw his chance and seized it."

"It's a lie!" cried Schnabel.

"You don't even know for certain that Krankl was really dead when you left the room." Holmes persisted. "Perhaps he was only stunned, and was finished off later by Schnabel, after you had gone to bed. It would of course suit his purposes perfectly to be rid of Krankl, who was a staunch proponent of the Austrian alliance."

"That's lie number two!" interrupted Schnabel, his voice hoarse, but Holmes's words had evidently plucked a cord in the young nobleman's memory.

"I had wondered about that," he said, "wondered if I had really killed him or not. For even in my shamefully drunken state, I had noticed that Krankl's wound did not appear to be bleeding at all, and nor was there any sign of blood on the floor the following morning."

Abruptly, the infuriated Schnabel attempted to launch an

attack on Holmes, but the latter levelled his pistol at him and he gave it up at once. "The only way to decide the matter is to examine the body," said Holmes. "Schnabel says it is buried out this way on the marsh. Will you show us where it is?" he asked, turning to the German. "No. You can find it yourself," Schnabel responded.

"Your lack of co-operation is disappointing," remarked Holmes. "I had only permitted you to drag us out here in the hope that you would lead us to the remains of the unfortunate Herr Krankl. However, we shall find them soon enough. First, though, I think we'll all get back to the inn, and notify the authorities of what has occurred."

When we reached The Wild Goose, Trunch was nowhere to be seen, but his absence was soon explained, as the serving-girl informed us that he had gone to fetch the local constable, after declaring with great vehemence that he wished he had never become involved with these people. Just a few minutes later we heard a trap pull up outside the inn and Trunch entered, with a policeman who was almost as massive as Trunch himself. Holmes quickly explained to the policeman all that had taken place. This interview ended with Schnabel in handcuffs, and he and von Stamm going off with Trunch and the constable.

"I can't imagine what Mr. and Mrs. Whittle will think when they learn what you have discovered," I remarked to Holmes later that day, as we took lunch at a hotel in Cromer.

My friend chuckled. "Yes, it will certainly be strange for them to discover that as their honeymoon was taking its no doubt blissfully happy course, they were, all unaware, sharing a roof with international intrigue and murder!"

I heard later that the body of Franz Krankl had been recovered from a shallow grave on the marsh, but the medical examination and inquest which followed proved inconclusive. The cause of death was established with certainty as being the wound to the head, but the medical examiner stated that he could not be certain whether Krankl had been struck once, or more than once, and in the end a verdict of accidental death was recorded. Trunch, Schnabel and von Stamm were all convicted on their own admission of attempting to conceal the death, but taking various circumstances into account, and with no doubt half an eye on the diplomatic aspects of the case, the court took a lenient view and handed down relatively light sentences. Trunch therefore returned, no doubt a chastened man, to the inn on the marsh where he continued to cater for the needs of keen bird-watchers, and von Stamm and Schnabel returned to their homelands, and never, so far as I am aware, visited these shores again.

The Adventure of the Traveling Orchestra

by Amy Thomas

My friend Sherlock Holmes, as I have observed on occasion, was at his best when investigations were at their zenith. With all of his senses and powers of observation engaged, he appeared lit from within, as if by some force neither known nor experienced by the rest of the world. In contrast, when too long a time elapsed in which a case had not presented itself – or, at least, no case possessing feature sufficient to keep his interest – that selfsame light was extinguished, progressively, until a dim shadow of the man remained, a repository of talent lacking an igniting catalyst. Such was Holmes's condition in the autumn of a year not many into our acquaintance.

We were partaking of dinner together in Baker Street, as was our usual custom, when a thought occurred to me. "Perhaps you might take up the violin tonight. Mrs. Hudson and I would be vastly amenable to a concert." I had observed the effect music had on my flatmate, a deeply calming one not unlike that of his seven-per-cent solution.

Holmes raised blank eyes to mine, his long, thin fingers closed around his glass. "I have no inspiration, Watson." Such was the exact source of my concern, for when his mind had reached that point, there was little else to expect but the drug. I fell silent, but fortunately, the lassitude was soon to be remedied.

As I finished my last morsel of sustenance, my friend rose abruptly from the table and went to the window, peering down into the darkening street. "If I am not mistaken, Watson, a client appears." His voice sounded hopeful for the first time in several weeks. I followed Holmes's gaze with my own and found it filled with the sight of a young man carrying an oblong object in his right hand.

"A musician," said my friend, and I realized that the object was of the size and shape of the sort of box that normally contains a small instrument such as a flute. Unlike many of our visitors, the man did not hesitate in the slightest to make his way to the entrance to the building.

Holmes already looked more vital than I had seen him in quite some time, and as we waited for the newcomer to join us, his energy only appeared to increase. Gone was the lethargy that had plagued him; it was instead replaced by the quickness of movement and glance that characterized the detective in his prime.

Within a moment or two, Mrs. Hudson admitted the young man to our dwelling. In the light, I could make out more of his appearance. He was tall but slight in build, of an age I put between twenty and thirty years, and possessed of dark brown hair. Now that he stood before us, he seemed no more tentative than he had previously. In fact, the air of confidence he conveyed made it seem as though his thin frame took up far more space than it actually occupied.

"Mr. Holmes?" His blue eyes passed across both my friend and myself.

"I have the honor to be thus addressed," said Holmes readily, motioning to the chair we kept for guests.

"I am Charles Green," he replied, before taking his seat, a smile on his lips. Rarely had I seen a client in such a perfect state of non-agitation. "I see that you've come to me about the theft of your instrument," said Holmes, taking his seat opposite Green, his eyes on the instrument case that rested on our visitor's lap.

"How?" asked the young man simply. Far from appearing put out, he grinned broadly at the deduction of the missing contents of a hard-sided, closed case that did not seem to betray anything about its contents or lack of such.

"The theft wasn't a brutal one," my friend replied, "but I see signs of the center clasp, which normally locks, being pried open, an unlikely action for the owner of the instrument to perform." Green handed over the case, and upon closer inspection, I, too, could see evidence that something had bent the clasp and then bent it back.

"I also deduce from your manner," continued Holmes, "that this theft was, if not welcomed, at least not overly troubling."

Our guest smiled again and leaned forward excitedly. "It was stolen from a concert hall, along with every other instrument in the entire orchestra. If they're not recovered, or are recovered damaged, the hall will have to pay us for the lot of them. I liked my flute well enough, but the payout would furnish me with a better one. I haven't been with the orchestra for long, and my instrument is hardly worthy of it." It occurred to me to wonder, if this were true, why he had chosen to consult my friend at all. He must have realized how he sounded, for he added, "Not all of us were so fortunate. A few of the instruments were valuable enough to be irreplaceable. I've come to you on behalf of friends for whom the losses are far more catastrophically felt than my own."

"Were all the cases, like yours, left behind?"

"Yes," answered Green, nodding emphatically. "That's the strange part. They took the trouble of taking every one of the instruments and leaving each case exactly as they found it."

"Which was how?"

"We are a traveling orchestra," the young man replied. "Our members are usually responsible for their own instruments, but most of us had left them behind for a single evening of dining out. We are not wealthy, and our manager had promised us a night of rest and good food, not something we are normally afforded for free."

"The hall itself was left in the care of a guard, and we locked our instruments into a dressing room and thought little of it. The few who refused to do this are, of course, relieved and filled with the glow of justification."

"All right," said my friend, "let me ascertain the timeline of events.

You and your fellow musicians arrived in London upon what day?" "Yesterday morning," he answered promptly. "We traveled from Edinburgh to begin a series of engagements in England. We lodge at a boardinghouse near Dorrigan Hall, which is in –"

"I know where it is," said Holmes brusquely. "Continue."

"We arrived by train in the early morning hours, and had only long enough to deposit our personal belongings in sparsely-furnished rooms before we were spirited away to rehearse in the hall, a schedule we are accustomed to keeping. We observed our usual agenda of four hours of practice, then a half hour for dining, and back to the grindstone in the afternoon."

"What did you do with your instruments during your midday meal?" I was gratified that the same question my friend asked had also occurred to me.

"We kept them with us," answered Green. "Food was brought to us from a local public house."

"Very well. What of your evening entertainment?"

"Before we recommenced our rehearsal, our manager, Mr. Pike, informed us that we were all to be his guests last evening at the Hotel Durrants on George Street, a fact that was met with a great deal of excitement by most members of the orchestra, who are little accustomed to such luxury, especially at Pike's expense."

"It is unlike him, then, to offer such a gift," murmured Holmes.

Green nodded. "I don't mean to imply he's an unfair employer. He's scrupulously conscientious in his dealings and, I think, errs more on the side of leniency than severity in most instances, but he is not a rich man. He's in a better way than most of us, but he's far from truly wealthy, at least as far as any of us have ever seen in his person or manner of living."

"I see," answered Holmes.

"As I said previously," Green kept on, "most of us left our instruments in a large dressing room on the right side of the hall, with the assurance of a sturdy lock, a competent guard, and the hall's responsibility for their safekeeping. Musicians, as a rule, care for our instruments, but only a few of us are so particular as to require them with us at all times, especially considering how little most of them are worth."

"The theft was discovered, I take it, upon your return," said Holmes.

I could tell that he was beginning to grow impatient with the repetitive part of Green's narrative.

"Yes," came the answer. "We returned to our boardinghouse after six hours of practice to prepare ourselves up for the evening. From there, we were taken by taxicab to Durrants, where we dined very well, drank good wine, and generally enjoyed ourselves. We returned in the late evening, determined to rehearse for one more hour, but we were greeted by a locked room of empty instrument cases and a guard who was at the other side of the building and claimed utter ignorance."

"Peculiar," said my friend. I hoped that this portended his willingness to take the case and finally escape from his recent malaise. "Why did you not consult me sooner?"

The young man sat back in his chair. "I had not – as you said before, I did not have the strongest incentive for approaching you. It was only after –"

"After the young woman with whom you are in love made her distress known to you." Green nodded wordlessly and did not ask for an explanation of Holmes's deduction.

After a moment of silence, he explained, "I became aware of your talents last year. I read about your exploits in the newspaper during our last trip to London, so when Doris – Miss Lake – told me of her distress over the loss of her viola, I spoke to Mr. Pike about consulting you."

"I'll admit –" He looked down at his interlaced fingers, "that I did not quite believe that you could be real or your reputation justified. However, Pike mentioned the idea of consulting you to Mr. Dorrigan, who owns the hall and will be out a great deal of money if our instruments remain lost, and he expressed great faith in you and tasked me with coming here straightaway to consult you about the matter."

"Very well," said Holmes. "Now I wish to see the scene of the robbery."

We engaged a taxi, and within minutes, found ourselves passing through the London streets toward a part of the city that might almost be called fashionable, except that the highest echelons of society were never seen there on account of it being too affordable for those they considered irrevocably beneath them. In other words, it was a place of social passage between the low and the high, where those who wished to climb rubbed shoulders with those who had fallen.

After a brisk ride, we arrived in front of a large, solid building that clearly belonged to its place in the city: Dorrigan Hall. I had never attended there, but I had certainly seen theatrical entertainments and heard concerts in similar places. It was of a new style, constructed, I thought, within the past decade. Eight entrances opened it to the street, and the tall façade was impressive with its arched doorways and massive windows.

We entered in the deepening dark of evening and found ourselves in a large vestibule designed to accommodate large crowds of patrons before a show. It was, like the outside, functional rather than opulent, but there was an impressive quality to its newness and scrupulous cleanliness.

"You're back." A soft, feminine voice spoke to us as we passed through the low-lighted lobby. Holmes, Green, and I were alone, save for the owner of the voice, who quickly joined us. Miss Doris Lake was a small, pale young woman with a shy smile. As we spoke our greetings, I fancied I could understand her association with Green, whose open and confident temperament was so much the opposite of her own. Nevertheless, her voice was low and lovely, and she had striking blue eyes that made her otherwise ordinary face attractive. She took Green's arm as soon as she could manage it and clung to him as we made our way about the premises, which were much as I had expected, avoiding the appearance of extreme opulence or extreme tawdriness. We were still standing in the front room while Green explained the basic layout of the hall, when a short, round, and extremely fast-moving man entered from somewhere in the deeper environs of the building.

"Charles!" he said breathlessly, as if he'd been exerting himself, "I'm glad to see you. Who are these gentlemen?"

"This is Dr. Watson and Mr. Holmes, the detective I was sent to seek."

"Oh, thank goodness," the other man replied. "I've had nothing but questions from every quarter the entire time you've been gone. The Misses Blake are threatening to – to leave us, after all these years!"

Holmes cleared his throat. "Mr. Pike, I believe?"

"Oh, yes, sir," said the agitated man. "I'm so pleased you've come." "Then please allow us to proceed on our tour of the premises," said my friend shortly, though I hardly blamed him. The man seemed harmless enough, but he was not in a helpful frame of mind.

Green, as calm as ever, picked up where he'd ceased and continued to explain the structure's simple design of main auditorium with wings on either side, the left of which contained practice rooms and the right dressing rooms, with offices in the back, behind the stage. The hall, while primarily concerned with musical entertainments, sometimes also hosted small dramatic productions, so its allotment of dressing rooms was greater than might be supposed necessary for an orchestra or an individual singer.

Once he'd finished his overview, Green led us through the vestibule and into the auditorium, which was illuminated but empty, save for a lone cellist who sat upon the stage and played his instrument without looking up as we entered. I thought that he had not heard us come in, so great was his concentration. It was curious, to my mind, that one of the remaining instruments was one so large and unwieldy. I tried to imagine him carrying it to a restaurant and had some difficulty in doing so.

"All right, Robert?" Once we were close enough to the stage to be heard, Green addressed the cellist in a loud voice. The auditorium held, by my estimation, about four hundred seats, so it did not take long for us to make our way down the center aisle to stand in front of the stage.

The man, who was white-haired and elderly, looked up and blinked, immediately ceasing his playing. "Aye, Charles. Can't get a moment of quiet in the wings. Everyone rushing this way and that. Came here to be alone."

"Ah, yes, yes, everyone's in a terrible roar," said Pike, who was trailing behind and seemed entirely ignorant of the fact that he was part of the commotion. Robert the cellist did not seem overly fond of his manager, for he did not answer and simply stared down at him from his place atop the stage.

I did, for a moment, wonder if the strange subversion of a flute player having more obvious authority than the manager of the orchestra was the normal way of things for this particular group, or if it had merely arisen out of the present circumstance.

Holmes was, as I would have expected, growing impatient by this time, and he simply strode toward the doorway on stage right, which opened into the left side hallway. Green,

Pike, and I followed along, and as we turned, I heard Robert's cello begin again, eerie in the emptiness.

"The room where it happened is this way," said Green, leading us to the third door on the right. When we reached it, Holmes studied the lock for a moment. "No sign of any sort of tampering or forcing," he said.

"None at all," answered Green, "but both keys to the room were accounted for the whole time – one with Pike and the other with the guard."

I followed Holmes inside the practice room, which was a large, bare space with nothing but rickety wooden chairs, upon which and against which were balanced all manner of instrument cases. It looked, to all intents, like the players had left them moments before.

"Once the theft was discovered, we asked everyone to leave things exactly as they'd been before, or as nearly as they could remember," Green offered.

"I take it the police haven't been here," said Holmes dismissively. "It looks far too unmolested."

"That's correct," offered Pike. "Mr. Dorrigan, the owner of the hall, doesn't want to involve them unless it's absolutely necessary, in order to avoid the terms of contract that force him to pay for the instruments."

Holmes rounded on him. "I should think you'd have something to say about that."

The man blanched. "I – didn't think there was any harm in it. No one's moved anything, and we sent Green to consult you when we realized there wasn't a simple explanation, like a joke of some kind."

"No matter," said my friend, almost to himself.

As I had many times before, I watched Holmes do his work. First, he walked around the room, as if to gain an understanding of it from every angle. Then, he moved through the rows of chairs without touching anything. Finally, he began a systematic examination of every instrument case in the room.

Green, Pike, and I stood behind, not saying anything while he did his work. By this time, it was quite late in the evening, and our inactivity led to drooping eyes and flagging energy. I was certainly eager to hear Holmes's opinion on the matter, but I could little discern of his thoughts from his actions.

Finally, when we had been at loose ends for many minutes, Holmes looked up from somewhere on the right side of the room. "Were any instruments moved to a new position in the room after the discovery, any at all?"

"None, for I watched the entire exercise," boomed a voice from behind me, and I looked back to see a tall, broad-shouldered man in the doorway. His face wore a sour expression.

"Mr. Dorrigan?" Holmes came over and gazed on the man without revealing any of his thoughts.

"Oh, sir, here is the detective," said Mr. Pike quickly, like a mouse addressing an intractable elephant.

"So I see," said the newcomer, fixing his eyes on my friend as if he didn't much care for what he saw. "I hope you'll be able to make an end of this ridiculous matter. Surely the theft of an entire orchestra's instruments is nothing but someone's idea of an unfortunate joke."

"Perhaps," said Holmes noncommittally. "Mr. Green informed us on the way here that the members of the orchestra are all on the premises. Please fetch the players of stringed instruments for me."

We were taken to another room, a slightly smaller space with a few tattered, cloth-covered chairs. "Would you like them sent in as a group or individually?" asked Green.

"One by one," answered Holmes. "Mr. Green, your assistance will not be required."

The first musician to enter the room was a middle-aged woman with long white hair, who slowly sat down opposite Holmes and me and smiled. "Come to find what's happened, have you?" she asked with a broadly northern accent.

"We hope to attempt it. Now, then, Mrs. Stoker, please tell me where your seat is in the orchestra and what instrument you play."

"If we go to the next room, I could show you," she said, inclining her head in the direction of the room we'd just exited.

"That will be unnecessary," said Holmes. "I am familiar with orchestral seating, and I have the room's layout stored in my memory."

"All right," she answered. "I'm a second violin. We're opposite the firsts. I'm third from the center."

Holmes wrote this down in a notebook he pulled from his jacket pocket. "That's all that will be necessary. Send in the next one." I looked over at my friend, mystified. Even I, with my limited powers of deduction, had surmised that if none of the instruments had been moved, Holmes really didn't need the musicians themselves to answer his questions. The evidence was already present, and surely Pike could have told him where they sat.

Nevertheless, I didn't have time to ask Holmes anything before we were joined by a middle-aged man with a slight limp. He took his seat and stared at the floor, a bit bleary, as if he'd been on the bottle.

Again, as before, Holmes asked incidental questions and was answered without issue. Finally, as the man prepared to leave the room, he turned back. "I hope you find my viola," he said.

This happened twice more, once with a young man of awkward disposition, and again with an elderly, emaciated male violinist. Each time, my friend asked the same questions and received simple answers. Each time, I was mystified as to his real purpose in asking.

Finally, after the fourth musician exited the room, there was a slight delay before the next entered, and I turned to my flatmate, who stared straight ahead in his uncomfortable chair and said nothing. "Holmes," I hissed, thinking we might be interrupted again at any second, "what on earth are you doing?"

He bent the full intensity of his gaze upon me and, unexpectedly, smiled, answering rapidly, "You're a medical man, Watson. I didn't think it could have escaped your notice."

"What do you mean?" I asked, but just then, Doris Lake entered the room. Compared to her fellow musicians, she was a burst of life, alert where they had been nearly somnambulant.

"Good evening, Miss Lake," said Holmes, smiling. "I apologize for the ceremony, but I didn't have a chance to ask you about your seating position in the orchestra. Mr. Green informed us of your instrument."

"In the chair right behind Mrs. Stoker's. You've already spoken to her, I believe."

"Yes," answered Holmes. "That's all I need from the string section. I would, however, like to speak to Mr. Pike and Mr. Dorrigan again."

Miss Lake nodded. "If you follow me, I'll take you to the office." I noticed as we exited that Green was nowhere to be found. The girl took us past a few clusters of gathered orchestra members, who stared openly. I wanted to pity them; surely it must be distressing, I thought, for so many to have lost the sources of their livelihood. But their gazes were strange, unnerving, as if they weren't quite right.

We went through the hallway, past other small, empty rooms and back toward the dark area behind the stage, where Dorrigan's office was located. The area wasn't large, but it had enough room to contain an outer and inner sanctum. Miss Lake knocked on the door of the outer office. It was opened by a young, dark-haired man with a moustache and pock-marked skin.

"They weren't expected yet, Doris," he said sharply. "Nevertheless," she answered meekly, "they're ready to see Pike and Dorrigan."

The secretary nodded and knocked on the inner door, which was soon opened by an irate Dorrigan, who frowned even more deeply than before when he saw us. "I had understood you as wanting to question members of the orchestra."

"So I have," said Holmes coolly, "and I am now finished."

"Pike isn't here," said the man tersely, "but if you'd like to speak to me, I suppose I can't prevent you."

"Just so," Holmes replied. "If I may, I would like to speak to you, Green, and Miss Lake together." Dorrigan's brows knitted together even more forcefully, but he nodded once and shouted for his secretary.

Miss Lake returned first, and it was another ten minutes before Green joined our awkwardly silent group. Upon entering the room, he immediately took the girl's hand. Dorrigan presided over his enormous wooden desk, and Holmes and I sat on its other side, with our chairs facing outward, toward the young people who stood before us.

"How long have you been obtaining opium for the members of Pike's orchestra, Miss Lake?" The girl's face went even paler than it usually was as the words of Holmes's question poured over her.

"I – we – Mr. Green is my fiancé. That is my only position of importance."

"No," said Holmes decidedly, though not cruelly, "he isn't. Or, if he is, that certainly isn't all he is, but you know the truth. I would like you to tell it to me now."

"How did you know?"

Holmes answered after contemplating her for a moment. "Your empty viola case was in the wrong section of the practice room. Every other instrument case in the orchestra was in its proper location; only yours was incorrect, obviously a signal of some kind. I could have attributed this to the confusion after the theft was discovered, but it wasn't a seat or two away from its place. It was in the middle of the woodwinds. Of course, when I first discovered the case,

I had no idea whose it was, but that was easy enough to ascertain by questioning members of your section."

She shook her head and gave Dorrigan a desperate look. "He said – he said that you wouldn't know about that. He was afraid the police would bring in a musical expert of some kind, but he said one detective wouldn't know difference, so I mustn't risk anyone seeing me move it back."

"My musical talents are less renowned than my others," Holmes replied, "but I certainly know how an orchestra is arranged." The irony was not lost on me, for I was well aware, as was Holmes, that if they had called in the official force, the likelihood of anyone noticing a detail of that nature would have been nearly nonexistent. They had bet on one man, but he was entirely the wrong man.

Holmes added, "Every member of the orchestra whom I've met up to this moment shows the effects of opium – not the most acute effects; Pike wouldn't have allowed that, but I recognized its lingering presence in their lethargy. It was too coincidental to assume that your instrument signal was uninvolved in something so unusual. Now," he continued firmly, "the truth."

She nodded, resigned. "I met James Dorrigan two years ago, when our orchestra was first engaged here. It was a good time for us. Pike was delighted, because this hall represented a step up in the world, a foothold in London. Green hadn't joined us yet – of course." I did not know what she meant by this, but Holmes obviously did.

"The night of our first concert here, Dorrigan caught me bringing the opium to our members, something Pike had paid me to do for three years previously, using the placement of my viola case to signal the members that the drug was available. He recruits members from opium dens, supplies them with the drug, and then pays them nearly nothing, supposedly because they owe their wages to him as payment. He makes a profit, and they don't know they're being cheated." Her contempt was palpable. "The only reason I did his work of giving out the drug once he obtained it was that he threatened to put me out on the street if I didn't, and I had nowhere else to go – I'm not accomplished enough to join a more important orchestra, if one would even take a woman, which is extremely rare, and I had joined this one without realizing its true nature."

"The night Dorrigan found out, he threatened to terminate the contract and cancel our remaining three performances on account of the disgrace of it. This would have been disastrous. Pike had already put up what little collateral he had to transport us to London, under the promise of a large profit. I knew that he would blame me for being indiscreet, so I offered Dorrigan a deal – part of the profits from the opium in exchange for being quiet and letting things go on as they had been. The potential of making money far eclipsed any scruples he might have had."

"I had to tell Pike, but I waited until I had things arranged with Dorrigan. Pike is – he's not an utterly unkind man, and he took a more charitable view than I'd expected. He offered to divide the loss of Dorrigan's share with me, so the three of us were, effectively, in business together."

She stared daggers at the owner of the hall. "Of course, we'd have liked to get rid of Dorrigan as part of the equation, but he had the upper hand. He threatened to spread the news publicly of our orchestra's particular – interest and destroy our careers just as they were beginning to improve. That was the reason for the theft. Pike stole the instruments in order to force Dorrigan to either pay for them or agree to relinquish his share in the opium. If Dorrigan refused, Pike intended to go to the police and force him to honor his contract. By then, the instruments would have been long destroyed. It was Green's idea to go and see you and ascertain your likelihood of solving the case. He was only to bring you if he thought you would be easily deceived." Holmes smiled at this, and I realized that not only had Green been trying to fool us, but Holmes had also been fooling him all along, using flattery and simple deduction to look as if he esteemed his own abilities as much greater than they were.

At that moment, someone yelled. I realized, after my initial surprise, that it had sounded like a male rather than a female voice. Miss Lake and I stared at each other for a few seconds, but Holmes wasn't paralyzed by surprise. He was at the door in an instant and nearly collided with a white-faced Robert the cellist. "It's Pike. He's – dead."

Holmes swore under his breath. I followed him out of the room, dazed, and into the dressing room wing. Sure enough, Pike lay in the middle of a deserted room with his throat slashed. From the look of things, I surmised that he'd been dead for at least a quarter of an hour.

Holmes turned to Miss Lake and Green. "No one may leave this building. I'll have the murderer contained presently." I could tell that he had no intention of concealing his purpose from any of the orchestra members, who stood around the corpse with wide eyes and horrified faces.

"Where is Mr. Dorrigan's assistant?" my friend continued. "I have need of his abilities."

In that moment, Green tried to flee the room and was only caught by the resourceful Robert, the cello player, who pinned him to the floor easily.

"Mr. Green," said Holmes, giving him a hard stare. "Your disguise was a good one, but not good enough."

Doris Lake looked as shocked as I've ever seen anyone be in my life. "Charles, you –"

"You weren't the only one with secrets, Doris," said Dorrigan. "Didn't you notice that Green joined you just after my discovery of your arrangement? I sent him to you to make sure you and that fool Pike didn't cheat me. I didn't order him to do a stupid thing like killing Pike, though," he said, utterly disgusted.

"Neither Pike nor Miss Lake appears to have made the connection to your secretary," said Holmes, "but I believe you did." He indicated Robert, who was still sitting on

Green with good cheer.

"He had me fooled at first," said Robert, "but it was just too ideal – the way he'd found the orchestra, settled in so easily. He did well to keep himself from being seen in his other guise, but he couldn't entirely avoid it."

Holmes nodded. "I recognized the connection between Miss Lake, Pike, and Dorrigan first, but then I realized Green's recent entry into the orchestra and swift courting of the lady couldn't be without significance. I didn't know what it portended until I saw that Dorrigan's secretary was the same man."

Robert the cellist smiled. "Most policemen don't get to use their musical talents. I suppose I should be grateful for the opportunity. I'm only sorry to have to go back to my usual duties after such a long and interesting digression. I'm also sorry, of course, that I didn't prevent Pike's death."

At this moment, Green, who had been silent, exploded. "I did it for Doris, to free her from this – imprisonment! No one was supposed to come to this wing. In the morning, when the body was discovered, Dorrigan would have been suspected."

"Contingent," said Holmes mildly, "on your identity as Dorrigan's secretary remaining undiscovered and on no one poking about the way Robert has. You wouldn't have come out of this well either way, but killing Pike was a fatal mistake, one I doubt you'd have made if you hadn't determined that I trusted you completely, as I intended you to believe when you visited my flat."

"My name is Williams," said the cellist, "Inspector Robert Williams, Scotland Yard. You may think little of us, Mr. Holmes, but one of my associates – Gregson – saw a pattern in the information he obtained from one of his informants in the opium business. I was tasked with joining this unfortunate group many months ago, and I have been trying to build a legal case against them for some time."

"Yes, Inspector Williams, you're free to give your report

to Scotland Yard. Your competence has been, frankly, a welcome surprise. Pike's death is a pity, but it's not your concern to anticipate the actions of a mentally unstable and narcissistic criminal."

"I agree," the man answered with a grin.

In the end, none of the participants in the orchestral case faced retribution except Miss Lake, Dorrigan, and Green. The lady stood trial, but since her precise level of knowledge of the opium operation beyond her activities as intermediary could not be determined, she was allowed to go free, with her broken heart as her only punishment. Dorrigan, who had possessed extensive knowledge of both the legal and illegal aspects of Pike's involvement in the opium business, faced an unsympathetic jury who were plied with tales of ruined lives. He was given a prison sentence likely to outlast his earthly life. Green, his guilt easily proven through evidence and his own angry admission, was sentenced to hang. I cannot say that the thought of him being removed from the earth bothered me a great deal, but I did ask my friend why anyone would engage in such a blatantly ridiculous act as murdering someone when Sherlock Holmes was on the premises.

"I have seen it before," Holmes answered placidly. "Some criminals crave being caught and appreciated for their deeds. You saw the man when he first approached us. I've never met a more perfectly narcissistic personality. I believe he thought he could not fail in his plan to frame Dorrigan and free the lady, and all the better to have the satisfaction of knowing he'd done it under my nose. Barring that, he seemed to think Doris would love him more as a result of his the murder." I shook my head in disbelief.

"Still, this must be the most quickly-solved case of your career," I said. "Though the details are ugly, your investigation was not."

Holmes, who enjoyed praise far more than he liked to let on, smiled. "Thank you, Watson. The details and mistakes of the participants aligned to give me an excellent foothold, to say nothing of Williams's ingenuity, but I believe I did well enough with what I was given."

A month after the closing of the sordid case of Pike's orchestra, Mrs. Hudson and I were finally treated to the concert I'd suggested prior to Green's fateful evening visit. For once, however, my friend did not play alone. He was accompanied by a middle-aged policeman whose cello seemed to fill up the room. Williams was not as accomplished a player as Holmes, but then, few were. Still, I could tell by Holmes's expression when they played that he found the man's efforts satisfactory. I hoped, temporarily, that their shared interest might lead to my friend engaging more in society, but that was never his preference at any point in our acquaintance, and his first evening of musical partnership was also his last.

The Haunting of Sherlock Holmes

by Kevin David Barratt

In the events that I have recorded elsewhere as "The Adventure of The Speckled Band", I wrote that the case had more singular features than any that I had encountered up to that time in the April of 1883. Six months passed and my days with Mr. Sherlock Holmes seemed to settle back into a familiar routine until the receipt of a letter in the October of that same year set off a train of events that brought the whole horrific episode back into my life once more.

I kept few secrets from Sherlock Holmes. Indeed, as he seemed able to glean facts from the littlest things that I said or did, I found it almost impossible to keep anything to myself. However, my family and its history were not subjects into which I wanted him to intrude, and until now I had succeeded in keeping them private. The letter that came was from my sister-in-law, who wrote to tell me that my brother, who was a gambler and a heavy drinking man, was currently in poor health because of his excesses and that she had reached her wits end with him. She begged for me to try and step in before he killed himself, or before one of his moneylenders did it for him. My brother had made and lost a substantial amount of money in the gold fields of Australia, and years back I had received a similar summons to the other side of the world to assist them in fleeing the country. They had now settled in Scotland, but a visit would mean being away from Baker Street for some time, and this was not a particularly good time to leave. Holmes had been behaving strangely of late. Cases had recently been in short supply and, knowing the ways that boredom affected him, I was convinced that his long-standing drug habits were again being employed, despite his attempts to hide them from me.

"You must go, Watson," Holmes declared, as I sat opposite him before the fire.

"Yes, I suppose that I must," I mumbled, lost in my thoughts. I then jerked myself back from them and said, "This habit of yours is beginning to get tiresome. How much have you deduced from my thoughts this time?"

"Very little," he admitted, "but it is obviously a summons for help from someone dear to you."

It was at this point that I told Sherlock Holmes a lie. "It is not from someone dear to me, actually, but from an old comrade from my university days who wishes me to spend some time in Scotland looking after his medical practice because he has to travel abroad on family business. I could be away for some time and, depending on the date of his return, I may not be able to get back to Baker Street in time for Christmas. That is why I am deep in thought."

If Holmes saw through my fabrications he was polite enough to not show it, but, as he had rightly said, I must go. I quickly made arrangements to travel as soon as possible. I left Mrs. Hudson with my brother's address in case she needed to contact me. I could hardly leave it with Holmes, now that I had lied to him, but I believed that I was not the only one keeping secrets. Holmes may have the greater intellect, but I have the greater medical skills, and I can spot the effects of drug misuse as easily as he can spot footprints.

My time in Scotland was spent in attempting to rehabilitate my poor brother and saving his marriage. His gambling and drinking had resulted in a spiralling descent into a sickness of body and mind such as to leave him unrecognisable as the loving husband and brother that I knew him to be. He had sunk so low into debt as to pawn our dear father's watch, a treasured heirloom that, as the oldest son, he had inherited some years ago. I believe that it was the death of our father that had first set him on this road to ruin.

By employing a generous amount of tender care and an equal portion of steely resolve, I succeeded in keeping my brother away from alcohol and gambling for two months. His spirits revived enough for him to recommence work and earn money again. As a sign of gratitude for his compliance and efforts, I presented him with a gift. I paid the pawnbroker for the return of our father's watch. My brother was so grateful that he broke down in tears and vowed never to return to his old ways. His wife was, of course, delighted, and she begged me to stay with them for Christmas. Despite my eagerness to return to Baker Street, I did not feel able to refuse her generous hospitality.

Unfortunately, I was soon forced to change my plans. A letter arrived from Mrs. Hudson and it was couched in words of distress. She expressed concern that Sherlock Holmes was ill. He was spending practically all his time indoors, forsaking company of any kind. She had tried to let in clients on a couple of occasions, only for Holmes to shout at her from the landing. Even Inspector Lestrade had been turned away. She wondered what it could all mean. I had an uncomfortable feeling that it meant trouble.

It also appeared that, despite Holmes's insistence on no visitors, he must have taken a new lodger into our rooms. The man who could go for days with little nourishment had suddenly taken to demanding more frequent and larger meals. He had also been heard shouting at someone, "You will not succeed with your plan, you devil! You will not!" This was often followed by the heavy sound of something being thrown at the wall. Things reached a head when Mrs. Hudson heard a fearful banging on our door. She reached the top of the stairs to find the door locked. When she called to Holmes, his voice screamed at her from the other side, "Help me! Find Watson! Please, find Watson!"

With a heavy heart I explained that I had to return home urgently. Feeling that I had done as much as I could for my brother, they both agreed with my plan to make a hasty return to London. I dare not begin to contemplate what I may find upon my return, but I was fearful for Holmes's safety from whomever, or whatever, now occupied our rooms.

It was Christmas Eve when I arrived back in the Metropolis. As I made my way from the train station back to Baker Street I saw shopkeepers and passers-by making the most of the festive season. Groups of singers stood on street corners, gloved and muffled against the cold. Everything appeared normal, in stark contrast to the thoughts running through my head. As I entered 221b, our landlady came running up to me, clearly in a state of distress. The anxious looks upon her face showed that she was both pleased and relieved that I had returned. Words tumbled from her, and I had to raise my hands to silence the torrent.

"Mrs. Hudson, please calm yourself. Firstly, let me thank you for sending for me. Secondly, I do not know what I will find, so I beg of you to return to your rooms until I have evaluated the situation."

She said, "Be careful, Doctor. Whoever this other person is, he must have some nasty hold over Mr. Holmes, or why hasn't he let me call the police and have him removed?"

With a promise to speak to our landlady later, I left my case and coat in the hall and ascended to our rooms. Each of the seventeen steps seemed to pull at my feet as if to prevent me from reaching the door. I was also aware that I was holding my breath, as if I was fearful to make a sound. However, I must have made some sound for, as I reached the landing, I heard the turn of a key, and our door was thrown open. Holmes stood on the threshold in his dressing gown.

Such a change had come over my friend. His face was

grey, sweat stood out upon his forehead, and he had a look of intense horror upon his face. His voice came as a croaking rattle as he said, "Oh, Watson! Watson! Thank God you've come."

Grasping my coat sleeve, he pulled me inside and quickly closed and locked the door once more. He stood with his back against it, and I could see that he was shaking, as if in a considerable state of anxiety.

"Holmes, you are shivering," I said, my voice filled with concern. "It is not cold which makes me shiver," Holmes said in a voice that seemed to come from a great distance. "It is fear. It is terror."

At these words, the hairs seemed to rise on the back of my neck, for I had heard these exact words before. In April, Helen Stoner of Stoke Moran had said the same in this very room before laying her story concerning the speckled band before us. Slowly, I approached Holmes, guided him to his armchair, and sat him down. I offered him a drink, but he made no reply.

As I poured him a large brandy, I looked around. The room was a mess, with a number of objects on the floor by the door to Holmes's bedroom, as if he had been throwing them at it and had left them where they fell. The table and sideboard were weighed down with a large number of dirty plates and dishes as if they had not been cleared for days. A strange thing was that it looked as if there had only been one diner. There was no fire in the hearth, and the whole room felt as cold as the grave.

I placed the glass to Holmes's lips and made him drink a little brandy. As he gave a choking cough a little colour seemed to return to his face. I poured myself a drink and sat across from him in my own chair.

"Holmes, you spoke just now of fear and terror. Fear and terror of your mysterious guest?"

"Guest, Watson? There is no guest. What is here has come uninvited."

"And what is here?" I asked quietly.

Holmes appeared to be looking over my shoulder towards his bedroom. When he spoke, although I recognised the voice, the words were not what I expected to hear from my friend.

"As you know, Watson, I am not a superstitious man, and logic tells me there are no such things as ghosts, and yet I say in all faith that I am being haunted by an evil spirit."

"Evil spirit? Surely –"

"An evil spirit with a name, Watson, and that name is Dr. Grimesby Roylott."

Despite the look of seriousness upon his face I had only one reaction to his announcement. I broke into a hearty laugh. As tears began to roll down my face, I saw tears of another sort roll down Holmes's face. I fell silent, and Holmes continued with words that again came from Miss Stoner, spoken in a high voice with an intensity that sent a thrill down my spine.

"Oh, sir, do you not think that you could help me, and at least throw a little light through the dense darkness which surrounds me?"

It was not the lack of a fire that suddenly chilled me. I leaned forward and looked into Holmes's vacant eyes. My heart seemed to stop until I saw a light return to them. When I spoke, it was in a voice that showed him that I no longer doubted that he was a troubled man.

"Holmes, I swear to do everything that I can to help you through this."

"Thank you, my friend," he replied, and again I saw tears well up in his eyes.

After another mouthful of brandy, Holmes proceeded to explain the events that had brought him to this singular position.

"At first it began as a feeling that something was approaching. I forbade Mrs. Hudson to let anyone into the house, but as time went on I knew it was already here. I began to hear Roylott's voice coming from my bedroom."

I asked what the voice had said, but I feared I knew the answer. He became animated and began to shout, "Meddler! Busybody! Scotland Yard Jack-in-office!" As he settled down again, he said, "At all times of day I heard him, but no matter what I threw at him, he kept on returning to taunt me. He warned me that day when he came here to keep myself out of his grip. Well, now he has me in that grip, and matters are approaching a climax."

"What makes you think that?" I asked.

His voice took on a distant sound again and the pitch rose as he said, "Because during the last few nights I have always, about three in the morning, heard a low, clear whistle." I remained silent as he continued, "I sprang up and lit the lamp, but nothing was to be seen in the room." The light then returned to his eyes and he looked at me.

"Holmes, this is intolerable. If you truly believe that someone is whistling in the night and menacing you with a snake, how does the snake get in and out of your room? There are no vents, no bell-ropes."

"Spirit snakes do not require bell-ropes."

"And spirit snakes do not attack the living in their beds. For Heaven's Sake, Holmes, return to your senses before it is too late."

"If these things are but fancies of an addled brain, Watson, how do you explain this?"

He got up from his chair and went over to his desk. He opened the drawer and returned with our poker. It had been bent in half, just as Roylott had done on his visit. I sat in silence. I knew now that any answer I made would not appease him. Instead I asked him what he needed me to do.

His eyes glazed over once more and in a hushed voice he said, "There is a distinct element of danger. Your presence might be invaluable." Then he seemed to return to himself again as he added, "For goodness' sake let us have a quiet pipe, and turn our minds for a few hours to something more cheerful." Instead of reaching for his pipe, his hands clenched into fists, his eyes seemed to roll up into his head and he lapsed into unconsciousness.

As Holmes slept for what might have been the first time in days, I built up a fire and tidied the room a little. I collected up as many dirty plates as I could and carried them down to Mrs. Hudson. I took tea with her and assured her that I would take good care of Holmes. I asked her to trust me when I said that I was sure that he would soon be returned to his old self.

I returned to our rooms to find Holmes was still unconscious. I unpacked my case then, washed and refreshed, I took a Clark Russell sea story from the bookcase and settled in for a long night ahead. As I read, the adventure took me onto the high seas far away from my friend's troubles and spirit snakes. I became so engrossed in my book that I lost track of the time and it was soon eleven o'clock.

As the clock struck the hour, Holmes opened his eyes. "That is our signal," he said, springing to his feet just as he had done at the Crown Inn many months ago.

Lighting a lamp, he crossed the room and put his ear to his bedroom door, then silently motioned me to him. Making a trumpet of his hand, he whispered in my ear. "The least sound would be fatal to our plans." With the lamp before him he slowly opened the door and stepped into the room. Of course, it was empty.

Holmes returned to himself again. "Good. Roylott is unlikely to try anything until I am in bed, so this is what we must do. Watson, you must stay with me tonight, keeping watch. As we know from the events at Stoke Moran, the snake does not strike every time and the victim may escape for nights. I have been lucky so far, but eventually it will kill me. Therefore you must be ready to kill it first."

Holmes removed his dressing gown and hung it behind the door. I placed a heavy chair against the same in order to bar any means of entry or exit. I set tables at both sides on which I placed a drink, my book, a lighted candle, some matches, and a stout stick. As I settled into the chair, Holmes climbed into bed and extinguished his lamp, leaving the flickering flame of my candle as the only illumination. It cast strange shadows across his anxious face.

"Do not go asleep, your very life may depend upon it," he whispered, his voice taking on that far away quality once more. "Have your pistol ready in case we should need it."

"And risk shooting you in the dark? If anything should appear I am sure my stick will suffice."

No answer came. Holmes had lapsed into unconsciousness once more. I took up my Clark Russell in the hopes that the thrill of the tale might keep me awake, but with the strain placed on my eyes from the dim light and the tiredness of a long day, I am ashamed to say that I fell asleep.

A sibilant sound penetrated my mind, like the hissing of a kettle. I opened my eyes but could see little for my candle had burned down to a stump and was barely flickering. The hissing stopped, and as my eyes grew accustomed to the gloom I could make out Holmes, resting up on his elbows and looking down his body.

"You see it, Watson?" he yelled. "You see it?"

Fear gripped me for upon Holmes's chest there was something long and thin in the shape of a letter 'S'. I could not make out any details in the dim light, but it appeared to be trying to move towards Holmes's neck as if to strike at it.

With no thought for my own safety I leapt across to the bed, grabbed the vile thing and hurled it into the corner of the room. Taking up my stick I followed it and beat it, and beat it, and beat it, until I was certain that it must be dead.

Quickly I lit the lamp on Holmes's bedside table. He was now sat upright in bed, his face ashen, sweating profusely. His eyes were fixed on the corner of the room, his lips quivered. "The band! The speckled band!" Holmes whispered, and then his eyes closed. He sank back onto his pillow and was asleep once more.

Turning away from him I approached the corner of the room and could now make out the coiled object on the floor against the wall where it had fallen. I could barely believe what I saw lying there. It was the cord from Holmes's dressing gown.

It was Christmas Day, and all the churches around were ringing out their glad tidings. It was now late morning and I was sat before a roaring fire with a cheery drink and pipe. When Holmes's bedroom door opened he was dressed, and I had to admit that he looked more like his old self than he had done on the previous night. He certainly sounded like his old self as he bellowed, "Merry Christmas, Watson, and the greetings of the season to you." Crossing to me, he handed me a box. As he stood warming himself before the hearth with a broad smile, I opened the box. Within it was the morocco case containing his syringe and bottles of drugs. I looked up at him.

"What does this mean, Holmes?"

"It means that it is all over," Holmes answered. As he prepared his first pipe of the day, he began to explain. "As you were aware before you left on your travels north, there had been little to stimulate my brain. As a result of this I began to use more and more drugs to counter the boredom that possessed me. Without your presence to keep me in check my intake grew to the point where I began to fear for my safety. One night I resolved to stop completely in order to surprise you with the news upon your return, and that is what I did. Unfortunately –"

I interrupted him. "Unfortunately, you suffered the consequences of your actions. As a medical man I have read much about the misuse of drugs and their effects upon the body, and I am well aware of the symptoms caused by sudden withdrawal from them. There is a growing feeling of agitation and much restless behaviour, and then paranoia sets in. This was why you began to believe that Dr. Roylott was haunting you, and explains why you shut yourself away from all visitors, even Lestrade. You became convinced that he was in your room, even believing that you could hear his voice. It was no wonder that Mrs. Hudson believed you had a new lodger, for as well as holding bizarre conversations, you were eating enough for two. An increased appetite is another symptom of sudden withdrawal. I think I am correct in saying that you began to suffer vivid and unpleasant dreams, and that during one of these dreams you walked in your sleep. Do you remember how, in April, you had the strength to straighten the poker again after Roylott had bent it?"

Holmes chuckled at the memory, but said nothing, to allow me to continue.

"It was you who bent the poker in half this time, and then returned to bed with no knowledge of your actions. Finally, we come to the events after my return. How long had it been since you last slept?"

Holmes lit his pipe and sank into the chair opposite me. "Two days, maybe three."

"And by that point you could not distinguish fantasy from reality. Hence, the drama that played out last night. I believe that you have been reading my notes on the Roylott case."

Holmes smiled. "How do you deduce that?"

"My notes are my memory of what was said and done, and thus may vary from the actual events. Yet, you quoted me word for word on many occasions."

Holmes gave a hearty laugh and clapped his hands. "Wonderful, Watson."

"Then the dressing gown cord arranged upon your chest to look like a snake, the hissing sound you made to waken me. Due to the flickering light of my guttering candle, I did think that I saw a snake slithering up your body, but I had been deceived. It was your conscience that created the entire illusion. You told me that you did not think that Roylott's death would weigh very heavily upon your conscience, but

I believe that it had more of an effect upon you than you realise."

"Perhaps it did, but thanks to you, I hope to have finally defeated my demons. Hence, my gift to you."

I looked once more at the case before me. It appeared that not only had I saved my brother from the path of self-destruction, I had now assisted in saving Holmes from his personal demons. But, I wondered, in both cases, for how long?

"Holmes, I cannot accept this gift. I will accept you as a patient and help you as much as I am able, but you must appreciate that only you can ultimately conquer this thing."

"But we have conquered it," Holmes replied.

"Not yet, Holmes. You must understand that this might not be the end of your troubles, and that dark days and nights may still lie ahead for the both of us."

"Nonsense, Watson. The ghost of Dr. Grimesby Roylott has been well and truly exorcised." As Holmes puffed on his pipe, he paused to add, "But there is one detail, however, that appears to have been overlooked within your theory."

"And that is?"

"The dressing gown cord."

"I have explained that," I replied.

Holmes shook his head. "Not at all, my friend. Consider this. How could I have got up from my bed, crossed the room, and taken the cord from my dressing gown without waking you? Remember, you were sat against the door and my dressing gown, with tables at both sides blocking my approach. It would have been impossible to reach without moving either a table or yourself, and what is it that I try to impress upon you? When you have eliminated the impossible, whatever remains, however improbable, must be the truth. Don't you agree, Watson?"

The Allegro Mystery

by Luke Benjamen Kuhns

As I glance over my notes between '82 and '90, I fondly remember those early years. I, having returned to London from my Afghan campaign with a Jezail bullet as a souvenir in my limb, was by no means ready for civilian life. I will always be grateful to Stamford for introducing me to that strange bohemian man, Sherlock Holmes, whose powers of observation and deduction continue to astonish for nearly quarter of a century.

It was in the autumn of 18 – when one of the strangest cases found its way to the doorstep of 221b. While the story received some press, a proper and accurate account of the event has yet to reach the public. I feel, also, that the parties concerned in the matter have reached a time of life where these events would be nothing more than a thrilling story of their youth. A wound long since healed as opposed to a freshly bandaged scrape.

"I have put her away for good, Watson. I have put her away for good!" said Sherlock Holmes with a sweeping entrance into the study. I folded the paper.

"Who have you put away?" I asked.

"Miss Susan Sutherland, my dear fellow! For months she's plagued chapels, music halls, theatres and busy streets, pick-pocketing any inattentive fool."

"Well, this is the first I have heard you mention her,

Holmes."

"Yes, well, you have had your own matters to attend to of late.

Though I deduce you aren't friendly with Miss Edwards any longer." "Good heavens, Holmes!" I barked. He smiled.

"She has kept you from our work the past few months, but looking at the state of your hair, the longest it's been since you met her, and the state of your whiskers, your personal grooming says there is no one to impress."

"Not that it is any of your business, but you are, as always, correct." I rubbed my face, my whiskers had become rather unruly and were in need of a good trim. "Tell me about this Miss Sutherland."

"Right!" Holmes began as he continued through the study and fell into his chair. "Sutherland, quite the villain I should say." Holmes picked up his pipe and filled it with tobacco from his Persian slipper. "I got word that men and women were being robbed in church services across London. And don't give me that look, Watson. The robbery was not the minister collecting the tithe. The robberies were from individual pockets and handbags. Change, watches, bracelets, and even rings were slipped off. Raptured away! I discovered that each of the robberies were on the person's right side. So, I was looking for a left-handed crook. Of course the difficult thing was finding the person hiding in plain sight. I had to find the disguise among the general public façades in the crowd."

"How on earth did you catch them, then?"

"Accessories, Watson. It all came down to simple muff."

"A muff?"

"Correct." Holmes took a deep inhale of his pipe before exhaling and continuing. "This is where I found Susan Sutherland. She always kept her left hand inside her muff."

"I thought you said the thief was left handed." Holmes raised his finger to me.

"So I planned my trick to take place at one of her places

of worship. Having disguised myself splendidly as an old woman with a monstrously huge bag ripe for the plucking, I sat and waited. Soon enough, she sat by me, just to my right and her left. Then I felt it!" Holmes said slapping his hand upon his knee. "Her hand was inside my bag. I peered over to see her left hand still in her muff. My assumptions were correct. I, too, had a similar plan. As she reached into the bag what she did not expect to find was my hand inside. I grabbed hers, threw off my disguise, and exposed her. Then one of Scotland Yard's finest came to cart her off to a cell." Setting down his pipe and pressing his fingers together, he leaned his head back and a smile of satisfaction stretched across his face. "Though, there is no guarantee that any or all the stolen belongings will ever be recovered. Most are likely lost to the pawnbrokers."

I clapped my hands together.

"Well done, Holmes!" I paused a moment. "And I am sorry for my absence of late. I pray you won't hold it against me?"

"Watson, all matters of love I leave in your hands. While I haven't the time or energy for such commitment, I can, at the very least, understand the game you play. For love is a game, maybe the most dangerous game of them all."

There was a ring on the bell followed by the sound of hurried steps up the stairs. A woman, my God, a woman burst into the study. I turned quickly, Holmes slowly lifted his head. The fairest creature I had ever seen stood there, pale faced and gasping for breath. There was a familiarity about her, I thought, as I marvelled at her tall slender frame. She wore a long green dress and large floral hat. Her dark blonde hair had fallen loose from under her hat. This porcelain woman, with striking rosy cheeks, darted her blue, gem-like eyes between myself and Holmes.

"I am looking for Mr. Sherlock Holmes," the woman asked in a French accent.

"I am he," Holmes returned

"Then you must help me, sir!" she pleaded, still standing in the doorway panting.

"My dear, won't you have a seat. You are flush," I said. She looked at me with a blank stare before nodding quickly. She glided across the floor, her green dress flowing with every step. I called for Mrs. Hudson to bring us some tea.

"Mademoiselle Dipin," Holmes said, "what can the West End's shining star need with my services?"

"You know me?'

"I know you are rising star, with a one-off stint at Her Majesty's Theatre performing an exotic ballet. No paper in London has missed the show."

"It is a beautiful story," Mademoiselle Dipin began. It seemed that whatever concerns she had upon entering our rooms vanished as her mind turned back to her art. "The movements, the music, oh it's...." She pressed her fingers to her soft lips and kissed them.

"So I've heard, though yet to see," said Holmes.

"And you might never get the chance." Her face turned to stone. "I cannot say how much longer I'll survive the show."

"Is your life in danger?" I asked. She looked at me, her eyes piercing.

"For the last two-and-a-half months we performed and all seemed fine, but it began with letters."

"Tell me all from the beginning. Leave no detail out, no matter how trivial you might think it," said Holmes.

"Then, to tell you of recent events, I need to tell you about my past. My stage fame has inspired many devoted followers. They attend more shows than the lead actor or actress themselves, it seems. They wait outside the stage door, they bring you flowers, chocolates, many different gifts. If you miss a show they send you a card. It's quite remarkable what the fanatics will do for you. A mutual appreciation for the art brings people together.

"I love these types of people, Mr. Holmes, those who

love the art and can discuss the art. But some," she paused and clasped her hands, and nervously twiddled her thumbs, "they see you as the embodiment of art, and assume you are the final authority on it, rather than one of the many channels by which one can demonstrate it's beauty. Back in France I had many admirers. Some were harmless. Some were more...forceful. "There was a man named Jean Javet. He believed he was in love with me. He started by offering flowers after performances. I thought nothing of it at the time. I graciously accepted his gifts. That was my first mistake. Next, he started sending letters. In the beginning, they spoke of his love for my art and how passionate my movements were. Saying how he'd never seen such marvellous style and superb technique.

"From time to time I would write very gracious letters in return, thanking him for his compliments and coming to see the performances. I started to become a concerned after a rather poor review was published in one of the local papers. The critic called our performance a disgrace, scandalous, and said it should be ended now. One never forgets a terrible review. I did my best to put it to the back of my mind. Some people will always hate your art.

"A few days after that the review, I received a letter. Monsieur Javet took great offence on my behalf for the review. He ranted about how terrible they were for saying such harsh things, and that the paper should know the error of their ways. I replied saying it was no issue and that we must move forward in our art. He replied with a single letter, 'Our art will be beautiful. I will make sure no one speaks of you and our art that way again.'

"I was slightly haunted by this response. What he meant I did not know, at the time. A few days later the paper that published the review was set on fire and burnt down! There was no evidence, no clues at all as to who started it or how it happened. It was passed off as an accident. Javet wrote me again, this time he said, 'Our art is saved'. I knew what he meant. I knew he was responsible, but I did not know if I should turn the letter over to the authorities. Would they believe me?

"I waited, foolishly. Mr. Holmes, I waited! That very night after my performance, I was the last to leave the theatre. When I left, Javet was outside the stage door. He rushed me and took me in his arms. He raved about our art and love. I pleaded with him to let me go. He continued to speak of our love and what love does to art. He said he loved me and forced a kiss on me. I was confused, frightened, and alone. I said I had no feelings for him.

"This angered him. He pushed me against the wall. My breath was taken from me. I tried to regain composure, but he held me gently and caressed my hair saying, 'No, no, you do love me, you do. I know it. We are both artists, and we'll make beautiful art.' I dug my nails into his face and tore his skin. He fell back holding his face, which began to drip with blood. I ran, he chased. Thankfully, a policeman was nearby and heard my cries. He stopped Javet and arrested him. He was tried and sentenced to jail for the fire and assault. That was three years ago this last July."

She paused a moment. "This brings me to now. At the end of the first week's performance here in London, I received a letter." The ballerina took out a piece of paper and handed it to Holmes. He took it and quickly read it before handing it over to me. It read thus:

> *My beautiful Mademoiselle, How I've missed your art. How I've missed your movements.*
>
> *How I've missed your touch. I am excited to see you on stage in London very soon.*
>
> *Keep a watchful eye, I will be there. J*

"I have been frightened terribly by this. I did not keep this letter a secret, but I was assured measures would be taken to ensure my, and the entire cast's, safety. During my second week's performance I got another letter. It was from Javet. He said how wonderful the show was and how I am the light of London. He promised he'd see more performances, and that I'd never be out of his sight again." Her eyes began to well and her lower lip quivered. But she remained strong. She straightened herself and fought back the tears.

"Two nights ago, I believe I saw him in the audience. He was not seated. He was standing in a doorway. He made a nod and hand gesture at me, like an American salute. It was the only time during a performance that I have ever stumbled! The next day he wrote again, saying how pleased he was to get that reaction. Then, last night on my way home, I was followed. A man, of similar stature to Javet, followed me from the theatre, through Leicester Square. It was heavily crowded and I took the opportunity to hurry my pace and get away. I made haste to Soho where I have lodging while I am here in London. Before I entered, I looked and took no notice of anyone else. I sat at my table and looked at the newspaper. An article in it spoke of you and your assistance to the Yard. I looked you up and thought if anyone could help me, it would be you!"

Holmes looked at the woman a few moments. "Well, well. You fear, then, that this Javet has escaped or been set loose from his cell in France and is here in London to watch you perform, and possibly more. Have you made enquiries with the France police to see if he is still there?"

"I have not, no," she admitted. Her cheeks flush with embarrassment.

"No need to blush. These are enquires I will make on your behalf. If this man is in London, and intends to cause you torment, I assure you he will be found and his deeds exposed."

"Mr. Sherlock Holmes!" she cried. "So you will help me?"

"I will." Holmes handed the woman a slip of paper. "Please write your address on here. Continue life as usual. Please know I might call upon you at various times and places if need be." She nodded excitedly as she scribbled down her address and handed it back to him. "Tell me, the letters you received here in London, have you kept them?"

"Yes, I have."

"Good. Then I will send Watson here to fetch them and bring them back to me," Holmes looked at me. "That is, if you have nothing else pressing, my good fellow."

"Indeed, I do not! I would be happy to get them." I passed a friendly smile at the ballerina. She smiled. The out-of-breath and frightened creature was gone. The woman who sat before us now was different, more confident, more enticing. It was no wonder she had driven a man to lunacy.

"And you won't mind if I keep this letter until the others arrive?" Holmes asked, holding up the document which she had presented to us.

"It is yours. I never wish to see it again."

"The last thing I would like to know, what does Javet look like?" The woman swallowed and jutted her chin slightly. "He is Lucifer," she said.

"Ah, but my dear woman, Lucifer, according to the holy text, is a beautiful being," interjected Holmes.

"Then Javet is a troll who belongs under a bridge," she returned.

"Let us not get carried away with bitterness. I want straight facts."

"Forgive me, Mr. Holmes."

My friend nodded and motioned for her to continue. "He is about your height, but stalky. Broad chest and thick skinned. He is not a fat man, though. He, last I saw, had thick whiskers on his cheeks, but his chin and upper lip were clean. He will now have the scars from three scratch marks on his left cheek from me. His hair is dark, black or dark brown. I've only seen it from under his hat and at night. I do remember him having a thin upper lip and a dot in the centre of his chin. He is a very strongly built man, Mr. Holmes."

"Thank you, Mademoiselle." Holmes turned to me. "Shall I retrieve those letters?" I asked.

"Yes, we can take a cab," replied our guest.

"If you will bind the letters with a thread and set it just outside your door, Watson will wait in in the cab collect them once you have set them out, I don't want anyone to see him go inside," said Holmes.

We were off in a hurry. I sat next to our alluring client. The crisp autumn air filled the cab as we bounced down the streets. I peered, causally, out the window to see if we had been followed. Nothing out of the ordinary caught my attention. Mademoiselle Dipin sat calm and quiet, keeping her face away from the windows. I would ask her questions about the show, but her responses reminded me of Holmes when he was busy with thought. Short and vague. We passed through Soho Square before coming to a stop a few yards behind the ballerina's door. I watched as she darted out, looking back and forth, before vanishing into her building. I stepped out of the cab just as the door opened enough for me to catch a glimpse of her dainty hand leaving a bundle of letters bound together. Putting them safely into my pocket, I returned to my cab and ordered the driver to return to Baker Street. When I did, Holmes was nowhere to be found. A note had been left which said he had gone to enquire about Javet and would return later. I did not see Holmes the remainder of the day. What exploits he had engaged himself with were not learned until I woke the next morning.

I found my friend lying on the floor on our bear rug. He gazed intensely at the ceiling. At his feet lay scraps of paper, and to one side lay the letters I had retrieved. I bade him good morning. He was, as on several occasions, unresponsive. I glanced the room for any sign of his cocaine usage, which had, at times, been the cause for his silence.

"Fret not, good fellow," he said. I turned to look at him. He remained unmoved except one hand extended into the air. Grasped between his index finger and thumb hung one of the letters. "I have been in engaged with this. I seek solace in cocaine when there is nothing to stimulate my mind." I rose an eyebrow at him. He finally turned his head slightly to look at me.

"What have you done?" I asked.

"Look at the floor and make a deduction," he encouraged. "It seems like you've created a mess," I said sarcastically.

"Beyond the most obvious, Watson," his tone became stern, which I found surprising.

"It looks like you have been comparing papers to the letters, given the different makes you've laid out."

"Well done!" He said cheerfully. "After I sent a message to the Continent to learn the whereabouts of Javet, I came back to find these letters. I immediately rushed back out, after having thoroughly examined then. The letters are all written in the same hand, of that I have no doubt, even the ink is the same, as was the pen that was used. The paper, dear Watson, on which our man scribbled, is not all the same. So I scoured the city to see where these types of papers are relatively found."

"What was your conclusion?" I pressed.

"The paper is off poor quality. Sold primarily through street vendors. Most vendors won't give you what you pay for and you run out of your sheets soon."

"So our culprit is new to town and grabbed cheap paper, which is why you know this man used it so quickly?"

"The ink, Watson, is a fine ink. Expensive to obtain. He is buying cheap paper from street vendors in order to avoid being recognised in more well established retailers. How I know he's using it quickly: On two of these letters there are three droplets of ink that correspond when the pages are placed together. The man dipped his pen in the ink and it splatted and stained both pages. What I do believe is that our man has set himself up in Islington, somewhere near Angel."

"How did you come to this?"

"Street vendors!" He exclaimed and shot up from the bear rug. He rifled through the paper and the letters. He matched the letters to the blank sheets of paper. I stood over him and looked down. Written on the new sheets at the top left corner was the name of the vendor and a street where they were sold. "It took me most of the day and into the evening but I found them all. There are three vendors who sell these papers in the Angel area. I took their information, and once I learn about Javet from the French authorities, I will go retrace that avenue if need be."

"When do you expect to hear back?"

"I sent a message to Monsieur Dubuque of the Paris police," Holmes was interrupted by a knock on the door.

"A message for you," said Mrs. Hudson, poking her head around the door. Taking it from her, I handed it to Holmes. In a single thrust he leapt to his feet from the floor.

"Come, Watson! The game is afoot!"

Silently we sat in the cab. My heart raced with excitement and curiosity. Mademoiselle's apartment had been ransacked during the late morning, between nine and eleven a.m., and Inspector Lestrade of the Metropolitan Police had called for our assistance. When we arrived, two police officers stood outside. They waved Holmes and me through.

The apartment was a devastating mess. Cabinets where toppled over, clothing was scattered and torn, pillows were thrown here and there.

Shreds of paper were under every step. Inspector Lestrade stood in the middle of a small lounge near Mademoiselle Dipin. Her face was buried in her hands for a moment before running them through her extraordinary hair, pulling it back away from her beautiful face. When she saw Holmes and me, she stood up and approached.

"I am so glad to see you, Mr. Holmes," she said.

"Yes, good of you to come in such a hurry," said Lestrade.

"What do you know?" Holmes asked making no time for pleasantries. Lestrade nodded at the lady.

"Nothing seemed out of the ordinary. I did not notice myself being followed or feel that someone was watching me. I've been about my daily business. I spent most of the morning at the theatre. I came home to relax for a few hours and freshen up before I returned this evening. When I got home, I found the place like this!"

"The lady here has told us about this Javet character. He seems a good suspect," said Lestrade.

"Yes, but we are not certain where he is at present," returned Holmes.

"He's certainly in London!" Lestrade said with a chuckle. "The girl told me about the letters and everything."

There was a commotion outside; officers were shouting. We could hear the sound of several feet thumping up the stairs.

"Where is she? Where is my daughter?" echoed the voice of a strong woman. She stood in the shadow of the doorway, majestic, towering some six feet tall. Glowing golden hair was fashionably tied up and styled on top of her head. She was certainly a woman who, in her prime, would have been stolen the hearts of every man. While still very handsome, she was the type of woman who now preferred softly lit rooms. Tucked under her arm was small box which she clung to tightly.

"*Mere!*" cried Mademoiselle Dipin. Her expression was of utter horror. "What are you doing here?"

"I have come to speak with you, and when I do, I find you caught up in a mess!" the matriarch returned. "Tell me what has happened!"

"It seems your daughter has caught some unwelcome attention by an enthusiast for her art," said Lestrade. Her mother scoffed. "We believe he's the one behind it all."

"It's Javet, *Mere.*"

"That man?" she roared. "This is why I come here, to beg your return to Paris at once."

"I won't leave, *Mere!*"

"But can't you see, this is punishment? Holy judgement for pursuing such an unholy profession!"

"You're wrong!" Mademoiselle Dipin yelled.

"Come now, ladies," Inspector Lestrade chimed in. "Let's just calm down." The tension between the two women slowly eased.

"What are you doing here?" Holmes asked our new arrival. "I am here to see my daughter," she replied.

"Yes, but why?" he pressed.

"To beg my daughter's return. Are you deaf, sir?" She rolled her eyes. "I would do anything to get her to come home where it is safe!" The ballerina's cheeks began to turn red.

"Do you know about Javet?" Holmes asked. The woman shook her head.

"Why do you have such a fervent aversion to her performing?" I asked.

"Look at it, already! She was stalked and attacked in Paris, now her home has been vandalised." She turned towards Lestrade. "And what you are doing to keep my girl safe? Scribbling in your notebook! "

"Mere, please. I beg you, stop!" asked Mademoiselle Dipin. "Ladies, calm down, shall we?" said Lestrade. "I assure you, Madam, that we will do our best to find the one responsible," assured Lestrade. Holmes let out a sigh.

"Have you questioned any of the *corps de ballet?"* the girl's mother asked. "It wouldn't be the first time an up-and-coming tried to push the *Prima* out!" Lestrade turned back towards the ballerina.

"I...I don't know."

"Have you noted any peculiar behaviour?" Lestrade asked.

"I have not, well...no. It was nothing." Mademoiselle Dipin trailed off, her face blank as if she recalled something.

"Very well, then," said Lestrade. "We will get to work on this Javet character. Mr. Holmes, a word outside, please."

We left the mother and daughter in the apartment and stood outside in the cool air. The mother had made the room warm with unease. I found the brisk air refreshing.

Lestrade stated, "What do you make of it?" Holmes replied, "The mother is an odd character."

"I shouldn't wonder if it was her who has done all this," said Lestrade. "What with coming here like this all the sudden, wanting her daughter to leave. She's probably organised it all."

"Javet is very much a possibility," said I. "We won't know until later," said Holmes.

"The young girl said you were currently looking for this Javet. Any leads?" Lestrade asked.

"Nothing that I can reveal."

"Holmes! You aren't you're own authority," snuffed Lestrade.

"Do remember, I am not employed by the Yard. It was the girl who hired me. My duty is to her and her safety. If there is any information that is beneficial to both parties, I will share. Presently there is not. I will keep you updated, Lestrade." Just then the girl's mother rushed out the front door and jumped into a cab. Her elegant face was distorted by a horrid expression of anger and grief. Her daughter followed, holding the box which her mother had held earlier. She only saw the back of the cab pull away. "Your mother has quite the temper, dear girl."

"She does. She hates my work, my art," she returned. "Has she always hated it?" I asked. She nodded. "She has, yes."

"What did she give you?" I pressed, looking at the box. She opened it to show us two ballet shoes tucked inside.

"For someone who hates your art, I'm a little surprised by her choice of gift," said I.

"She said she picked them up from the theatre. A gift." I nodded. "Might I have a solitary word?" asked Holmes to the ballerina. The two walked off a moment. I stood there,

Holmes's back to me, watching our client answer whatever mysterious questions he posed to her.

"He's bloody brilliant, but he boils my blood sometimes," scoffed Lestrade. Holmes and the girl turned and came back towards us.

"For now, Watson and I must go. We have other business to attend." I gave Holmes an inquisitive look. Without so much as a nod or wink he took off in a fast walk. I jogged behind a moment to catch up, leaving Lestrade and Mademoiselle Dipin behind.

Holmes and I arrived that Her Majesty's Theatre and walked inside. During our cab ride, Holmes told me about the brief conversation had with Mademoiselle Dipin. He, too, noticed her uneasy expression when her mother asked about the *Corps*. The girl admitted that one of the fellow dancers, Esther Daines, who would be first in line to replace her, should anything happen, ducked out of a rehearsal about two hours before she came home. Mademoiselle Dipin said that she hadn't been close to Miss Daines and didn't pay her much attention, but noted her acting uneasy before she left.

"If ever there was a motivation, Miss Daines would have it, Holmes," said I, as we walked the backstage halls of the theatre. "Mademoiselle Dipin is a remarkably handsome and elegant woman. I'm sure jealously follows her wherever she treads."

"Jealously, Watson. A waste of an emotion. It spurs people and drives them to ludicrous decisions that never reveal a positive outcome.

Look at David and Bathsheba, jealous for another man's wife, so he sends that man to the frontline of war, and he's slain."

"It is a monstrous emotion, but do you mean to tell me you do not feel it?" Holmes did not reply. "Truly, Holmes?"

"I suppose I have had my experiences with it, yes." Holmes stopped. "Ah," said he tapped his knuckles repeatedly upon a closed door. It swung open and a short

"Is her life in danger?"

"Go to her now!"

I went off immediately to find our ballerina and relay Holmes's instruction. It was not unlike Holmes to keep his plans to himself. As much as he criticised my apparent romanticising of his adventures, he, too, had a flair for the dramatic when he drew a case to a close. This was no exception. Holmes was playing this so very close to his chest. But his reasons were always valid. Holmes was an endless enigma. His methods were strategic but unpredictable. What the game was rolled over in my mind again and again as I made haste to our client.

Arriving at the theatre, I found Mademoiselle Dipin. She was in mid-rehearsal. The stage was full of ballerinas in tutus, their legs bound by white stockings. They bent and twirled this way and that with impeccable timing. They flowed together, and everything was natural, like the movements of the oceans as tides comes and go. Mademoiselle Dipin was glorious. She wore her outfit with pride and seduction. She was a magnificent sight to behold! Everything about her was a masterpiece. She eyes lit when she looked out into the auditorium and saw me. She waved her hands and the productions stopped. She floated towards me.

"Doctor Watson, what brings you here?"

"Holmes has sent me with word," said I. Her expression suddenly tensed. "He's said the game is over. It is best for your safety that you stop performing and leave the show."

"I demand a reason. What is happening?" she snapped.

"He hasn't informed me. He's just told me to come and tell you at once. He's asked that you pack and leave by morning." The woman look at me with horror. Her breathing increased. Was it panic or anger? I could not fully tell, perhaps a combination of the two. Watching this fine artist be told she must abandon her art for her safety – when has an artist done such a thing truly?

"No!" she roared. "I won't go. I won't do it. This is what

my mother wants. This is what the villain who is chasing me wants, to ruin my life." She stormed off. I began to follow her. She darted onto the stage again. She called Miss Daines over. Our sweet ballerina looked at Miss Daines and instructed her to do something. She snapped her fingers and Miss Daines went off. I was taken aback by this. The woman, so gentle before, seemed tense and fierce. Miss Daines returned, looking most unhappy. She carried a pair of ballet shoes.

"I've brought these like you asked," I heard her say. Mademoiselle Dipin took them into her hands, slipped off her old shoes and put the new on. She looked at them a moment and balanced herself momentarily. She clapped her hands then the rehearsal began. She began to move and glide across the stage. She was picked up and twirled. The soft shuffle of feet could be heard against rhythm of the orchestra. She began to twirl furiously around, the clicking of her shoes echoed as she balanced between spins. Suddenly she slipped, her legs buckled and she fell, letting out a cry of pain. I stood. A crowd rushed around her. She was escorted off stage and taken to her dressing room. As I followed, I caught a glimpse of Miss Daines, who looked to be smirking. I found Mademoiselle Dipin in her private room with her leg propped up. Her shoes were on the floor. I examined her leg and foot. She has sprained her ankle, at least several day's rest would be in order.

"I should have left," she said to me. "What happened?"

"A problem with the shoe." She turned her head towards them. I picked them up.

"Heeled? Unusual."

"I wanted to try them. They are like the shoes of old."

"Looks like the heel broke," I observed. I examined it closely and sniffed the heel. I attempted to put Holmes's own power of deduction to use. I ran my finger along the broken edge. "Who gave you these shoes?" I asked.

"My mother. She said they were left for me here."

"By who?"

"Miss Daines got them as a gift."

"Excuse me," came a mouse-like voice from behind. It was Miss Daines. She looked at me with surprise. In her hand she held a letter. "Don't I know you?" she asked.

"I believe we met," I returned.

"Yes, the shy man. Your friend was very talkative."

"What do you want?" Mademoiselle Dipin snapped.

"I wanted to say sorry. The shoes. I was told they were strong, I didn't know they would do that." She fiddled with a slip of paper in her hands.' "

"What is that?" I asked.

"This came for her just now." She handed her the letter, which was read immediately. Mademoiselle Dipin looked at me with despair.

"Miss Daines, leave us please." When the girl had gone I looked over the letter.

I hope the shoes fit J

"It's him," she said, with an exhale.

"I must let Holmes know what has happened." She looked at me longingly as if to say, "Don't leave me alone here." I put my hand on the lady's hand. "I will make sure no more harm befalls you. Give me a moment." Leaving the shoes, I spoke with a young stage hand and asked him to stand watch outside her rooms and see that she went nowhere. As I walked through the theatre, I saw Miss Daines. She was with a tall, dark-haired man. Tears ran down her face and he embraced her. A man wearing flat cap with a bucket and mop shuffled past the two, bumping into them.

"Watch where you're going, geezer!" the dark-haired man shouted. "My apologies, my apologies," the old man echoed, shuffling past me. I exited the theatre and found a police officer outside. I begged his assistance and told him to go inside and watch over the ballerina. When I said I was working with Sherlock Holmes, he did not hesitate. We both rushed inside, but when we got to her dressing room she has vanished. The young man who I instructed to watch her was unconscious on the floor. We revived him, but he had no recollection of what happened. On her table was a note the said she was leaving and not returning. My heart sank. I needed Holmes. I looked for the broken ballet shoes but they were nowhere to be found! I took my leave and raced to Baker Street.

When I arrived, I ran up the stairs and into the study. I called out for my friend. Holmes came out his room, quickly shutting the door behind him. He held a rag and was wiping his face. I took a moment to catch my breath.

"Sit down, man," he said to me.

"We have a problem," said I. "At the theatre, Mademoiselle was hurt. The shoes her mother brought to her...."

"They were tampered with. The heel was weak and bound by cheap glue, with the intent of causing physical harm to our dear ballerina," Holmes finished. I look upon him with utter amazement.

"Holmes! You are magician! How can you know?" He picked something up from his chair and tossed it over to me. It was a flat cap. "That was you?" I asked. "Tell me what you know!"

"Let the night play out, Watson. I have a few things left to arrange. Tomorrow morning all will be revealed. Tonight, though, you and I will attend the ballet."

We did just as Holmes said. The crowed was buzzed with excitement. Murmurs of Mademoiselle's departure was talked about by almost everyone we passed. Miss Daines had finally slipped into the lead. As for the performance began, she was elegant and graceful with her movements. Watching, one would think she had always been the lead. Holmes watched the stage, not as a spectator, but like a hawk. He disappeared after intermission, leaving me to watch the remainder on my own. After the show, as I made my way through the lobby, my arm was grabbed. It was Holmes.

"Where have you been?"

"Putting the final pieces in place," he smirked.

"You are enjoying this too much, Holmes!"

"Well, aren't you the detective who was meant to look after my daughter?" I looked to see Madam Dipin.

"I am," said Holmes.

"And now she's vanished, abandoned all. I hear she's even sustained a sprain."

"And why aren't you looking for her?" I interjected.

"I told that girl this life would end her, and so it has. And I wanted to see how her replacement did."

"Some might think you ended it for her," said I. The woman's eyes blazed with anger. She puffed her cheeks and stormed off.

"Come now, Watson," said Holmes. I gave him a curious look. "Oh, dear boy, she's not our culprit."

"The shoes though, she could have tampered with them!"

"I know who tampered with them. It wasn't her," Holmes confirmed. "I've dropped the net, and now we pull our catch in! Come and watch." I followed my friend outside the theatre and around the back. There was a police Maria and two officers. Lestrade had Miss Daines cuffed and was escorting her into the carriage. I couldn't believe my eyes. I thought back to when Holmes and I met with her. The mouse-like girl. Then I remembered her smirk when the injury occurred.

"This church-mouse of a girl is responsible for such horrible acts, fueled solely by jealousy."

"Come, let's return to Baker Street. We don't have much time."

Holmes told me to take a seat upon entering. He darted into his bedroom quickly shutting the door behind him. I heard a murmur as if he was speaking to himself. There was as sudden beat upon the door. Holmes shot out of his room. I stood. The door swung open and a dark haired man stood there. It was the same man who I saw hugging Miss Daines.

"I got your note, Mr. Holmes!"

"Why don't you take a seat and explain yourself?" Holmes asked.

"Why don't you explain why you framed my darling sister!"

"Don't make threats unless you have solid evidence," Holmes said coolly. The man pressed forward.

"You have no evidence against her. She's done nothing!" The man's face turned beet red.

"Your sister wanted the spotlight and she got it, at a high price I might add."

"She is a saint! She deserves that light, not some French *Prima Donna!*" The man lashed out and charged at Holmes. With a swift and graceful movement Holmes took hold of the man's extended arm spun him around and tossed him into a chair. He sat there shocked to have not caught his prey. Holmes motioned for me to stay back, but I remained ready to come to his aid.

"You will admit the truth, or you sister will suffer," said Holmes.

"Admit what?"

"This is no time to play games." Then Holmes gave three taps on the floor. His bedroom door opened and there stood Mademoiselle Dipin! Her presence only inflamed the man's rage. He shot from his chair and Mademoiselle Dipin held her hand up. Grasped in it were the letters. Suddenly the man's rage withdrew and his face turned white with panic.

"I suppose you know what's in her hand?" Holmes asked. He shook his head.

"It's...nothing."

"It's everything," she said. The man fell back into the chair. "I...it was all done for my sister," he said.

"Miss Daines?" I questions. He nodded.

"I got carried away. It was meant to be harmless."

"You tried to run me out of town! You tried to foil my

work! You send me letters pretending to be Javet. You followed me, you destroyed my apartment! How is any of that harmless you...you beast!"

"This isn't over, Mr. Holmes. You have yet to prove a single thing. This is all conjecture and blackmail!" The colour began to return to his face.

"Shall I lay it out so that even you can understand?" Holmes said sharply. "You might have got away with the entire operation should you have done one thing differently." The man looked at Holmes. "Typed out the letters." Holmes paused a moment, and Mr. Daines suddenly looked sheepish. "Being familiar with the study of the written hand, when I spoke with your sister I noticed on her dresser that there was a letter on her table. I recognised the hand which had written it. I was able to take a quick glimpse at the letter," which Holmes withdrew from his pocket. "It was an invitation from you for her to join you for dinner." Holmes walked over to Mademoiselle Dipin and took a letter from her. "It's the way you swoop your L's and looped your E's that gave it all away initially when I examined the papers.

"So, I followed your sister to her dinner date. I watched you like a hawk. I found where you live, a nice place in Angel. Inside your house, I found papers bought from local sellers, all of whom remember selling to you. Types of paper that match the letters received by Mademoiselle Dipin. I also noticed a particular brand of ink on your desk which happens to be the exact ink on the letters, and a particular pen which was used to script the letters." Holmes looked at the man who now cowered in the chair. "Harmless, you say? Was it harmless when you sent the shoes to Mademoiselle Dipin with a weak heel? Your sister already said how you gave them to her, to try and win favour with Mademoiselle. Or when you placed the final letter at the front desk for her about the shoes? Oh, don't look surprised. You might remember an 'old geezer' who was mopping the floors. Yes, that was me. Give it up, Mr. Daines, the game is over."

There was a ring at the bell, and Lestrade came in with Miss Daines. She look horrified to see her brother standing there.

"Darling, I'm sorry," he said to his sister, as tears welled in her eyes. "I didn't want to believe them, brother!"

"Lestrade, we have your man," said Holmes. Mr. Daines looked confused, as all his elaborate planning to see his sister take the spot lot foiled around him. In the coming months, not only would his actions end up ruining his life, but they would also ruin her career simply by association.

"Come now, Mr. Daines, you're coming with us," said Lestrade, taking them man by the arm and escorting him out of 221b Baker Street. His sister followed sobbing behind.

"Mr. Holmes, I can't thank you enough," said Mademoiselle Dipin. "It was my pleasure to assist."

"As to your fee...." she insisted.

"Why don't you treat Watson and me to your next performance, when your foot has healed." She smiled and nodded cheerfully. She grabbed Holmes by the hands and squeezed.

"Until next time," said I. She touched my arm and made her way out. When she had left, Holmes walked over to the window and looked out at the street below.

"You surprise me, Watson," said he. "Why is that?"

"She was a splendid woman, as far as women go. I gave you plenty of opportunities to be in her presence without me."

"I don't understand?" said I.

"I thought you would have invited her for meal. I liked her better than the last."

"Good gracious, man. Were you trying to arrange something between us then?" He smiled, reached for his pipe and lit it. A few puffs and smoke lifted from the cherrywood pipe.

"Maybe we'll find you a wife with one of these cases."

The Deadly Soldier

by Summer Perkins

Someone was trying to kill him. Of that, Professor James Moriarty was certain. For three nights now he'd seen the shadow of a man standing outside his Conduit Street residence. The man stood just out of the way of the gas lamps that lined the street, so only the long silhouette of him was discernable in the light.

When a carriage passed by, it disrupted the play of light on the cobblestones, throwing the shadow into long contrast against the walkway to Moriarty's home, as if the shadow itself was an insidious beast, lengthening and reaching out to take Moriarty within its grasp.

However, Moriarty was a scientist and believed in nothing of the terror to be found in beasts and shadows. He was rational above all else, and though his pursuer had been careful to keep his face well hidden, his unmoving, attentive posture was that of an army man.

Moriarty had no personal quarrels with Her Majesty's Army, nor had he recently done business with anyone who had a bone to pick with a man from the service, which made him conclude that this man had been hired by someone else altogether.

While in the practice of thinking, and especially when puzzling over some incredibly intricate piece of mathematics or trying to decide in just such a way how he would deliver a certain client's request, he had taken to pacing long, sure strides along the floor of his library. The movement of his legs helped energise his brain, and occasionally his fingers would twitch about the window coverings, pulling them back to view the city's comings and goings.

It was a pity that the gas lamps gave off too much light to accurately see the stars; the view of such a thing would have settled his mind much more than watching the scurrying to-and-fro of the citizens of London as they rode by in hansom cabs or walked arm in arm as lovers – all inconsequential to him, like so many ants upon a hill.

Yet, the stars were obscured from him, so he contented himself with stalking his rooms, thinking and watching. It was during just such an evening days ago that he'd first noticed that shadow of the man standing too still and purposefully ensconced in darkness.

The sight had amused Moriarty; for if the man had been sent to watch him, he'd have a long evening ahead of himself indeed, as the professor had no plans to leave his home that evening.

By the time he'd risen the next morning, the spot on the sidewalk where the man had stood was vacant, and while not putting the situation out of his mind, he filed it away carefully to be recalled if need be, though he had far more important things to think about than mysterious men standing on sidewalks.

Yet the long shadow of the man was back the very next night, and then again the next. Moriarty had noticed him again in one of his pacing turns about his library when he'd pulled aside the curtain to imperiously view his little spot of earth.

As he stood with black silk curtains still grasped in one hand and in full view of the window, he imagined the man must be stalking him, and perhaps compiling information upon his whereabouts to present to a third party. Then Moriarty noticed the silver glint of a gun as it was aimed and *oh*, wasn't that just the thing to spice up a dreary evening?

Moriarty was a tall man, nearing fifty, though slender as a matchstick with viper-fast reflexes. The very sight of the gun had sent off the impulse in him to duck before his conscious mind had caught up, and rightly so – his pursuer fired once, then twice, straight through the window.

The glass gave way with a powerful crack and shatter, raining down upon him in slivers like razor-sharp snowflakes. Moriarty, flat on his stomach, face pressed into the dull pattern of the Persian rug that carpeted his library, pulled himself away from the window, not risking raising his head to look out. He scuttled further into the room to reach his own weapon.

Despite being a man of books and cunning, it would be folly of him to not carry a piece for these such very reasons. In the decade since he'd got into his particular brand of criminal acts, he'd made a laundry list of enemies, and attempts on his life had run the gamut from poisoned tea to an attempted kidnapping. Though the latter had been botched from the start and ended rather abruptly when, having been tied to a chair and threatened with the red hot tip of a fire poker, he calmly inquired to the man holding it if he was going to attempt to burn the soul from him. He'd wondered aloud if such a thing were possible if he were lacking a soul to begin with.

Whether it was his perfectly calm demeanor at the question, as if they were discussing something of no more importance than the weather over tea, or the fact that the pupils of Moriarty's eyes were coal black and betrayed no fear, he found the poker being dropped and his kidnapper backing away, muttering something about "This ain't worth it – the crazy bastard," under his breath. At the time, he'd laughed.

He laughed again, crawling across his floor three hours after sunset with broken glass crunching under his knees and the elbows of his jacket. The laugh was a low, unholy rumble, mad and lacking in any real mirth. It was a laugh that cautioned *you'll be sorry*. He got to his knees when he reached his piano, deft fingers feeling across the wooden seat, finding the catch underneath. Once opened, he lifted up the false bottom to unearth an opening the length of the seat in which he kept a loaded rifle.

Outside he heard voices. There had been shrieks at the shot and the tramping of feet – probably someone running to call a constable. He lived in too respectable a neighbourhood not to warrant the concern of the police when something as alarming as gunshots occurred.

How disappointing. I'd have liked to deal with him himself, Moriarty mused from his crouched position; his long spindly fingers still wrapped around the handle of the gun aimed directly at his window. He only stood once he'd heard an authoritative voice call, "Is there anyone inside?" with the accompanying light from a shining torch.

He rose in a fluid, near-serpentine movement, lowering his gun slightly – though not all the way in case the soldier was only pretending to be police – and took stock of his own countenance. His jacket and trousers were rumpled from his abrupt movements and a fine layer of white dust coated the dark garments. This he immediately tried to brush from his clothing, disliking the way it marred the fabric.

His features, too, he schooled into the look of bewildered apprehension he assumed the situation called for, his brow furrowing, eyes widening slightly. His lips, already a rather thin slash in his face, going even thinner with faux fear. By the time the constable peered in at him through the window, Moriarty was playing his part quite well.

"Alright in there, sir?" the constable inquired, reaching in through the broken glass of the window with his torch to widen the gap in the curtains. As his ruddy looking face came further into view, Moriarty lowered his gun completely and abandoned it on the closed piano bench, giving a nod.

"Quite alright now," he assured the policeman. "Though

those gunshots were indeed a shock. Would you like to come in?"

The officer nodded his agreement and Moriarty crossed the room to let him in the front door. He showed the man into the library where the assault had taken place.

After a cursory glance around the room, both men's eyes followed the trajectory of the bullets, both of which were lodged into the spines of books upon Moriarty's shelf opposite the window. One had even pierced the spine of his own work, *Dynamics of an Asteroid*, and *oh*, whoever this shooter was would pay dearly for that.

"Do you have any idea who might want you dead?" the constable inquired, head tilted up to look into Moriarty's eyes.

Moriarty pretended to pause momentarily, as if to consider the question before replying in the negative. "I'm afraid not. I don't have any enemies as far as I'm aware. I suppose this means you weren't able to apprehend the suspect?"

The constable shook his head. "The ruffian must've fled the scene before I arrived."

"Pity, that."

Again, the constable glanced around, taking in the opulence of the room. Though Moriarty's upper-class residence wasn't out of place in Westminster, he did own rather a large collection of both ancient and new texts, not to mention a nice looking piano and a telescope in the corner of the room.

"Could be a thwarted robbery," the constable mused. "That wouldn't be uncommon in a neighbourhood like this. Thieves prey upon the wealthy."

Moriarty suppressed an eye roll. A thief, this assailant was not, nor could he imagine there being much call for astronomy books and scientific apparatuses to fence on the black market.

His gaze once again drew to the bullet holes. Judging

by their relative height, the first shot would've struck him square in the chest had he not ducked, and the second was likely the assailant's second attempt to get him before he hit the floor. The fact that the man had got off two quick shots in succession like that spoke of his experience, which further bolstered Moriarty's suspicion that the man responsible had a military background.

The constable pulled him out of his musings by speaking once more. "I could have some of my boys do a patrol of your street if you'd like, to make sure he doesn't come back."

"No, no," Moriarty waved the suggestion away. "I'm sure I'll be perfectly alright here." He did have use for a police officer, but he'd already had one in his employ who understood the sort of business he conducted. "If I have further need for the police, I'll speak with Inspector Turner at the CID."

The constable's brows rose nearly to his hairline at the mention of the name. "Oh sure, of course, sir. I didn't know you were friends with the higher ups."

Moriarty just gave him a tight nod, growing bored and impatient with the constable's dull, bumbling presence, and crossed the room, opening his front door swiftly for him in an effective dismissal.

That night Moriarty was unable to sleep. The boarded up window marred the perfection of his library, looking crude and out of place, like a scar marring otherwise perfect skin. He shut the curtains to block it from view, but even having retired to his bedroom, he still could not rest for knowing it was there, so back down to the library he went, resuming his pacing. Upon every turn of his heel he glared at the window, eyes narrowed and full of simmering fury that doubled with each passing hour.

At the first light of dawn, he decided he could wait no longer to leave the house. He'd go to Clapham and see Andrew Turner right away. Turner had been a former client of his. At the time, the up and coming constable had been aiming for the job of detective and it had come down to he and another man in the end. The other man, a Mr. Charles Woodlite, had at least a decade in age on Turner, and had been working as a constable a handful of years longer. That was where Moriarty had come in. At Turner's behest, Moriarty had arranged for Woodlite to be struck by a runaway carriage, killing him and leaving Turner as the only available candidate for the job.

Moriarty had been pleased to take on work for a member of the police and had waved away payment, telling him instead that if the time arose when Moriarty needed his particular services, he would call upon him. That had been a good eight months back, and they'd thus far parted ways without any contact, though with the attempt on his life, Moriarty now saw need for him.

When he came to the row house in which Turner lived, he gave three solemn raps on the door, and then waited a few moments before repeating the action when he heard no movement from within.

He imagined Turner and his family were still asleep upstairs, though that was no concern of his. He needed a job done and he expected his wishes to be attended to posthaste.

Finally, the door opened, revealing a sleep-rumpled Turner, his short blond hair tousled and sticking up on end. He was still in pyjamas and a plain navy blue cotton dressing gown, the sash of which he was still tying as he opened the door.

Upon seeing Moriarty, his posture immediately changed, eyes widening first in recognition, then apprehension, back straightening as though he were a marionette whose strings had suddenly been jerked. "Professor...." he trailed off, seemingly at a loss, before swallowing thickly. When he spoke again, his voice was hushed. "It's early, what can I do for you?"

Moriarty made no mention of the time, though he was pleased to see the immediate deference and subtle hint of fear Turner gave off at the sight of him. "You can invite me in, for a start."

Immediately, Turner stepped back, allowing Moriarty into his home. "Can I get you anything?" he asked. "Tea?" He hesitated and added, "My wife and child are still asleep upstairs," by way of explanation for his lowered voice.

Moriarty took no care to lower his own tone, speaking instead in the same cold commanding note as ever. "No tea. This isn't a social call. We have business to discuss."

"Right." Turner nodded, his Adam's Apple bobbing again as he swallowed apprehensively, taking Moriarty's coat and hat before leading him into a sparsely decorated parlour. He immediately set about starting a fire in the fireplace while he beckoned Moriarty to take a seat on the sofa. "What can I do for you?"

Moriarty perched on the edge of the sofa, noticing the stitching worn threadbare in places. His lip curled up in a sneer of distaste, the lack of sleep he'd suffered only serving to make him all the more impatient and demanding. He explained the events of the previous evening in few words before arriving at the point of his visit. "I believe my assailant will try again. I'll need you to tail me over the next few days and keep an eye out for anyone else who might be doing the same."

He spoke the words to Turner's back, watching him stoke the fire with a poker before the man finally stood, turning to face Moriarty again. "Have you filed a report on it? I could try my best to get assigned to your case."

Moriarty's head swiveled on his neck, turning from one side to the other slowly, as if to stretch his muscles, though his eyes never left Turner's. It gave the appearance of a snake sizing up a rodent it was about to devour. "I'm not interested in filing a report," he answered at length, his tone clipped. "When my pursuer is apprehended, I'll not be handing him over to the police. I'd far prefer to deal with him myself."

The threat within those words were unmistakable, and

Turner, of anyone, should know just what sort of things Moriarty did when he'd decided to deal with someone on his own terms. Turner nodded again, though he still looked unsure, his hands toying once more with the sash of his dressing gown. "Westminster isn't in my division. I'm not allowed to patrol whichever part of London I choose. Perhaps there is something else I could –"

Moriarty had heard enough and cut him off before he was able to get another word out. "The man pursuing me is clearly dangerous. Is it not your job to make London a safer place for all citizens?" he inquired. "With a wife and child, I'd imagine you'd want our streets to be free of murderers."

Turner swallowed again. "I –"

"It's just that it would be a shame," Moriarty continued smoothly, as if the Inspector hadn't spoken, "if something were to happen to your child. An infant girl, am I correct? Rebecca." He hummed the name out, a slow smile spreading his severe, bloodless lips even thinner.

Colour bloomed high on Turner's cheeks; anger and fear making him gawp at Moriarty wordlessly for a moment, before he reached up to run a shaking hand through his unkempt hair. "I – I can start as soon as you need me to."

"Glad to hear you've come around to the idea. Get dressed, Inspector. You have a long day ahead of you."

Moriarty's pursuer was more intelligent than he'd originally given him credit, because after employing Turner to tail him, he saw neither hide nor hair of anyone following him or acting suspiciously.

He would have assumed the soldier had given it up as a bad job now that Moriarty had an Inspector watching out for him, if not for the fact that the last three men he'd had appointments with had turned up murdered.

The first, a Mr. Jonathon March, a banker who had a case of sticky fingers and decided he'd wanted to start pocketing some of the money from his bank's safe, had been found dead in his home. Nothing from his residence had been stolen, but a single bullet had pierced his chest, straight through his heart.

After March had neglected to show up for his appointment, Moriarty decided to pay him a visit, because people did not back out on their appointments with him without consequence. When he arrived, he saw a swarm of policemen at March's residence and turned back, not wanting to get himself involved in a police matter in which he didn't control all the players. In the evening paper, he read of the murder, and though such a thing could be discounted as a coincidence, after having just survived an attempt on his own life, it didn't seem likely.

His assailant was clearly still on his tail and watching him close enough to know with whom Moriarty did business. Yet, why kill one of his clients? Beyond the minor inconvenience of it, Moriarty cared little for their lives, and the loss of money from March's business was minimal.

He shrugged it off as a desperate attempt on the soldier's behalf to rile him, and continued on as usual, instructing Turner to keep following him in case the soldier decided to show himself again.

Then, his next client was murdered three days later, and another two days after that. The papers started calling it the work of a deranged killer, though they were unable to find any connection between the murders. Each man was killed with a single shot through the heart, without any other assault or robbery of his person and an absolute lack of evidence as to who had done it.

It was starting to become...inconvenient. One murdered client didn't bother Moriarty overmuch, but if the murders continued, it would be only a matter of time until a connection between the men led back to him, and word would get around that anyone who hired him wound up dead.

Not to mention that the police, even as incompetent as most of them were, would eventually find the connection, and while he had Turner in his pocket and didn't doubt his ability to find weaknesses in the others to bend them to his will, it would take an amount of effort in which he did not wish to partake.

As ambitious as he was in things that interested him, he didn't appreciate feeling as though someone else was forcing his hand, and as Turner was proving worse than useless as a tail, Moriarty decided to approach this from a different angle. It was about time he did something to draw the solider out.

First thing the next morning, he invited Turner in and gave him a rundown of their new goal, before walking him to his door to dismiss him. He waited until the Inspector was on his doorstep in plain view of the street before arranging his features into his a scowl; brows knitted together, dark eyes narrowed in cool dissatisfaction, mouth curled into a sneer, as he informed the Inspector in a clipped tone, "Since you've been unable to find the man who attacked me, I have no choice but to relieve you from your duty."

Turner gave a nervous jerk of his head, Adam's Apple once again bobbing as he swallowed reflexively in fear. The sheer terror on the man's face amused Moriarty. Though this playacting was part of his plan, the Inspector looked genuinely terrified at Moriarty's cold fury.

When Turner spoke, his voice was hesitant and wheedling. "I'm sorry, Mr. Moriarty. I've been following you day and night as requested. I just haven't seen anyone that I'd consider suspicious, I –"

"I'm not interested in your excuses," Moriarty interrupted. "I made myself quite clear when I told you what I expected."

Turner's pallour faded almost to Moriarty's own near paper white tones. "Yes, but –"

"No." Moriarty gave a jerk of his head, cutting off any more excuses before they could issue from the Turner's lips. "I believe I told you what the price would be for your failure."

Turner's eyes widened. "Please, sir, don't hurt my family...."

Moriarty watched the man dispassionately, tilting his head to one side and then the other slowly, stretching his neck out. "Then catch my assailant, Inspector." He reached into his pocket, withdrawing a small leather-bound appointment book and handing it to the other man. "In here you'll find the addresses of my clients and the dates of our appointments. Catch this man before he can kill another one of them. You have twenty-four hours."

He watched Turner take the book and then continue standing there, gripping it so hard that his blunt nails left small indents in the leather.

"Well? Off you go," Moriarty prompted, jerking Turner into action again.

He gave a start and then nodded, pocketing the book. "I won't let you down again," he promised, fitting his hat on and all but fleeing from the house.

"See that you don't." Moriarty smirked, watching him hurry off, before stepping back and shutting the door after him with a decisive click. Everything was going to plan so far. He'd just hoped the soldier had been lurking out of sight to witness that performance.

Most people's motives, Moriarty found, were easy to suss out – greed, malice, simple stupidity – they all drove men to act in ways that were tiresomely predictable, and this soldier of his was no different, he assumed. Greedy, yes, as he'd likely been hired to do this job and was therefore motivated by money. Malicious? Perhaps. The pattern of the bullets made for a quick death, and the use of a rifle meant he preferred to work from a distance, though Moriarty assumed that to be from his military training more than from any preference to not get his hands dirty.

As for stupidity? There'd been a surprising lack of it, thus far. The man had been careful not to get himself caught by police, nor noticed by Turner, and he'd been patient enough not to fire off another shot at Moriarty too soon after his failed first time.

Truth be told, he was the sort of man who Moriarty wouldn't mind having in his employ himself. Though Moriarty relished in his own intimidation tactics, usually needing little more than a few discrete, well-placed threats and a narrowing of his eyes, even he could admit that sometimes more drastic measures had to be taken. Having a trained muscle that was proficient with a gun had its advantages.

It really would be a pity for his assailant to be shot as Moriarty's plan came to fruition, but sometimes these things couldn't always be planned for. He was perfectly willing to pull the trigger if he deemed the man unreasonable after having a proper chat, but first he had to lure him in. Getting rid of Turner had only been the first step. Now to put the rest of the plan in motion

The soldier hadn't shot a single person in public thus far, preferring to take them down in their homes. As his first long range attempt had failed, Moriarty could only assume this time it would be something a little more close and personal.

So, to give the man time, Moriarty left his home quickly as if he had business with which to attend, immediately setting off for Regent Street. In his purported haste he neglected to turn the lock on his front door. If this soldier were to break into his home to await his return, he'd much rather there be as little destruction upon his property as possible. He didn't fancy another boarded up window.

Once on Regent Street, he allowed himself to get lost in the flow of pedestrians clamouring in and out of shops. His upper lip curled in distaste at the mass of swirling humanity around him; the cacophony of voices, the clomping of horses' hooves as carriages passed by, and a squeaking out-of-tune piano-organ ground by a boy looking for change. The boy gained nothing but a withering look from Moriarty as the professor passed by him.

A glance to his pocket watch told him it was barely nine in the morning; if this soldier were any sort of criminal at all, he'd surely wait until nightfall to make his move. He had hours upon hours to waste before then.

While it had been his plan to lose himself in the press of bodies along Regent Street, making it impossible to murder him without someone seeing, he quickly found being among that many people intolerable.

Surely, risking a bullet to the chest would be preferable to being amongst that much constant braying humanity, and after barely an hour he'd returned to Conduit Street once more, heading for Saunders, Otley & Co., a circulating library not too far from his home.

In addition to frivolous dramas and works of poetry, the library also had a large collection of practical and scientific texts. The professor whiled away the rest of the morning and much of the afternoon reading up on the management and keeping of bees, while pondering just how many stings it would take to overload a man's body, forcing it to shut down. It would be a waste for the bee to die as well, however inefficient insects that they were. He made a mental note to research the keeping of wasps instead.

When it was approaching dusk, he ate at a local pub before checking his pocket watch once again and meeting Turner outside. At precisely their agreed meeting time, Turner made his way through the crowd, a subdued expression making his cornflower blue eyes appear dull.

"Hello, Mr. Moriarty," he inclined his head in greeting. Despite his many shortcomings, at least he was punctual. That was a trait Moriarty valued highly. Men who kept him waiting tended not to live long.

"Mr. Turner," Moriarty answered, voice cool. "I take it you've brought the cuffs I requested?"

Turner nodded, reaching into the pocket of his overcoat to pull out a set of silver handcuffs. He produced a small revolver as well, which he dutifully handed over to Moriarty.

After a cursory glance, Moriarty slipped both items into the pocket of his own coat and then shrugged the garment off, handing it over to Turner along with his top hat. Turner followed suit and soon Moriarty pulled on the other man's coat, looking down in brief distaste at the poor quality of the fabric compared to that which he was used to. He nodded for Turner to lead the way while he kept back at a discrete distance.

The plan was simple enough; Moriarty was banking on his assailant waiting for him in his home, and though Turner lacked Moriarty's tall, slim stature, in the poor light, Moriarty assumed the soldier would mistake Turner for him. Once the solider made a move, Turner would disarm and cuff him. He had explicit instructions not to fire upon the soldier unless absolutely necessary, but it would be foolhardy to not at least have brought a gun in preparation.

Moriarty watched Turner's back as they walked in silence toward his home; the professor taking care to keep well back and into the shadows. Turner walked up to his front door, opening it as if he were the owner of the place and stepped inside.

Moments later, Moriarty saw the light in his library shine through the curtains; Turner obviously had lit the gas lamp once he was inside. All was silent and he resolved to give the Inspector a few minutes before approaching the house himself to see how he was getting on. As soon as the thought had entered his mind, the unmistakable crack of a gunshot pierced the air.

Moriarty's head snapped up in attention. He hurried toward the house, hoping that Turner had been wise enough to follow his instructions. Had he killed the soldier before Moriarty himself could get his hands on him, there would be consequences.

As Moriarty's hand reached for the doorknob, he saw it turn before he could grasp it and the door was pulled open from the inside. The gestured revealed a man a bit shorter than himself but nearly twice as wide, compact with solid muscle. The man's sandy blond hair was cut in a short military style and smoothed down with wax, and he had a bushy moustache the same colour; it twitched as his lips pulled up into a smile. The gesture of amusement didn't reach the man's hard green eyes.

"Professor," he addressed Moriarty, stepping back so Moriarty could enter. "You've proven difficult to hunt down."

The smell of gunpowder was pungent in the air. Behind the soldier laid Turner, a spreading red stain across the front of his vest, soaking into his white cotton shirt. He drew in a shallow breath, moaning as he exhaled.

Moriarty's eyes slid from Turner's body on the floor back to the solider and he stepped inside. The man was still holding his military issue Webley revolver, though Moriarty just tilted his chin up in defiance, unafraid.

"And you've proven a nuisance," he answered dispassionately, stepping over Turner. "How disappointed you must be that you've still not taken me down. I'll bet your employer is most displeased."

The soldier laughed, raising his gun at Moriarty. "What makes you think I won't shoot you right now and be done with it?"

Moriarty watched the silver muzzle of the revolver point directly at his chest, though if he felt any sliver of fear it didn't show on his face. He just slowly tilted his head from one side to the other, stretching his neck out in his usual serpentine movement. "You could," he agreed, "But then you'd never hear my business proposition, and you'd be the poorer for it."

He watched the soldier cock his weapon, finger sliding to the trigger, though the man then hesitated a beat and Moriarty took advantage of the hesitation, adding, "I'm not sure what your employer has told you about me, but just by this brief meeting, I can gather a few things about you. Judging by your posture and the type of weapon you carry, you are a military man. Your skin is far too tan for someone who has spent much time recently in London, which means you've been abroad. Perhaps in Kabul, the Battle of Sherpur? Yet your decision to dabble in crime is a curious one. Maybe you've been recently discharged and found yourself unsuitable for a life which doesn't include wielding a gun."

As Moriarty spoke, the cruel, self-satisfied smile slid from the soldier's face, to be replaced with a look that was first weary, then begrudgingly bordering on awe. "You've deciphered all that from just looking at me?"

Moriarty inclined his head in agreement. "I have. Yet I find one thing about your methods very curious."

Despite the look of awe on the soldier's face, his revolver didn't waver from Moriarty's chest. "And what's that?"

"If you've been hired to kill me, what purpose did the murder of my clients serve?"

The soldier's smile returned, and he let out a hearty laugh as though Moriarty had just told a particularly funny joke. "That, Professor, was just for my own amusement. You've proven more difficult to get to than I'd planned, and instead of trifling with the Inspector tailing you, it was far more entertaining to follow home the men you had meetings with and dispatch of them. I knew you'd eventually grow tired of the damage it was doing to your business and try to lure me out."

He let out another small chuckle, shaking his head, "It was quite a nice touch with the Inspector wearing your overcoat as well. Perhaps a lesser man might've fallen for the gag, but I recognised his gait the moment he walked up to your house."

As if on cue, another moan of pain issued from Turner on the floor. Without taking his eyes off Moriarty, the soldier turned his revolver on the Inspector, delivering a fatal shot.

The heartlessness of the action impressed Moriarty, as did

the soldier's cleverness. Though he clearly wasn't as good at reading people as the professor himself, he was a great deal smarter than most men Moriarty employed. Moriarty could use someone skilled with a gun, since Turner was now no longer drawing breath.

"I have to commend you on your work," Moriarty told him. "You're far from the first man hired to take my life, but out of them all, you've got the closest."

"Closest?" The solider echoed with a raise of his brows. "My good sir, between the two of us I'm the only one with a weapon in hand and I've just ended another man's life. Whatever makes you think that I won't be successful in ending yours?"

It was a fair point and a lesser man might've conceded defeat and started to beg for his life, but Moriarty was not a lesser man. He only watched the solider intently, reaching up to remove the top hat he'd not had the chance to divest himself of earlier, what with the commotion he'd met upon entering his home. His overcoat was shed next and he took his time, drawing out the silence between them. He enjoyed the way the soldier's attention never left him as he waited for Moriarty's reply.

Whether the man realised it or not, he was already in Moriarty's thrall, and when Moriarty felt the tension in the room increase to such a level that the solider was about to speak again, Moriarty opened his mouth to reply. "I suppose you would be successful in your objective, if that's what you so choose, but you've just killed someone of use to me, and as such, a job opening has become available.

Whatever the solider had been expecting him to say, that clearly was far from the mark. He gaped at Moriarty, brows rising again this time nearly to his hairline. Slowly, he lowered his gun to his side. "Are you telling me you're looking to hire me?"

"I am," Moriarty confirmed.

"What makes you think I'd betray my boss to work for

you?" he scoffed, though he didn't raise the gun again.

This time, Moriarty didn't even pretend to draw out the silence before answering. He already knew he'd won. The solider having lowered his gun was as good as a yes already. "It's steady work, and whatever you're currently being paid, I'll double it."

The solider stood motionless for a breath, thinking it over before slipping his gun back into its holster.

Moriarty added, "You can start by disposing of the Inspector's body. Then pay a little visit to your boss and bring him to me. Do we have a deal?"

He put out his hand to shake on it, like the start of all gentlemanly agreements. The soldier's brows knitted as he looked down at that hand, as though shaking it would be akin to making a pact with the devil.

"I'll even triple your pay, if you manage to impress me," Moriarty added, and the man's hand met his in a firm grip.

After they shook, Moriarty spoke once more. "Another thing. If you're going to work for me, I'll need to know your name."

The man nodded, reaching up to stroke his moustache before standing up straighter, heels clicking together. It was the move of someone used to standing at attention in front of a superior officer. "Of course. It's Colonel Sebastian Moran, sir. At your service."

The Case of the Vanishing Stars

by Deanna Baran

My friend Holmes was never happier than when his formidable intellect was captivated by some abstruse problem. Contrariwise, ennui was abhorrent to him. October of 1885 was an intense month for Holmes. After the adventure of the cyclist's cipher came quick upon the heels of the problem of the change-ringers' society and the Armenian carpet affair, the comparative sluggishness of November left him morose and dissatisfied. Only so many hours could be filled by cutting articles from the papers and updating scrap-books. Although the weather was hardly conducive to such outings, and my wound ached at every change in the glass, I found myself taking wholly unnecessary turns through Regent's Park to escape the oppressive atmosphere of Baker Street, as the steely November skies had nothing on the gloom of a Holmes without a challenge. He had work, mind you, for rarely a day passed without the page admitting some colorful individual or another to our sitting room, but the parade of petty problems that beleaguer humanity did little to stimulate his mental machinery.

Thus it was, when I descended to breakfast early in December, that I was pleasantly surprised to find Holmes in better spirits than I had seen for several weeks. The night before, we had taken an evening's entertainment at St. James's Hall, and he was anxious to resume conversation on the subject.

"Mind you," he said, "I don't care much for Gallic glitter. Give me German introspection on the program any night. Still, that was rather a unique interpretation. Berlioz clearly specified *agitato*. One might even tread towards *vivacci* territory. Yet to give his *Fantastique* such an *andante* delivery – the character of the piece was completely transformed, and I doubt Berlioz would have thanked him for it."

The succeeding meal consisted of his humming of passages from four or five different interpretations of the piece in question, punctuated with approving or disapproving comparative analyses of the varying approaches. While I enjoy music, I have not the musician's brain that permits one to reduce a concert piece from its whole into its parts, as though there were no difference between the performance hall and the dissecting-room, and I found the majority of his criticisms too technical to appreciate. Still, I was heartened by this spark of enthusiasm on an otherwise dreary morning, and I did all I could to encourage his exuberant opining.

So it was, that after the meal was cleared away, and he had substituted his violin for his egg-spoon for the purpose of illustrating his points, and the subject of conversation had meandered into the influences of French Romanticism upon Wagner, and from there upon programme music versus Gesammtkunstwerk, that when the bell rang to indicate a caller, he was visibly annoyed at this check upon his discourse. But he was ever the gentleman, and by the time our visitor had been shown into the room, she would never have suspected her timing was unwelcome or inconvenient.

She divided a cautious smile between the two of us. As I made my greeting and offered her a seat by the fire, it occurred to me that she must have been quite the beauty in her day. Holmes gave her fashionable appearance his customary swift analysis. "Watson and I were just discussing programme music," he said amicably. "How serendipitous to find someone who has trod the boards in our midst.

Although now, perhaps, you seem to busy yourself with costuming, although that is not your primary occupation?"

Just as the jackdaw cannot maintain its charade once it speaks, neither could her charming appearance survive speech. For all the expense of her costume and the glitter of her ornaments, she possessed the harsh metallic twang of a costermonger.

"I toured the Continent and America in the '60's and '70's," she said. "Perhaps you remember 'Daddy, If You Love Me.' It was my big hit on the music-hall circuits, though some prefer 'The Big Noise at Brighton'. I don't mind taking a turn onstage to give the audience a treat, though I've run my own music hall these last ten years. I've worked both sides of the lights, and I knows what things belongs. A woman must always have an eye for tomorrow, what 'as no one's showered with diamonds forever."

It was hard to imagine this woman as a chanteuse, showered with jewels by an adoring public. But Holmes's cordiality didn't waver. "That is a very practical mindset –"

"Mrs. Hughes," she supplied. "The posters say another, and my Jimmy's gone to glory, but it's Mrs. Hughes all the same."

"Perhaps you can tell us what has brought you so far from Mile End on such a chill morning, Mrs. Hughes?"

Our guest's visible surprise confirmed the accuracy of his statement, but, never one to deny an audience's request, she launched upon her narrative. She possessed the singular inability of her class to relate a sequence of events in linear fashion. Yet Holmes was patient with her, permitting her to drift into side channels of expository, but always drawing the threads of narration back towards their original point, here summarized for expediency.

Having spent the better part of fifteen years on stage, Mrs. Hughes determined to yield the limelight to a younger generation of performers. Although she had married a stolid, sensible stockbroker, she wished to additionally secure her future. She discovered a song-and-supper room for sale in Mile End, whose owner wished to forsake the overcrowding of the East End in favor of market gardening in Fulham. She purchased the premises, and between the depth of her purse and her considerable experience, launched a successful business providing cheap edibles and entertainment for the immigrants and laborers of the area.

There was a fire and a subsequent renovation. Her husband passed away one winter of double pleuro-pneumonia. The economic depression that began five years ago took its toll on the box office receipts. Overall, however, business proceeded as normally as it could for several years.

On the other hand, life was never ordinary when one's business model involved the employment of a motley variety of artistes. Just in the last fortnight, she'd dealt with the acrobat who'd attempted to climb the walls, the conjuror who lost his pigeons, prowlers at the basement window, and the police-whistle that interrupted a canine act. There were other peculiar things, like the matter of the drapers who had come to measure the curtains, yet she had placed no orders; or the gasfitters who had come to fix the lights, yet the lights were in perfect condition and no one admitted to having summoned them. But nothing ever happened that would require the services of a consulting detective.

However, around Martinmas, abnormalities began to accumulate. Her faithful right hand, Mr. Jacobs, who was had been with her a decade to schedule talent and oversee the technicalities of stage management, had passed away from blood poisoning at the beginning of the month. The new manager was competent enough, and had arranged for a number of intriguing performers, yet the performers themselves tended to be chronically unreliable. It was common in the business for an artiste to book his little ten-minute act, leave home fully made-up to take his turn, receive his pay, and then rush off to repeat the process at three or four establishments in one night. Despite this ambitious schedule, she rarely had a problem with individuals who failed to fulfill their contract. Recently, however, as many as a full third of the advertised "turns" on her program would fail to report for the curtain, much to the chagrin of her paying customers. Word was going around, and attendance, usually consisting of five to six hundred heads per night, had plummeted in response to the wagging of critical tongues. In a matter of weeks, she had come to a point where she was hesitant to advertise a particular program ahead of time, for fear of not being able to fulfill the audience's expectations.

The Christmas pantomime season was normally a busy and profitable time of year, and although *harlequinades* were no longer as fashionable as they had been mid-century, and she herself rarely ventured into dramatics duc to licensing issues, those who patronized her hall would "never say 'no' to a good piece of business with a policeman and a string of sausages," as she expressed it. Although she had made some small economies by doing much of the costume design and tailoring herself, she still had invested a not-insignificant sum into costumes and set-pieces. Yet just last night, the entire cast of "Harlequin and Cinderella" had reported for the curtain, then without a word, vanished! Neither Harlequin nor Columbine nor anyone had remained to take the stage. The audience was in an uproar at her attempts to make substitutions for the climax of the night's program, and she'd had to refund the entire evening's receipts. If she'd known that her reputation would be in shreds, she would have sold it at a tidy profit to the stranger who had offered to buy her music hall back at Hallowtide.

"How many marriage proposals have you received since the beginning of autumn?" inquired Holmes.

This was not the question Mrs. Hughes was expecting. "Three," she said. "One, by letter, from an admirer who claimed to remember me from my 'Daddy, If You Love Me' days, but who never actually spoke to me in person. One from my new manager, about two weeks into his employment, but he was only fishing, and I told him what was what. One from a friendly rival from down the road. Mr. William Ferguson, of Bill's Cyder Cellar." She hesitated a moment. "I handed them all the mitten, of course. Not a one of them has a head on his shoulders, including the manager, and I intend to give him notice after Christmas."

"And, apart from those three, the rest of the year?"

"I had my share of fortune hunters after I lost Jimmy. I made things clear enough then. It's got around that it's not worth the effort, so it's rare what as I have to deal with unwanted attentions these days. I generally keeps to myself and my scrapbooks and don't pay much attention to the other places."

"Splendid. And, pray tell, when did the fire occur?"

"I bought the Aoede in January that year. It was late February. Someone placed a candle too close to the curtain. My plan was to space things out, so as it could pay for its own fix-up, seeing as the previous owner hadn't kept up with the place at all. It cost me a pretty sum, what with the painters and the carpenters and the plasterers and half of London crawling over the place. We got the scaffolding out by March's end, though, and was back in business by the beginning of April."

"Half of London?"

"More like one person. He was a relative of the former owner, by name of Tull, but didn't know the place had been sold. Came running in there with the police on his heels one day. Caused a lot of trouble."

Holmes rose. "Thank you for your information, Mrs. Hughes. Who is generally around, and when?"

"I live in rooms onsite, sir, so it's rare what as I'm over a moment away. I had enough of the fast life back in my day, and the fizz don't taste so good when it's your own shilling. The manager interviews performers on Mondays. Meals are available daily, though most grab a bun through the window as they pass. We offer a program of music and entertainment four nights a week, and a matinee on Saturday, so there's the hands and the performers then, as well as the kitchen staff and the waiters."

"Most excellent. I hope to bring your problems to a tidy end before a week is through."

Mrs. Hughes looked disappointed. "I don't know if the Aoede's reputation can survive another week, especially after 'Harlequin and Cinderella.'"

"Even a conjuror needs time to collect his pigeons," said Holmes, with perfect tranquility. "There are at least nine different explanations for your recent events, and it will take a small amount of investigation to determine the cause at its root. If fortune is on your side, you may be able to make up most of your losses before Christmas. One piece of advice before you depart, however: even should a position come vacant, whether cook or waiter or anyone else, I beg you leave it unfilled for at least the week."

The door had scarcely shut on our mystified client before I turned to Holmes. "Surely, Holmes, that was going a bit too far. You know the artistic temperament for what it is. It's rather ungentlemanly of you to give her hopes, when you can't possibly do a thing to transform what is undoubtedly an unreliable segment of the population into sober and dependable human beings."

"And yet she has spent the last ten years with a perfectly sound business built upon the entertainment they provide, and had spent previous decades moving in those selfsame circles herself. She 'knows what things belongs', as she so quaintly put it."

"Speaking of which, how on earth did you know she was on the stage? It seemed a charitable guess, between the expense of her clothes and her dreadful accents, yet you had her labeled before she said a word."

"Surely you remarked upon her complexion, my dear Watson. Years of greasepaint for the stage will have an effect on the pores in a way mere powder never could."

"And the costuming? Yet you knew she was not a seamstress?"

"Surely you spotted those stray threads which clung unheeded to her skirts, Watson. One could hardly walk around a room where sewing activity is taking place without some of the materials adhering to one's hems, and she was distracted enough to not notice. Then there was the consideration of her cuffs. They were made of quite the extravagant silk plush, and are most excellent for retaining impressions. From the patterns of wear, one could spot the marks of long hours at the sewing machine upon the left cuff, but not both, as one would expect with, say, a professional typist. Add to that the fact that such a walking dress is unlikely to be found for less than fifty guineas, and, judging by the shape of the bustle, is quite the latest, and you have a woman far more affluent than most hirelings, especially with the economy in its current straits."

"And Mile End?"

"I had briefly considered Bethnal Green. Even the most recent newcomer to London could not have failed to place her in the East End, merely on the strength of her abuse of phonetics and idiom. But you know I've made a study of the unique characteristics of the various soils to be found in the districts of London. It is the rare person who does not have crusted dirt clinging to their boots at this time of year, with the rainy days of winter upon us."

"What do you propose to do?"

"Right now? I propose to peruse the papers. This afternoon, however, I intend to travel to Mile End."

"To lay eyes upon the Aoede?"

"Rather, to lay eyes upon Bill's Cyder Cellar. Would you care to come along?"

The odors of tobacco, perspiration, and onions mingled in a poisonous miasma at our destination. There was not a drop of decent wine upon the premises, but the waiters mingled through the crowds in the pauses between turns, noisily advertising the availability of gin, whiskey, and rum. Although it was presumably a supper-club, the only foods that appeared to be available were common breakfast foodstuffs: sausages, fried ham and eggs, kidneys. There were perhaps one hundred persons, of mixed company, crowded around tables, all eating and drinking with vigor and conversing loudly. A handful of infants slumbered or nursed through the proceedings; the number of children present was shocking. Most of the company present ignored the entertainment at the opposite end of the long, narrow gallery, where a stage had been erected. A pair of violinists – one blind, the other with a wooden leg – and a pianist accompanied a vocalist whose song, or as much as I could catch of it, was more crude than comic. A placard on a stand beside him suggested that this was the fifth act of the evening; I did not feel as though I had missed much by arriving late.

Holmes had tasked me with discovering what information I could from the masses, while he pursued his own separate inquiries. Disguised, he had entered the premises a full ten minutes before I did, and I felt quite out of place alone amidst this raffish crew. I sidestepped a waiter peddling the sheet-music that had accompanied Number Five's performance and settled down in a vacant seat. I had changed my customary garments for shabbier clothing, but was uncomfortable in the knowledge that I had no place amongst this society. I ordered a whiskey for which I had little desire, just as Number Six took the stage, coughed for attention, and the waiters scuttered from the floor. There was a slight decrease in the din, and he commenced an act whereupon he juggled an assortment of loaded pistols. I found I could not take my eyes from the foolhardy spectacle, and all thoughts of striking up conversation with my neighbors fled for the duration of his act. Soon enough, however, he finished his performance, relinquished the stage, and the waiters buzzed through the room once more, calling for orders, while the few whose attention had been captured by his turn resumed conversation with their neighbors once more.

Fortified by a draught, which I suspected of having been somewhat watered, I turned to my own neighbors and attempted to make conversation with them. Yet what would have proven a singularly difficult undertaking under ideal circumstances proved nigh impossible amidst the noise and smoke of this crowded hall. Realizing I would get little insight from the party of cabmen I had originally sat next to, I circulated around the room in the hopes of attaching myself to some lone individual who would be amenable to casual conversation. But my approaches were generally received without encouragement, forcing me to move on, and thus I passed my time through a series of performing cats, an American comedian, and a Scotsman in kilt and sporran.

"Buy me my liquor?" I was approached by a very free and forward woman, and I automatically acquiesced to her request – gin, neat. "Out slummin', are we?"

"Perhaps," I said, not a little discomfited. "In fact, I had heard of Bill's Cyder Cellar, and I wished to see it for myself."

"It's a far cry from the Alhambra," said the woman, with a braying laugh, "but it's all the same at the bottom."

"I had also heard of the Aoede," I pressed. "And I wished to make a comparison of the two."

"Writing for the guidebooks, what?" joked a male neighbor, who had ignored me until this point.

"Er. More like, an investment," I said. "Suppose I wanted to invest in a music hall or a supper club. Is the Cyder Cellar an example of a successful enterprise?"

"Comic singers do best on stage," said the woman promptly, "but the music halls would be empty if it weren't for the people what comes to them."

"Yes, I believe that's rather self-evident," I began. Another braying laugh.

"Take this act, for example," I pressed on hurriedly,

indicating the one-legged dancer who capered onstage. "Suppose he has booked himself in three different venues on one night, one of which was mine. How can he be relied upon to faithfully make his appearance at all three locations? That's rather a hectic schedule. Surely the Cyder Cellar must have an appreciable number of no-shows, merely due to unavoidable obstacles that life places in one's way."

The woman appeared unconcerned. "We all like to eat, don't we? If he don't perform, he don't get paid, and if he don't get paid, he don't eat."

"My brother did turns in music halls for years," said the man. "The stories he had! The problem was, the music halls don't pay enough to keep body an' soul together, so you needs to stack 'em. The music halls complain that the same turn appears three times on the same street. They needs to pay more if they wants an exclusive."

Once the conversation had started upon this path of remuneration and employers, there was no retrieving it, despite numerous attempts. It was with relief that I escaped from the oppressive atmosphere of the hall to the chill of the overcast winter night and met Holmes outside the coffee house two blocks away at our designated time. Yet again, he had transformed himself with his usual deftness. Slouching about in a suit of third-hand clothes, his accent as unintelligible as any other in that shabby den, I felt a pang of envy at the realization he was always at ease, whether in the midst of kings or costermongers.

"All I could determine was that Bill's seems to have no trouble with irresponsible artistes," I reported. "I could find no instances of turns listed upon the programme, where the artiste failed to appear."

"Of course not," said Holmes. "You'll find this specific trouble is endemic to Mrs. Hughes' establishment, and will not be found plaguing her neighbors."

"Then I can't say I see the point of this wasted evening," I said, with some asperity. "Unless you discovered something you would care to share."

"We'll see how the Aoede is on Monday," he replied, "and that will give me a better idea of the facts in play."

By "we", Holmes obviously meant "I". He emerged from his room before dawn, this time dressed as one who had seen former affluence, but had come down in the world. He disappeared, violin case in hand, not to be seen again until the lamps had been lit.

"Congratulate me, friend Watson," he said, "for I am to make my stage debut on Friday evening at the Aoede. Or rather, congratulate James Gray, if all goes well."

"Whatever for, Holmes?"

"A simple experiment which may help us determine what outside forces may be meddling with the Aoede's contracted artistes, or if, perhaps, there is an explanation closer to home for Mrs. Hughes."

"And if nothing comes of it?"

"Then perhaps the labourers of London will enjoy ten minutes' worth of Mendelssohn, or what they can hear of it, and then I shall be followed by an adagio act and quickly forgotten," came the tranquil reply. "I spent several hours of my time observing the day's auditions and contracts. Next, I visited a jeweler's shop. Then, I placed an advertisement for the services of a reliable wall-paperer. The remainder of my day was spent investigating records of the area's criminal activity. Matters proceed in a satisfactory manner."

Contrary to expectations, however, by Friday afternoon, nothing had interfered that would cause any cancellation of plans. Holmes, under his alias, took the stage as Number Eight on the evening's bill, and executed his piece with much gravity. As Holmes is in the indulgent habit of compensating my patience with flurries of Mendelssohn and other favored melodies, I privately sorrowed over the indifference that met his performance.

The Aoede, even in its current state of disfavor, still held more than treble the number of patrons that Bill's Cyder

Cellar had boasted. The atmosphere, with its high ceilings and glittering chandeliers and heavy velvet drapes, held pretensions of affluence which contrasted sharply with the dinginess of the Cellar. The ventilation was also distinctly superior, although the class of individuals who frequented the hall were still of the poor and humble sort, and crudity and double entendre abounded throughout the evening's entertainment.

Three of the twenty billed performers were unable to make their advertised appearances: Sevastyanov the Russian illusionist; the Barzotti Brothers, who performed feats of strength; and "Hamlet in Eight Minutes, performed with the greatest possible success" by Henry Jones. They were all key pieces, and despite the audience's apparent lack of attentiveness, the subtraction of these three turns from the programme was met with great hostility. Although I had little fondness for music halls, it saddened me to see our client's livelihood in such unfavourable straits.

It was quite late by the time the hall closed and the crowd dispersed. The staff was left to clean and tidy. Holmes gestured for the manager and Mrs. Hughes to join him in conference, and we all seated ourselves around a table. He introduced the manager as Mr. Munby; Mr. Munby seemed quite at a loss as to why Number Eight had called a meeting, but despite his bull-like appearance, he followed his employer's lead with docility.

"I hope things have been quiet these last few days? No intruders?" inquired Holmes.

"Nothing's come to my attention," said Mrs. Hughes, glancing at Mr. Munby for affirmation.

Holmes nodded his approval. "One will find, with observation, that there has been an increase in the foot-traffic around your establishment these last few nights. It cost but a trifle and makes prowlers cautious. Have you had any defectors amongst your staff?"

"Wednesday, one of the waiters quit without notice,"

said Mr. Munby. "We've been shorthanded as a result, but I was instructed to leave the vacancy until further notice."

"Most excellent," said Holmes. "If you don't mind, I believe half of your problem could be solved by fresh wall-paper. I have taken the liberty of advertising around, and am in communication with four wall-paperers. They will come by in the morning, take measurements, and give their price. We will be here at nine in the morning to meet them."

"That's absurd!" exclaimed Mr. Munby. "We'll shut our doors before Christmas at this rate; this is no time for foolish spending."

"I believe the other half of the problem," continued Holmes, unperturbed by this interruption, "would be solved by the immediate termination of your employment, Munby."

Munby turned quite pink. "I've been here a month and am doing my best under the circumstances."

Holmes directed his conversation to Mrs. Hughes and myself, with the occasional gesture towards Mr. Munby as though he were some scientific specimen of mild interest. "You will recall that Mr. Jacobs passed on at the beginning of November. Concurrently with his illness and passing, you received an offer from an anonymous purchaser, which you refused. By midmonth, you had hired on Mr. Munby, and from the moment Mr. Munby took the reins, your artistes have begun to fail to appear in ways they had not hitherto."

"I say, that's not –" interrupted Mr. Munby.

"And not just small artistes who would be easily missed. Not a sentimental singer, or one juggler who is very much like another. Intriguing artistes with acts that capture the imagination, such as, say, a Russian magician, or an amusing interpretation of The Bard, or a comic skit. It is my assertion that there never was a Sevastyanov; there never were any Barzotti Brothers; and while I'm sure London is full of Henry Joneses, I doubt any of them is capable of performing 'Hamlet in Eight Minutes' with the greatest possible success.

Certainly, none of them auditioned on Monday. I posit to you that all of these acts were fictions, created with the sole purpose of disappointing the audience by their failure to materialize."

"What of 'Harlequin and Cinderella'?" demanded Mrs. Hughes. "Surely I didn't wear my fingers to the bone stitching costumes for no one."

"Oh! Surely they were real enough flesh-and-blood humans. Perhaps they even had acquired a genuine script to rehearse. But they were mere confederates, and there was never any intention of bringing their *harlequinade* to opening night. You yourself said they had reported for the curtain, yet had turned around and promptly disappeared moments later. If merely Pantaloon had turned up missing, or you had mislaid a policeman, one might consider the possibilities. But to have your entire cast vanish into the night minutes before taking the stage! How can that be anything but deliberate? Especially when occurring as part of a pattern that has continued for a month now? London has its share of the criminal class, but I doubt there's much profit in the chronic kidnapping of stage magicians and songsters, especially when it's only from one stage on one street."

"I don't see –"

"Which brings us to motive," continued Holmes. "Mrs. Hughes lives a quiet, isolated life. She is content to focus on her business, which thrives under the care she and Mr. Jacobs had invested in its success. There are other similar businesses as well. All know the Alhambra, the Argyle, the Barnes – but they are geographically remote and may be, for the moment, disregarded. Looking within the immediate neighborhood, who would benefit if the Aoede closed its doors? There are numerous victuallers, of course, but Bill's Cyder Cellar is the only local establishment in direct competition for the cheap dining-and-entertainment crowd.

"Having visited the Cyder Cellar earlier this week, it was easy to tell that it is doing a poor business these days.

At the peak of the evening, there were hardly a hundred individuals upon the premises, and of those, a tenth or more were children and infants! The spirits were adulterated; the food was lacking; the atmosphere was fetid; the cleanliness left everything to be desired. Bill is not the proprietor of a successful establishment; Bill is the captain of a sinking ship.

"Mrs. Hughes has told us she has no interest in marriage and is content to live quietly, yet she has received three propositions for marriage in the last six weeks, each, presumably, from a man who knows little or nothing of the woman to whom he proposed. One anonymous letter-writer; one from Mr. Ferguson himself; and one, as it happens, from you, Mr. Munby. When a man proposes marriage to a woman who is nearly a stranger, it is rarely from honorable motivations. Perhaps it is cynical of me, but ninety-nine times of a hundred, it is to gain access and control of whatever property she might bring to the union. And Mrs. Hughes is a prosperous, practical widow, having cultivated the diamonds of her youth into a tidy income. When Mr. Ferguson sensed his competition's vulnerability, upon Mr. Jacobs' illness and death, he attempted to buy her out for whatever pittance he could. When that failed, he attempted to again play upon the abandonment and isolation of a widow who has lost a trusted friend. And when that approach was rebuffed, he sent you in, Mr. Munby, to destroy from within as a ship-worm sabotages a ship. You made a halfhearted effort at a proposal yourself, but as that had failed twice before, it obviously did not work the third time it was tried. Instead, you concentrated your attack on her purse-strings. You advertised creative, inventive acts which could not possibly appear on stage, and attempted to destroy the credibility of her establishment, in the hopes that it would drive more patrons to Bill's Cyder Cellar, which, I've discovered, is unlikely to keep its doors open more than three months. He has enough bills from creditors to paper his office."

"It sounds plausible, but why should Mr. Munby go through all that effort?" I asked.

"Watson, you know that the study of physiognomy is just as important to me as the study of tobacco-ash or soil particles," said Holmes. "I had the opportunity to observe Mr. Ferguson himself earlier this week. He possessed a strong forehead with very square eyebrows. His earlobes were quite attached to the side of his head; he has a very square jaw; and there were seven or eight other unique points about his appearance. Looking at our friend Mr. Munby, you can easily observe that same phenotype, suggesting hereditary characteristics."

"He has no children. I'm not his son," said Munby sullenly. "Perhaps. Perhaps not. You may be a nephew of his, or something else, but the pair of you certainly share the same blood," said Holmes. "I wonder what he could have offered that made you think it prudent to partake in such an infantile scheme."

Munby arose abruptly and stalked past three waiters, who had spent the last ten minutes rubbing down tables nearby with more care than was strictly necessary. "I'll not take this abuse any longer. Unfounded, that's what it is," he shouted over his shoulder as he departed the room.

"Of all the – !" exclaimed Mrs. Hughes, who was still processing the torrent of explanation. "What can I do about it?"

"Munby may or may not be his real name," said Holmes. "And there's no physical evidence, of course, to bring him to a court of law. No phonograph recordings of him and Mr. Ferguson plotting against you, or a useful outline of 'Steps to Destroy One's Competitor' in their own hand. Still, I believe you can take solace in the fact that Bill's shall be a distant memory soon enough. The wicked do not always prosper. Now, this shall suffice for tonight. Let us retire, as the wall-paperers will be here soon enough."

"The wall-paperers! Surely that was a joke," said Mrs. Hughes.

"As I said, ridding yourself of Munby was only half your problem," said Holmes. "This has been slow enough to play out, but things must be done in the proper order."

It seemed like no time before we were back at the Aoede, the chilly grey mist swirling through the streets. Mrs. Hughes was instructed regarding her part, and Holmes and I stationed ourselves behind the heavy drape of the closed curtain, where we could see but not be seen in turn.

Three different wall-paperers arrived in succession. Each time, Mrs. Hughes would go up to her office to take care of some papers while they and their assistants took measurements of the room. Mrs. Hughes would return after an interval. They conversed with Mrs. Hughes; she thanked them and they took their leave. Holmes sat quietly and made no movement.

With the fourth set of wall-paperers, however, it was different. As soon as Mrs. Hughes had departed, he scooted his ladder from its station by the wall, and dragged it to the center of the room while his assistant stood watch near the door. The one with the ladder then commenced a thorough investigation of each of the large chandeliers which depended from the ceiling. He gave a muffled cry of excitement as he found something. Holmes stepped calmly from behind the curtain, stick in hand, and said, "Don't get too excited, friend. It's only paste."

The wall-paperer nearly fell from his ladder, but quickly recovered himself. He looked at the glittering handful he had pulled from the profusion of crystal swags, then tossed it across the room in disgust. His companion had already bolted from the scene.

"I presume you're looking for the jewels that Philip Tull hid there ten years ago," said Holmes. "I assure you, they have been found and are returned to their lawful possessor."

Mrs. Hughes had re-entered the room during this exchange. "What, and diamonds, too?"

"While you were explaining your initial problem, I

couldn't help remarking upon the additional oddities that had plagued you of late. Not just the prowlers, but the acrobat. The gas-fitters. The drapers. In each of those cases, random outsiders were finding every excuse to investigate the very ceilings of this particular room. Yet it didn't make sense to lay it at Mr. Munby's feet, as he had perfect access to this room 'round the clock, and had no reason to make elaborate excuses to investigate it with either acrobats or sham drapers. Therefore, there seemed to be a second issue at play, and it was my task to separate the threads of two independent problems.

"Imagine, if you will, ten years ago. You are a young man named Philip Tull, who has recently involved himself in some sort of criminal activity involving the possession of stolen property. With the police hot on your trail, you run to seek refuge on the premises belonging to a relative, but you are unaware that relative has relocated, and sold the property to another. You enter the premises; you see scaffolding has been erected for the post-fire renovation. You scramble up the scaffolding and hide sparkling jewels amongst a chandelier full of sparkling crystals. By the time the police capture you, 'the goods' are no longer in your possession, and they cannot arrest you on that...but there are other excuses for your detainment, as your existence has not been an honest one, and you find yourself in prison, where you die of influenza a few years into your term." Looking at the wall-paperer, he added, "I presume that is where you heard of the diamonds?"

"He knew he wouldn't make it out alive," said the wall-paperer gruffly. "There was three of 'em, and not as careful as they could be. His companions were caught with the goods on 'em, and met their ends on the scaffold. The jewelers got back everything in the end, excepting that piece. Its secrets would have died with him, if it weren't for his bragging."

"A collet necklace of considerable value," said Holmes, retrieving the dummy and pocketing it. "An odd subject to contemplate upon one's death-bed. Now that you know Philip Tull's ill-gotten goods have been returned to their rightful owners, and you have no further reason to pester this establishment, I will give you three minutes' head start before I call the nearest policeman."

The wall-paperer did not require a second suggestion. He fled the scene. Mrs. Hughes was more interested in examining the substitute necklace, which Holmes permitted.

"Holmes! You seem to have had a good grasp of the situation before you left your arm-chair!" I said.

"Although the main points were relatively straightforward, it was merely a matter of filling in the details," said Holmes.

"These ain't paste!" exclaimed Mrs. Hughes, looking up from the diamonds in her hands.

"Indeed, they are not," said Holmes, retrieving them gently. "Just as our friends had difficulty in accessing premises which were so heavily occupied 'round the clock, I, too, would have had difficulty in hunting these down and performing a substitution without exciting attention. And I especially did not want to do anything that would make Munby suspect anything was afoot. It was easier to leave them in place and allow others an opportunity to direct us to their location. Come along, Watson. I noted a German seller of sheet-music the next street over. Perhaps he may have something of interest for solo violin."

The Song of the Mudlark

by Shane Simmons

Before you says a word, I'll tell you I know. My writing ain't so pretty as what Doctor Watson puts down on his pages, but then I'm not a learned medical man, am I? So why's he not writing up this adventure of his friend and fellow, Sherlock Holmes, you're likely to say. Well he don't know half as much about it as I do, and even Mister Holmes don't know all the details, smart as he is, knowing everything as he usually does. But me, I know the whole lot. I was there from the start and to the finish. Who am I then, to be so well informed? If you say, as people do, that Doctor Watson's always been Mister Holmes's right-hand man, I expect that makes me his left-hand man. Or boy. There's a few years to go yet before people see me as a man, even though I've been on my own, taking care of myself and my mates, since I was old enough to walk and run the streets of London.

The name's Wiggins. I'd tell you my given name, but then we ain't so well acquainted, you and me. I'm writing up this here story, and you're reading it, which is all well and good. But if I don't know your name, you only get "Wiggins" for mine and that'll have to do.

I might have writ this tale earlier, only my words weren't so good then as they is now, which is to say they was a whole lot more horrible back when these events first happened and was fresh to me. Nah, don't you worry. I remember all the whys and wherefores just fine, like it were only yesterday. I remember because nobody ever forgets the time they brought a big mystery to the doorstep of the great Sherlock Holmes. How big a mystery? Well, let's just say it was so mysterious a mystery, Mr. Holmes agreed to look into it right away, and that don't happen much. It's got to be quite a teaser to get him interested, otherwise he'll take one look and solve it, quick as a fiddle, and where's the fun in that, I ask you. It was early one morning when me and the boys dropped by Baker Street. Mr. Holmes had a package come in on one of the ships at the dock, and he had sent me, personally, to fetch it. As it so happens, it was two packages I brought back – the one he was so anxious about, and another I hoped he would take on once I explained the situation.

I left the rest of the boys waiting in the lane out back. Mrs. Hudson was the name of the landlady, and she didn't much care for any of us tracking dirt inside and all over her nice clean floors. She was always claiming she'd just mopped them, even though I never saw her lay a hand to a mop or a broom except to chase us out of her rooms.

"He's upstairs and he's in a mood," she said when she saw it was only me coming in and my shoes weren't in such a sorry state.

She pointed the way, like I didn't already know it, like I hadn't been up there a hundred times before.

"Enter!" I heard Mr. Holmes shout after my first knock on the door.

He didn't sound none too patient. I didn't bother announcing it was me who'd come up. He would've already deduced that ages ago.

"Ah, Wiggins, at last," he said when he saw the wrapped bundle tied up under my arm.

"The package you been waiting on, Mr. Holmes," I announced.

He took it from me right off and tossed a shilling I had to

grab out of the air.

"What package is this, then?" Dr. Watson wanted to know as he looked up from the morning paper.

"Oh, merely something for my chemistry experiments," Mr. Holmes told him. "A perplexing puzzle in its own right, and something to occupy my mind while London is beset with this wave of inexorably dull, unimaginative crime."

He cut the string on the package with a pair of scissors and brought it over to his work bench that was stacked high with all sorts of glass bottles and tubes filled with who-knows-what for reasons I couldn't guess at.

"All the way from South America is what the cabin boy told me," I said.

"Barring one side trip to Germany for refinement, but yes, quite right."

Mr. Holmes looked in one of his drawers and came up with a small leather case. He opened it and I spotted a needle inside, the kind I'd expect to see in a doctor's hand, not a consulting detective's. I figure maybe he swiped it from Dr. Watson without asking first because he seemed to not want the doctor to see what he was up to.

"Off you go, Wiggins. You have your shilling. I will send word if I have anything else for you."

I nearly left right when he told me to, but stopped in the door. I didn't want to waste his time, but then I weren't so sure if what else I brought him was a waste or not, was I?

"Mr. Holmes, there's something more."

"Is there? Well, out with it, Wiggins. What do you want?"

"It ain't what I want. It's what I have for you. A mystery."

I saw Mr. Holmes swap a look with Dr. Watson, and for a moment I thought they might laugh at me. But then Mr. Holmes must have seen how I looked so serious, and knew it wasn't any childish riddle I was on about.

"Best I introduce you in person," I said to them.

I stepped out of the room, to the top of the stairs, and whistled loud as I could. The back door opened and I could hear footsteps stomping on up, with Mrs. Hudson complaining about each one. I led my guest inside and shut the door so we didn't have to listen to the landlady no more.

"Another one!" said Dr. Watson, not at all happy when he saw who I'd brought into their home. "Well, better than him leading in the whole lot as he usually does."

It was another young urchin to be sure, even more ragged than the ones he'd seen Mr. Holmes deal with before. I was about to explain what was special about this one, but Mr. Holmes was ahead of me.

"Now there's an irregular Irregular!" he said. "The ranks swell and diminish, Watson, lads come and they go, but this one is quite different. Not your usual recruit I would say, Wiggins."

"No sir, you're right there."

"How so, Holmes?" said Dr. Watson. "He seems to fit right in with the other street Arabs."

"Several factors exclude him from the rest," said Mr. Holmes, looking the child next to me up and down. "Firstly, this lad is at least a year or two younger than the rest. The jacket, cap and trousers are considerably rougher than what Wiggins and his crew wear, as though salvaged further down the line of poverty and despair. And there has been some grief of late, I perceive. The tears are not flowing this moment, but the last ones carved twin ditches down those dirty cheeks too recently to have been filled in by fresh dirt. Though the dust is no different than what might be routinely kicked up in a busy London street, the mud on those shoes is another matter. That is not from any puddle or pit in the city. It comes from the banks of the river. I should say this is one of the mudlarks of the Thames standing before us."

The mudlarks were the lowest of the low, and children the lot of them, either with no parents at all, or mothers and fathers too drunk or worse to take care of them. They worked the banks of the Thames when the tide was out, picking through the muck for anything they could sell for a ha'penny. Scraps and rubbish mostly, but worth something to someone somewhere, if only a farthing or a bite to eat. Compared to the mudlarks, we street urchins were the tip-top of high society.

"Right you are, Mr. Holmes," I said, "though you've missed out on one detail."

"Have I? Do enlighten us then, Wiggins."

"She ain't no lad."

Mr. Holmes raised my companion's cap off her head and studied the face more closely.

"I do believe you are correct," he said at last. "An easy enough detail to miss under so much filth."

"Her name is Beth," I said. "I've seen her working down by the water before, but today I found her in such a state."

"Me da's been killed!" Beth cried out when she couldn't keep silent any longer. "Washed up in the Thames and bleeding money like he were made of it!"

Fresh tears carved new ditches through the dirt on her face. "Bleeding money, you say?" said Mr. Holmes, picking out the one detail that weren't all too common. Poor folks drowning in the Thames was hardly worth a mention otherwise.

"The girl is imagining fairy stories, Holmes," said Dr. Watson and made to stick his nose back in his paper.

But Mr. Holmes, he didn't look so sure. "Wiggins, have you seen this yourself?"

"No sir," I said. "But word is out that a body's been spat out of the river with the low tide and's lying on the banks. The mudlarks all know it, but the police haven't come 'round for a look. Not yet at any rate. And I figure since you seem to always know so much about dead bodies . . . ." I had told Beth I knew a man who might help, but I didn't want to push my luck too far and endanger my job. Without Mr. Holmes paying us a regular salary, The Baker Street Irregulars would have a hard time of it, I know that much.

Mr. Holmes looked back to his work bench and his new

experiment and I knew we was losing him.

"No, Wiggins. There is nothing to it for me. Best let the police sort the matter out. It sounds like a routine drowning, or perhaps an altercation that ended in the river."

Regular wages or not, I didn't let it stand there.

"Show it to him," I nudged Beth and she dug deep into her one pocket that didn't already have holes in it.

"Show me what?" Mr. Holmes wanted to know.

"A clue," I said.

Beth came up with a small hunk of metal, not unlike the old bolts and nails she scavenged along the water's edge. At first glance it looked like any other scrap, but Mr. Holmes took it in hand and saw what was so special about it at once.

"Where did you get this?" he asked Beth.

"It was stuck in Da. I shook him and it fell out."

"What do you make of this, Watson," said Mr. Holmes, handing the thing over.

"Why, it's a gold sovereign!" Dr. Watson declared after having his look.

"Yes, I can see that for myself," said Mr. Holmes. "But what does it tell you?"

"Well, it is certainly mangled. Not the usual wear and tear I would expect to see on such a denomination. And it is far more money than some unfortunate mudlark could ever make."

"Not in a year or more of hard labour, even if they should they live long enough to procure a better occupation," agreed Mr. Holmes. "What else?"

Dr. Watson had another look because Mr. Holmes was suggesting he missed something. Something important.

"It's all rusty," he said at last.

"No Watson, not rusty, but imbued with the stuff. Gold neither rusts nor tarnishes, yet this piece is absolutely caked with both."

"So what does that tell you?" asked Dr. Watson of his friend. "What indeed?" was all Mr. Holmes had to say on the matter.

That got him interested. It made him stop and think for a moment, at any rate. And when he didn't come right back with an explanation, I dared figure I might have him.

"You'll have a look, though, won't you Mr. Holmes?"

Mr. Holmes had always done right by the Irregulars, and he gave me a bit of a nod and a smile and agreed.

"Watson, be the good doctor and see to our new client. If Mrs. Hudson has a soup on the stove, pour some into her. She's all skin and bones. Wiggins and I will take a hansom down to the water and see what we shall see."

After I dismissed the rest of The Irregulars for that day, me and Mr. Holmes caught ourselves a cab that took us straight down to the spot Beth had told me about. Once we were there, we saw the crowd that had gathered along the embankment. Somebody other than a mudlark had spotted Beth's dead father, and now the police were there, keeping everyone back.

It only took a word from Mr. Holmes to get past the two Bobbies blocking off the steps to the river. If they didn't know his face, they knew his name and reputation and that was enough. A third was standing at the water's edge, next to a fellow lying face-down on the rocks. The man on guard was a big peeler from The Yard – the kind what runs the likes of The Irregulars off the street if they get a notion we's up to something they don't approve of. He would have chased me off right quick if Mr. Holmes hadn't vouched for me.

"My name is Sherlock Holmes," he said, "and this is my associate, Mr. Wiggins."

I tipped my hat at the introduction, polite whenever I must.

"Mr. Holmes," said the officer in charge of the scene, "always a pleasure to hear you're on the job. Though what interest this sort of vagrant might have for you is beyond me."

"Even the lowest among us may suffer an intriguing

demise that warrants investigation."

"Take a look as you care, but he seems just another drowned shoreman to me. If anyone's at fault, I would point at the man who poured him his last drink."

It didn't take Mr. Holmes more than a moment to disagree with the policeman once he stooped down and began making all those deductions he's so good at.

"He is quite soaked through, but not drowned," he concluded. "No water has been inhaled. Dead men do not gasp for breath, above or below the water."

The man in charge didn't look so in charge once he heard it was a killing he was standing over.

"Hello, what have we here?" said Mr. Holmes, brushing aside the sopping tangle of hair at the back of the dead man's head. Beth had been right. Her father was bleeding money.

There, sticking out of an ugly hole punched through the back of his skull, was a tidy sum of money, all clumped together in a rusty chunk, with every coin stuck to their mates like they was all minted that way.

Mr. Holmes began the messy task of picking the pieces out as they would come. Some coins were loose, but most were massed in groups, with as many as a dozen at a time joined together. You'd need a hammer and long hours to break them all apart to spend. There weren't no more gold sovereigns like the one Beth had plucked out, but every other coin of the realm, copper or silver, made an appearance. All told, Mr. Holmes figured it to be at least three pounds worth – enough to have bought the eyes and ears of The Irregulars for a good long time, I'll tell you.

When he was done, the wound lay open and bare and it was sure as anything that that was what killed him. The bobby looked confused, and I'm not one to see eye-to-eye with the police most times, but it didn't make no sense to me neither.

"Who would kill a man and then, rather than stealing from him, deposit a sum of money in his body before throwing the corpse into the water? Surely he wasn't trying to sink it."

It was a foolish notion, but Mr. Holmes let it pass.

"Many a murdered man has been weighed down and sent to the bottom of the Thames. But not with only a handful of pocket change. And certainly not stuffed into a wound in his head. I would expect to see stones or perhaps heavy scraps of metal in his pockets, but there is nothing."

"What's the truth of it then, Mr. Holmes?" I asked.

"He was a shoreman most certainly, a tosher more specifically, but this has only been his occupation in recent years. The configuration of the callouses on his hands tell me of the tools he worked with. Not a long hoe, as a tosher might employ, but more likely shovels and picks. You can still see the discolouration in his skin from the coal dust to this day. He quit the mines after an injury left him with a broken arm that never set right, and came to the city to pursue a better life he failed to find. Fallen on hard times with a young child to support, he turned to toshing and may have come to more success at it than he wished."

Toshers were like mudlarks, all grown up but after bigger stakes. Their scavenging took them to much more dangerous, awful places. There were rewards to be had, sure enough, but it took a desperate man to try his hand at it.

"Was it murder?" was all the peeler wanted to know.

"I cannot say for the moment. Another man was involved at least. Of that much I am certain. Observe the heels of his boots, scuffed to the point of very nearly being worn through. The man was dragged here, pulled through the streets by his arms, and deposited along the banks of the Thames by someone in the middle of the night. He is wet, true, but from the morning rain, not the river. And the muck that covers his boots and trousers – how foul and fetid! I know every variety of mud than can be trodden in and tracked anywhere in London. I can tell you precisely which district a sample of soil is from and how fresh it is. But this! This I have never encountered. I am not acquainted with it nor, I suspect, do I wish to be. And yet, it shall be key to discovering the precise location where this man met his demise."

"What can my men do to help?" asked the policeman.

"Nothing at all. It is the assistance of young Wiggins I need now. As for the concerns of Scotland Yard, you may remove the body. It has told me all it can."

Mr. Holmes took me aside as the police prepared to carry the dead fellow to the wagon that had only just arrived. Beth's father would be filling a pauper's grave before another day had passed.

"We shall need a finer nose than mine to detect one scent amongst the myriad of fragrances we will face in the city streets," Mr. Holmes said to me. I knew straight off who he was talking about.

"Take a cab and have it wait for you," he said, giving me another shilling to cover expenses. "Pick up our mutual acquaintance and be back here as quick as you can. The longer we delay, the more the trail will be obscured by the regular traffic of London. I shall ask after any witnesses while you are gone, but our greatest hope lies with you and the best nose in England."

"Number Three, Pinchin Lane in Lambeth," was the address I gave to the first cab that would stop for me.

The journey wasn't a long one, and I soon found myself outside a row of shabby houses, picking out the one on the street filled with the calls and cries of a whole menagerie of animals.

"Can I borrow your dog?" I asked the man who came to the door.

I knew the reputation of this man who fancied himself a trainer of any beast he could lay his hands on, but he didn't know me from any other beggar.

"My dogs are not for rent," he said and tried to shut the door in my face. Only my foot in the frame kept him from kicking me out.

"Did I say anything about paying? No, I'm here to borrow on strict orders from Mister Sherlock Holmes."

And it was like I had said a magic word.

"Sherlock Holmes, you say? Then it must be Toby in number seven he's after."

It certainly was. Toby, ugly as sin, a shaggy mess if I'm completely honest, was the finest tracker dog to be had. Not that I had much cause to compare, but Mr. Holmes always swore by him, and we were soon reacquainted once his owner handed me the leash.

The hansom driver I left waiting didn't like carting around a boy of the street, even though I paid him good money. He liked it even less once I brought an unkempt mutt into his cab. Grumbling all the way or not, he got us back to the water in a short enough time.

Mr. Holmes took the leash from me as soon as we joined him and let the dog have a good sniff around. The body was gone, but the stink of his boots lingered and Toby soon had the scent. Didn't much care for it neither. Never did I see a dog recoil from a smell like that. For a dog what made it his business to put his nose to all sorts of dreadful things, this was one odour that seemed to outright offend him.

"I know, Toby," said Mr. Holmes. "Not the most pleasant aroma I have ever set you to follow, but follow it we must. There's a boy!"

Mr. Holmes's words of encouragement were enough to spark the dog's interest and he put his nose to the ground and hunted for which way the trail might lead. Through walkways and streets, around corners and down alleys we went. Toby kept us on the path that was invisible to the human eye but plain as day to the nose of an expert tracker dog.

Toby was so sure of himself as we wove our way into the city, it was a surprise when he started zigging and zagging, suddenly not so clear which way to go next.

"The trail splits in two, it seems," said Mr. Holmes.

"The man who dragged Beth's father to the river may well have doubled back on his own path and then on to a new destination. Whether we trace this to the man himself or the origin of his crime will have to be Toby's decision."

At last, Toby picked a branch and on we went for a few blocks more until we came to an east-end pub that was a short-walk local to anybody within a few doors. Anyone much farther away would have picked a better place to drink their worries away. It looked to be a rough place, home to nightly bare-knuckled matches, scheduled or not, but all of them bet on just the same. Mr. Holmes walked right on in like he belonged there, so I followed in case he needed my protection.

"You there! Get that dirty little mongrel out of here!" the barkeep shouted at us as soon as we stepped inside.

"I assure you, sir, he is very well trained, devoid of fleas, and will refrain from relieving himself indoors," said Mr. Holmes.

"I weren't talkin' about the dog! I meant the boy."

"As did I."

"Beggars and thieves, the lot of them!"

"He is with me, and neither of us will be staying long."

The barkeep made no move to toss us out on his own. You don't give the bum's rush to a gentleman like Sherlock Holmes.

"I won't serve him," he growled instead.

"We won't be drinkin' the piss you serve," I informed him.

Mr. Holmes looked down at me, pardoned my French, and agreed. "Quite."

He led Toby around the pub, from table to table, seeing which one the dog liked best. It didn't take him a moment to bring us to a man sitting at a booth in the corner, working his way through a pint glass I'd wager had been refilled a few times already.

Toby seemed pleased to have come upon a pair of boots

that matched the smell he'd been tracking, but he still took a step back when he caught a whiff of the fresh muck crusted there.

"What have you trodden in, I wonder," said Mr. Holmes to the man. "What business is that of yours?"

"I am Sherlock Holmes and this is Mr. Wiggins. The dog's name is Toby, if that is of any concern to you. Where you have been and what you have been up to is very much our business when you leave corpses lying about in public places."

The man made a move like he might bolt, but Mr. Holmes stood in his way, blocking him in the booth.

"You can talk to us, or you can be arrested for murder. It is entirely up to you."

That settled the man down a bit. Mr. Holmes handed me Toby's leash and sat down across from him.

"We have introduced ourselves. Who do we have the pleasure of addressing?"

"The name's Seaver. Edward Seaver."

"And the dead man?"

"That would be Albert Ewart. A good friend, he was."

It was the first time either of us had heard Beth's father called anything other than "Da."

"A tosher of late," said Mr. Holmes, "but formerly a coal miner, was he not?"

"Aye, he was in the mines. And it was coal in the end, once the ore mine he was in ran dry and closed. Mining is dark, dangerous work any way you look at it. But ore don't give you the black lung like coal does. Old Bert couldn't take it more than two or three years before he got out and came here."

"Tell me, did Mr. Ewart keep in touch with any of his fellows?"

"He did. One of them came through town only a few days ago."

"Bringing more than news from the mines, I expect. You

Mr. Holmes held the lantern over the dark hole so we could peer down into it. I could see the excavation went straight down through the dirt and broke through an arch of brickwork, offering entry into the sewer line that ran right under the building.

"This is the sort of vandalism toshers have been reduced to since the new London sewer system was completed. Rather before your time, Wiggins, but access used to be a far simpler matter when it ran freely into the Thames. Now such intrusions are forbidden by law, and if they're caught in the act, they face fines they can ill-afford to pay."

"What's so worth the risk and the stink of rummaging down there?"

"We shall see in short order," said Mr. Holmes, bidding me to help him lower the punt into the stream of filthy water below us.

The climb down was precarious, but we were cautious every foothold of the way, making sure nobody took a dip we'd long regret. Mr. Holmes carried Toby down in his arms, mangy but manageable in size as he was. We were soon all aboard the punt. A long pole tucked inside let Mr. Holmes push us off the side and set us down the slow-moving stream.

"Let us ascertain what befell Albert Ewart while he was seeking his fortune. Here is a new scent for you, Toby. See if you can sniff it out amongst all the other odours down here."

Mr. Holmes took a thumb-sized item from his pocket and held it under Toby's nose.

"What's that?" I asked him.

"Something the dead man had tucked under his belt. It is a vital tool in the mining industry, and was recently supplied to Beth's late father by his visiting friend. Undoubtedly he wrote to request it and several more just like it. It is called a blasting cap."

"What does it do?"

"Why, it explodes, of course. Not as grandly as dynamite, for instance, but it offers a smaller controlled charge to set off its more devastating cousins when much stone needs to be moved. Used on its own, it can still produce quite a powerful bang."

Drifting on a punt, Toby couldn't put his nose to the ground, yet he seemed able to catch the scent of recently detonated powder in the tunnel as he perched on the bow. It lingered in the still air, even hours later, and I thought I could smell it mixed in with the strong ammonia stink myself. When Toby seemed excited about a certain bend in the tunnel, Mr. Holmes poled us in that direction, taking us down a split lane. The current seemed to be picking up as the rain water from above filtered down into the sewer. Mr. Holmes had to work the pole harder to keep us from being swept along too quickly to give the tunnel a thorough search by lantern light.

After Toby's keen sense directed us to make a couple more turns, we happened upon a dark mass jutting out of the water. I might have missed it entirely, but Mr. Holmes seemed to know what he was looking for.

"There it lies, Wiggins. Riches more than we could hope to have to our names combined and multiplied. Who would have thought that such a treasure trove would be found in so foul a place!"

I leaned in for a closer look by the light of the lantern. There was more money in front of me than I ever dreamt existed, all fused together into one rusted mass – an entire boulder of it, jutting out of the sewage like a monument a madman might have sculpted for no one to ever see.

"I don't understand, Mr. Holmes. How could such a thing even exist?"

Mr. Holmes had an explanation, sure enough. He always had everything figured out.

"Think of all the coins that are dropped and lost in the streets of London each day. Some are discovered and picked up again, but many others are washed away into the gutter, down drains and into the sewers. All it takes is for one or two of them to get their edges caught in the gap between bricks under the waterline and they will collect others, like silt in a steady flow. They gather and rust together there for years, even decades, until they create a vast structure like this one, tempting to the toshers who come down here looking for lost valuables, but impossible to move. Such a waste."

"I'll not waste a penny of it! That you can be sure of!"

There was a lamp approaching us from down the tunnel, with footsteps splashing through the water beneath it. We couldn't see the face behind the bright light, but we recognized the voice of Edward Seaver.

"It's not the first lump of rusted coinage toshers have come across down here, but it's the grandest. And can we ever profit from any of them? No! Even if we could break them free, they're too heavy to drag up top."

Mr. Holmes was expecting he'd turn up, and turn up he did.

"Albert Ewart had a solution, did he not? A certain expertise that came from his mining days."

Closer now, I could see Seaver had the lamp fixed to his coat to light his way no matter where he turned or bent. He had his tosher's hoe with him, but had no plans to go raking for lost valuables ever again if he could come away with the pile of money that didn't want to go anywhere.

"He thought we could break it up, blow it into smaller pieces we could carry off," he said.

"With a number of these," said Mr. Holmes, holding up the blasting cap for Seaver. "As you can see, you failed to pilfer all of them from your fallen friend."

"It were his poor luck the one piece he blew loose came right at him when the fuse burned too quick and he couldn't run far enough. Shot down the tunnel like a bullet it did, with only his head to stop it. I couldn't leave him down here for the rats, but I couldn't leave him in the flophouse neither. Not looking like that for his own daughter to see. So I dragged him down to the river to let the tide take him away. A long, heavy trip it was, in the dark and rain. By the time we made it to the banks, the rain had let up and the morning sun was coming out. People would spot us, I was sure, and think I done it."

I looked at the mass of coins again. Near the top, you could see the spot where the charge went off. It looked like a bite had been taken out of it, but only a nibble compared to how much remained.

"If you want your proof I weren't the one that killed him, the piece that struck him down must be here somewhere," said Seaver, turning this way and that, shining his light around the water and walls.

"Your evening might have been more profitable if only you had bothered to examine Albert Ewart's wound," said Mr. Holmes. "I found a fair sum imbedded there this morning."

"Oh, I see now," Seaver hissed suspiciously. "You come to take the rest for yourselves! Well it's mine, I tell you, and I'll have at it by hammer and chisel till I'm old and grey if I must!"

Seaver came at us with his hoe raised as if he might try to beat us away from his treasure. Even as he pushed forward through water up to his knees, he seemed to make hardly any progress.

Mr. Holmes had his punting pole jammed into the side of the mound of money, keeping us anchored in place even as the flow of water picked up its pace. I'd hardly noticed the lazy current go from a steady trickle to a rapid river while the two men talked, but when Seaver, standing right in the middle of the flow, started to lose his footing, I knew something was wrong.

"The water's gone quick on us, Mr. Holmes, and I can see it rising up the walls!" I said, suddenly frightened. "We don't want to get caught in here come high tide!"

"No, it is far too early for high tide," said Mr. Holmes, seeing the same danger as me. "This is rain water. A deluge, in fact!"

With a terrible shout of anger and terror, Seaver tipped back into the flood and was swept away down the tunnel and into darkness. The last I saw of him was the tiny point of light from his lamp that blinked out once water pushed through the glass.

"Perilous occupation, toshing," declared Mr. Holmes. "It will see the end of us next if we aren't quick!"

Mr. Holmes cast off from the monument of lost money and tried to keep the punt weighed with himself, me and Toby from getting turned over in the swell. We flew down the tunnel at a quick pace and I kept counting and recounting the layers of brick between the surface of the water and the top of the sewer. That number kept getting smaller.

"The water's rising fast, Mr. Holmes!" I cried over the gushing cascade. Pointing out the obvious to Sherlock Holmes is a waste of his time and yours, but I was scared silly.

"We are too close to the river!" he said. "All the water flowing into the sewers uphill is converging here. The entire tunnel will be filled to the top in moments."

Mr. Holmes soon had to duck his head to keep from scraping it across the arched brick ceiling. I was sure the rising water would squash us to jam against the roof before spilling over the sides of the boat and dragging us to the bottom. We'd be drowned for certain.

"This is what we are looking for!" Mr. Holmes announced, jamming his pole into the wall and turning us towards a dead-end route that was capped with a huge iron door, sealed shut with no means to be opened. "The river lies just beyond."

"I thought you said sewer water don't flow into the Thames no more!"

"It does, but away from the city and too many miles

down river to save us now. We must rely on the emergency overflow outlets. They are designed to open when the sewer is over capacity to prevent flooding in the streets."

Mr. Holmes lay down at the bottom of the punt next to me and Toby. I gripped on tight to Toby's long, tangled mane and whispered to him, "Don't you worry, Mr. Holmes will see us through." But I wasn't so sure as the edges of the low boat floated high enough to touch the very top of the tunnel.

Just when I was certain we were all done for, there was a loud clatter that echoed through what bits of the tunnel weren't already under water. The next thing I knew, we were thrown forward and blown through the door as it flew open under all the pressure. I knew then what it was like to be fired out of a pistol. We were soaking wet in an instant, but not by sewer water sinking our little boat. It was rain, pouring down on us in sheets, and when I realized that I knew we were outside again.

I dared look up and saw we were adrift in the Thames. It was almost as dark out as it had been by lantern light in the tunnel, so black were the skies. Flashes of lightning lit up the shore enough for me to judge we'd been pushed all the way out to the middle of the flow, the tiniest ship on the whole river. Mr. Holmes stood up and surveyed our situation.

"We shan't be punting through waters as deep as the Thames," said Mr. Holmes, casting the useless pole down into our boat. "Make yourself useful, Wiggins, and help me flag down a passing vessel that might throw us a line."

I did as I was told, and it weren't too long before we was rescued, the three of us, and brought to the docks by a passing pusher tug. None were spared a thorough drenching, and me and Mr. Holmes had to return a stinking wet dog to his owner in Lambeth. We didn't tell him Toby might have ended the day smelling much worse had our venture into the London sewers gone badly.

"How has our houseguest been?" Mr. Holmes asked Dr. Watson back at Baker Street, once he'd gotten out of his wet clothes and into his robe.

"Ravenous," reported Dr. Watson. "I think we may go hungry in the coming week. Mrs. Hudson's pantry is down to crumbs."

Beth was sitting quietly by the window, humming softly to herself, trying to put the bad memories of the day aside with song.

"And how did your investigation go?" Dr. Watson asked.

"Well," said Mr. Holmes. "Wet but well."

"Back early enough to see to your chemistry experiments then, Holmes?"

Mr. Holmes took a long look at his work bench and then waved it away with his hand.

"No, Watson. I have had enough stimulation for the day. Perhaps tomorrow. At any rate, there is the girl, Beth, to attend to. Although I have solved the questions related to her father's death, she is too young to appreciate the case history, and there is no comfort for her to be had in the details. All that matters to her is that he is gone. "

"We should see about returning the girl to her mother," agreed Dr. Watson.

"Alas, there is no mother, Watson. Albert Ewart was a widower. A strip of clear skin around one finger told me of a ring that was there during his coal mining days, protecting that lone spot from the dust. It seems to have vanished years ago. Hard times or not, no living wife would let her husband pawn his wedding band."

Beth came out of her humming stupor and spoke up. "Mum's been dead so long, I can't hardly remember her."

"Another lost soul in London," said Mr. Holmes of the girl. "So many much too young for such a fate."

"I would say you already employ half of them, Holmes."

Dr. Watson was referring to me, standing out on a rug in the hall where I'd been told to stay, still dripping wet from the day, so I wouldn't stain the floorboards.

"Ah, if only that were so, Watson," said Mr. Holmes,

giving me a grin. "Not a criminal in the city could lift a finger without my knowing of it."

"A single sovereign is hardly an inheritance that will keep her forever," said Dr. Watson. "Inquiries will have to be made at London orphanages to find one that can take her in,"

I had to raise an objection to that suggestion straight off. "Some of the lads have been in and out of those places, and horrible they are. Like a prison for children whose only crime is being on their own."

"I am afraid it is the best we can offer her, Wiggins," said Mr. Holmes, even though I could tell he agreed with me.

"I understand," I nodded. "It's the best you can offer." I, on the other hand, figured I could do better.

"Do not be so downtrodden, boy," said Dr. Watson. "She may yet be adopted."

But when Dr. Watson turned to address me, all he found were wet footprints across the floor to the window and back again.

"I believe she already has been," I heard Mr. Holmes say upstairs as I led Beth out the back door and away from Baker Street.

The rest of the lads were waiting for me at our usual spot, in an empty lot out behind a tanner's shop, just a few blocks away. The rain had let up and it looked like the weather had decided to behave itself again.

"Meet our new recruit," I said to them as I approached. "You can call him Ben."

"Ben," I repeated to Beth, making sure she understood her new name, "these are The Baker Street Irregulars. You're one of us now."

Not all of them were so quick to accept new faces. Mullin was the first to protest.

"He's not one of the boys. He don't even look like a boy."

"He's one of us because I says so," I told him, "and he's a boy if I says that, too. You want to argue with me, open wide so's I can knock out a tooth or two while I'm knocking some sense into you."

Mullin backed down as soon as he saw me make a fist, but some of the others weren't so easy to bend.

"You been playin' a little too thick at bein' the boss of late, Wiggins," another dared to say.

"Yeah? Well how many of you have gone on an adventure with Mister Sherlock Holmes and helped him solve a big mystery? None, that's right. Because there's Dr. Watson and then there's me."

And that seemed to settle it. I didn't mention Toby in the list of Mr. Holmes's partners, just in case they thought I might rank third behind a dog. Once the matter of expanding our ranks was decided, I felt Beth tugging on my sleeve.

"What do I do?" she wanted to know, now that she'd given up a life of mudlarking to become an Irregular.

"You do as the rest of us does," I instructed. "You watch and you listen. We're the eyes and ears of London, we lot. And whatever we know, whatever we learn, it's Sherlock Holmes who'll put it to good use."

She was young, the youngest we'd ever taken in, but she understood straight away. I couldn't honestly say that meant she had a bright future ahead of her, but she had a future with us, and that was something.

About the Contributors

The following contributors appear in this volume
The MX Book of New Sherlock Holmes Stories
Part I – 1881-1889

Hugh Ashton was born in the UK, and moved to Japan in 1988, where he has remained since then, living with his wife Yoshiko in the historic city of Kamakura, a little to the south of Yokohama. In the past, he has worked in the technology and financial services industries, which have provided him with material for some of his books set in the 21st century. He currently works as a writer: novelist, copywriter (his work for large Japanese corporations appears in international business journals), and journalist, as well as producing industry reports on various aspects of the financial services industry. Recently, however, his lifelong interest in Sherlock Holmes has developed into an acclaimed series of adventures featuring the world's most famous detective, written in the style of the originals, and published by Inknbeans Press. In addition to these, he has also published historical and alternate historical novels, short stories, and thrillers. Together with artist Andy Boerger, he has produced the Sherlock Ferret series of stories for children, featuring the world's cutest detective.

Deanna Baran lives in a remote part of Texas where cowboys may still be seen in their natural habitat. A librarian and former museum curator, she writes in between cups of tea, playing Go, and trading postcards with people around the world. This is her first venture into the foggy streets of gaslit London.

Kevin David Barratt became a fan of Sherlock Holmes whilst at school. He is an active member of the The Scandalous Bohemians, a group who meet regularly in Leeds and for whom Kevin has contributed an essay on Sherlock Holmes and Drugs (which can be read at www.scandalousbohemians.com). Kevin is also a member of The Sherlock Holmes Society of London. He is married with two grown-up children and lives in Yorkshire.

Summer Perkins is a film student who lives in Portland, Oregon, and has been a fan of the various incarnations of Sherlock Holmes for many years. Though no stranger to writing in the world of Holmes, this is Summer's first published piece. In addition to writing, Summer can be found reading, watching films, and studying various eras in history.

Sir Arthur Conan Doyle (1859-1930) Holmes Chronicler Emeritus. If not for him, this anthology would not exist. Author, physician, patriot, sportsman, spiritualist, husband and father, and advocate for the oppressed. He is remembered and honored for the purposes of this collection by being the man who introduced Sherlock Holmes to the world. Through fifty-six Holmes short stories, four novels, and additional Apocryphal entries, Doyle revolutionized mystery stories and also greatly influenced and improved police forensic methods and techniques for the betterment of all. Steel True Blade Straight

Steve Emecz's main field is technology, in which he has been working for about twenty years. Following multiple senior roles at Xerox, where he grew their European eCommerce from $6m to $200m, Steve joined platform provider Venda, and moved across to Powa Technologies in 2010. Steve is a regular trade show speaker on the subject of mobile commerce, and his time at Powa has taken him to more than forty countries – so he's no stranger to planes and airports. He wrote two novels (one bestseller) in the 1990's and a screenplay in 2001. Shortly after he set up MX Publishing, specialising in NLP books. In 2008, MX published its first Sherlock Holmes book, and MX has gone on to become the largest specialist Holmes publisher in the world, with around one hundred authors and over two hundred books. Profits from MX go towards his second passion – a children's rescue project in Nairobi, Kenya, where he and his wife, Sharon, spend every Christmas at the rescue centre in Kasarani. In 2014, they wrote a short book about the project, The Happy Life Story.

Jayantika Ganguly is the General Secretary and Editor of the Sherlock Holmes Society of India, a member of the Sherlock Holmes Society of London, and the Czech Sherlock Holmes Society. She is the author of The Holmes Sutra (MX 2014). She is a corporate lawyer working with one of the Big Six law firms.

Dr. John Hall has written widely on Holmes. His books includes Sidelights on Holmes, a commentary on the Canon, The Abominable Wife, on the unrecorded cases, Unexplored Possibilities, a study of Dr. John H. Watson, and a monograph on Professor Moriarty, "The Dynamics of a Falling Star". (Most of these are now out of print.) His novels include Sherlock Holmes and the Adler Papers, The Travels of Sherlock Holmes, Sherlock Holmes and the Boulevard Assassin, Sherlock Holmes and the Disgraced Inspector, Sherlock Holmes and the Telephone Mystery, Sherlock Holmes and the

Hammerford Will, Sherlock Holmes and the Abbey School Mystery, and Sherlock Holmes at the Raffles Hotel. John is a member of the International Pipe-smoker's Hall of Fame, and lives in Yorkshire, England.

Luke Benjamen Kuhns is a crime writer who lives in London. He has authored several Sherlock Holmes collections including The Untold Adventures of Sherlock Holmes (published in India & Italy), Sherlock Holmes Studies in Legacy, and the graphic novel Sherlock Holmes and the Horror of Frankenstein. He has written and spoken on the various forms of pastiche writing, which can be found in the Fan Phenomena Series: Sherlock Holmes.

David Marcum first discovered Sherlock Holmes in 1975, at the age of ten, when he received an abridged version of The Adventures during a trade. Since that time, David has collected literally thousands of traditional Holmes pastiches in the form of novels, short stories, radio and television episodes, movies and scripts, comics, fan-fiction, and unpublished manuscripts. He is the author of The Papers of Sherlock Holmes Vol.'s I and II (2011, 2013), Sherlock Holmes and A Quantity of Debt (2013) and Sherlock Holmes – Tangled Skeins (2015). Additionally, he is the editor of the three-volume set Sherlock Holmes in Montague Street (2014, recasting Arthur Morrison's Martin Hewitt stories as early Holmes adventures,) and most recently this current collection, The MX Book of New Sherlock Holmes Stories (2015). He has contributed essays to the Baker Street Journal and The Gazette, the journal of the Nero Wolfe Wolfe Pack. He began his adult work life as a Federal Investigator for an obscure U.S. Government agency, before the organization was eliminated. He returned to school for a second degree, and is now a licensed Civil Engineer, living in Tennessee with his wife and son. He is a member of The Sherlock Holmes Society of London, The John H. Watson Society ("Marker"), The Praed Street Irregulars ("The Obrisset Snuff Box"), The Solar Pons Society of London, and The Diogenes Club West (East Tennessee Annex), a curious and unofficial Scion of one. Since the age of nineteen, he has worn a deerstalker as his regular-and-only hat from autumn to spring. In 2013, he and his deerstalker were finally able make a trip-of-a-lifetime Holmes Pilgrimage to England, where you may have spotted him. If you ever run into him and his deerstalker out and about, feel free to say hello!

Adrian Middleton is a Staffordshire born independent publisher. The son of a real-world detective, he is a former civil servant and policy adviser who now writes and edits science fiction, fantasy, and a popular series of steampunked Sherlock Holmes stories.

Shane Simmons is a multi-award-winning screenwriter and graphic novelist whose work has appeared in international film festivals, museums and lectures about design and structure. His best-known piece of fiction, The Long and Unlearned Life of Roland Gethers, has been discussed in multiple books and academic journals about sequential art, and his short stories have been printed in critically praised anthologies of history, crime and horror. He lives in Montreal with his wife and too many cats. Follow him at eyestrainproductions.com and @Shane_Eyestrain

Denis O. Smith's first published story of Sherlock Holmes and Doctor Watson, "The Adventure of The Purple Hand", appeared in 1982. Since then, numerous other such accounts have been published in magazines and anthologies both in the U.K. and the U.S. In the 1990's, four volumes of his stories were published under the general title of The Chronicles of Sherlock Holmes, and, more recently, a dozen of his stories, most not previously published in book form, appeared as The Lost Chronicles of Sherlock Holmes (2014), and he wrote a new story for the anthology, Sherlock Holmes Abroad (2015). Born in Yorkshire, in the north of England, Denis Smith has lived and worked in various parts of the country, including London, and has now been resident in Norfolk for many years. His interests range widely, but apart from his dedication to the career of Sherlock Holmes, he has a passion for historical mysteries of all kinds, the railways of Britain and the history of London.

Amy Thomas is a member of the Baker Street Babes Podcast, and the author of The Detective and The Woman mystery novels featuring Sherlock Holmes and Irene Adler. She blogs at girlmeetssherlock.wordpress.com, and she writes and edits professionally from her home in Fort Myers, Florida.

Sidney Paget (1860-1908), a few of whose illustrations are used within this anthology, was born in London, and like his two older brothers, became a famed illustrator and painter. He completed over three-hundred-and-fifty drawings for the Sherlock Holmes stories first published in The Strand magazine, defining Holmes's image forever after in the public mind.

JAICO PUBLISHING HOUSE

Elevate Your Life. Transform Your World.

ESTABLISHED IN 1946, Jaico Publishing House is home to world-transforming authors such as Sri Sri Paramahansa Yogananda, Osho, the Dalai Lama, Sri Sri Ravi Shankar, Sadhguru, Robin Sharma, Deepak Chopra, Jack Canfield, Eknath Easwaran, Devdutt Pattanaik, Khushwant Singh, John Maxwell, Brian Tracy, and Stephen Hawking.

Our late founder Mr. Jaman Shah first established Jaico as a book distribution company. Sensing that independence was around the corner, he aptly named his company Jaico ('Jai' means victory in Hindi). In order to service the significant demand for affordable books in a developing nation, Mr. Shah initiated Jaico's own publications. Jaico was India's first publisher of paperback books in the English language.

While self-help, religion and philosophy, mind/body/spirit, and business titles form the cornerstone of our non-fiction list, we publish an exciting range of travel, current affairs, biography, and popular science books as well. Our renewed focus on popular fiction is evident in our new titles by a host of fresh young talent from India and abroad. Jaico's recently established translations division translates selected English content into nine regional languages.

Jaico distributes its own titles. With its headquarters in Mumbai, Jaico has branches in Ahmedabad, Bangalore, Chennai, Delhi, Hyderabad, and Kolkata.

SINCE 1946